Son of a Pioneer Family of Kaua'i,

Eric Knudsen spent most of his life as rancher, hunter of wild cattle, lawyer, and legislator

Teller of Hawaiian Tales

by ERIC A. KNUDSEN

Foreword by A. Grove Day

MUTUAL PUBLISHING PAPERBACK SERIES
TALES OF THE PACIFIC
HONOLULU • HAWAII

THIS BOOK CONTAINS THE COMPLETE TEXT
OF THE ORIGINAL HARDBOUND EDITION

Elika the Taleteller

BLACKED out for the night in Hawaii during World War II, we turned on our screeching radio speakers and listened to shrill news of battles. More relaxing was the calm voice of "Elika" Knudsen as he narrated his tales of men and ghosts; his memories of native cowboys and journeys on knife-edged mountain trails; and and his versions of legends of the olden time when gods and goddesses mingled on daily terms with the Polynesians of the North Pacific. For a while, the placid voice over the air from Station KTOH at Lihue made us forget the evening toll of fighting around the globe.

A feature of Elika's program, "Teller of Hawaiian Tales," was an offer by its sponsor, the Coco-Cola Bottling Co. of Honolulu, Ltd., to send out free reprints of each story told on the radio. During a one-year period of weekly broadcasts, more than fifty thousand reprints were mailed in response to requests.

The stories of Eric Alfred Knudsen were not forgotten after V-J Day was celebrated and the end of hostilities came in sight. To meet the continuing demand for the complete series from schools and libraries throughout Hawaii and from many parts of the mainland, the tales were collected and published in book form in February, 1946. They are here reprinted, in a more modern format, for the enjoyment of another generation or two of "listeners," young and older.

The author of *Teller of Hawaiian Tales* comes from a Kauai family early prominent in island history. Eric's father, Valdemar Knudsen (1820-1898), was born at Kristiansand, Norway, son of the president of that Scandinavian country. With a university education, Valdemar emigrated to New York and was connected with book publishing. He joined the California gold rush of 1849, and with his gains from mining started a business at Sacramento. When returning from a visit to Norway, he contracted Panama fever and it was impossible for him to remain in California. By chance his ship stopped at Kauai and, hearing that he had been cheated of his mainland holdings, he began a third career by pioneering in the growth of sugar cane on the Garden Island. For some time he was manager of Grove Farm at Lihue, but gradually he acquired properties in southern Kauai that are still retained in the family. Valdemar served in the legislature of the kingdom, but was one of the first to pledge allegiance to the Provisional Government in 1893. Eric's Viking father appears in several roles among the pages of *Teller of Hawaiian Tales* — as Papa, as hunter, as lawyer, and as legislator.

The son, Eric Alfred Knudsen (1872-1957), was born on Kauai and educated at Auckland, New Zealand; Vienna; Berlin; and Massachusetts, where he graduated from the Harvard Law School in 1897. He returned to Hawaii in 1900 and became manager of Knudsen Brothers' Ranch. He first entered politics as vice speaker of the Territorial House of Representatives in 1903 and was a senator from 1907 to 1915. He was a member of the Kauai Board of Supervisors from 1923 to 1932. He was an authority on the game animals and mountain trails of Kauai, and blazed one of the earliest routes to the top of Mount Waialeale, "wettest spot on earth." Knudsen married Cecilie L'Orange in 1905, a daughter of the Sinclair-Robinson clan that bought the island of Niihau in 1864. They had three daughters and a son, Valdemar L'Orange Knudsen. Aside from *Teller of Hawaiian Tales*, Eric Knudsen was author, with Gurry P. Noble, of *Kanuka of Kauai* (1945), about the Knudsen and Robinson families of that charming island.

Teller of Hawaiian Tales is not a textbook or a suspense novel, but may be enjoyed by browsers. You can rove through the pages as you will, sampling from some sixty stories a myth here an an anecdote there. You might favor at first the yarns of camping adventure, or the recollections of a bullock hunter of the woods. You might start, on the other hand, with legends of the demigod Maui, who saved mankind from darkness and hauled up, on his enchanted fish-hook, an entire island. Told with simple strength, these tales of a vanished era on Kauai evoke memories of life in those early days on all the isles of Hawaii Nei.

The radio scripts appearing in the original edition of *Teller of Hawaiian Tales* have been edited to conform to current literary style. Since there is no authority for printing some Hawaiian words in italic type but not others, all such words appear in roman type. A reader unfamiliar with Hawaii, reading a book about Hawaii, can assume that the occasional strange terms come from that language. To assist such a reader, a "Glossary of Hawaiian Words" appears as an appendix to the book. O wau ka mea!

A. GROVE DAY
University of Hawaii

Contents

The One-Eyed Akua

WE HAD just finished breakfast and all of us children were out on the lawn. Makaawaawa, the cook, and his wife Makae, our nurse, were washing dishes. The sun was shining through the trees; early to bed and early to rise was an old Hawaiian custom and Papa ran the camp on that rule. The days were wonderful but the nights cold and dark, and the woods were not a good place to be in when night came on.

The natives said they were full of evil spirits and we children believed that and although Papa used to laugh at the stories we knew the natives were right. Hadn't they lived in the mountains for thousands of years before the white man came? They ought to know.

Suddenly Papa came out of the camp carrying his Winchester rifle, the good old .44. Something was going to happen. "Makaawaawa," he called and the cook came out of the kitchen wiping his hands. "Take my rifle and go kill a wild cow or calf. We have no fresh meat in camp."

Makaawaawa's eyes sparkled. To go hunting wild cattle was fun. He quickly took the rifle, stuck the hunting knife in his belt, called the big dog, Liona, and off he strode up the trail and was soon out of sight. That excitement over, we children settled down and went playing in the woods.

Lunch time came and the hunter was still away, but no one worried, for sometimes one had to hunt a long time before one found cattle. Then afternoon began to lengthen out and the sun dipped toward the west. Makae began to look out towards the hills, and finally she confided to us children that something terrible had happened to her man; he should have been back long before this. We children ran and told Papa but he only laughed and told us not to listen to such nonsense.

But when the sun disappeared behind Pu Hina Hina, Papa began to agree with us that something might have gone wrong and, when the sun set, he walked to the top of Halemanu Ridge and shouted long and loud, hoping to get an answer from the valleys and ridges that sloped away to the west. No answer came. He returned to camp and sent two big native boys up the trail towards the north to shout, but they soon came back. It was getting dark and they were afraid to be out in the woods. Poor old Makae sat in the servants' house and wept long and loud. She knew her man was dead and was not to be consoled.

Black night settled over the mountains and you couldn't see your hand before your face. We lit the lamps and gathered round the little stove. Mama made us some tea and toast, and finally the camp settled down for the night with only the chirping of the crickets and the low sobbing of Makae.

Early next morning we were all up and out. Two of the boys were saddling their horses to go and look for the lost man. Mama and Makae were getting breakfast for us children when we heard footsteps, and looking up the trail to the north we saw Makaawaawa coming down the road as fast as he could trot. We all gave a shout and ran to meet him as if he had come back from the dead. "Where have you been?" we all asked at once. "What happened?"

Leaning his rifle against the wall, he told us this story.

"As you know," he said, "I went off yesterday, and as soon as I reached the high ridge I plunged down into the great koa forests and Kopakaka, a favorite place of the wild cattle, but I saw none so on I went. Hour after hour I tramped along their trails. I looked into Tauhau, crossed the Makaha Valley, hunted through the Milolii valleys. Up and down I went but I saw nothing, and had just decided to go home when to my surprise I saw a big black cow standing right in front of me. I took good aim and fired and down she dropped. I walked up to her, laid down my gun, and drew my knife, when she jumped to her feet and dashed off through the brush. My dog and I had no trouble following her tracks, for she was badly wounded and left a trail of blood on the ferns. But she seemed tireless and led me up the ridges and into the valleys, always farther and farther away. I forgot all about time and I was so determined to get that cow that I trailed her away over into the Nuailolo woods, and finally I came upon her. She was standing quite still. I fired again and this time she was dead. I drew my knife and was going to butcher her when I realized I was tired. No wonder, for as I looked the sun was setting low over the ocean. I had no time to get meat—I must get home. I ran as fast as I could, but the sun sank into the sea and, as you know how quickly the night falls, I knew I could never get home. I was on a wide ridge all covered with lehua and koa trees, but the cattle road ran through a nice little open glade and at the upper end was a big koa tree. I just had time to gather a pile of dead sticks and build a fire near the tree. Then I leaned my gun against the

3

tree and sat down with my back against the trunk, and with my dog by my side settled down for the night.

"It was getting dark in the woods, but there was still light enough in the glade to see objects quite distinctly when my dog began to growl and the hair on his back stood straight up. He was gazing down the glade with terror in his eyes. I looked also and to my horror I saw a huge monster coming out of the woods. He was about seven feet tall, with a great tuft of hair on his head. His big arms swung at his sides as he walked towards me and his large hands almost touched the ground. He came slinking up to me, and my dog lay as if dead by my side.

"Hurriedly I put more wood on the fire, and then I saw that he had but one great big eye, large as a saucer, right in the middle of his face, and a great big mouth with teeth showing through the lips. I recognized him for one of the cruel akuas that live in the woods and kill every human being they can get hold of. My father had told me about them when I was a boy.

"Slowly he came, and luckily for me the fire burned up brightly, for they are afraid of fire, but he sat down opposite me and looked at me with his one big eye. There he sat all night long waiting for me to go to sleep. Then the fire would go out and he could come around and kill me. I sat and watched him, and every time the fire began to die down I put on more wood, praying my pile would last the night, for as I glanced down at it, it didn't seem so large. Woe to me if it ran out! All night long we sat and watched each other and the night seemed endless.

"The night wind was blowing softly through the

4

trees and I saw the akua turn his eye toward the stars. I looked up quickly and to my joy saw they were fading; dawn was coming and night would end at last. Still he sat and watched me, but the light began to come and the stars faded away. The akua had to go, for the sun would soon be up and its deadly rays would kill the akua. He rose to his feet, giving me one last ugly look, and then slunk slowly across the little glade, swinging his huge arms, almost touching the ground with his huge hands, and disappeared into the dark jungle.

"I waited a little while, then grabbed my rifle and ran up the trail, my dog at my heels. And here I am, lucky to be alive!"

Land of the Living Water

ONE DAY in the long, dim past, a Hawaiian king was taken seriously ill. All his family and friends gathered about the large grass house where he lay, whispering anxiously together, for they were afraid the king was soon going to die. The king's three sons stood together outside the door, wailing because of their grief.

A strange little old man stopped to ask the reason for their sadness. One of the king's sons replied, "Our father soon will die. There is no hope."

The stranger looked at the young men a long time before he spoke. "There is something that will make your father well again. He must drink of the water of life of Kane." And with those words he vanished.

The eldest son then said, "I am going to find this

5

water of life and save our father's life. I shall then become my father's favorite and shall have the kingdom for my own."

Taking his water calabash, he set out on his journey. As he walked along a path in the woods, he was suddenly confronted by a queer-looking man, a dwarf, or an a'a, as the Hawaiians call them. The dwarf demanded to know where the prince was going and why he was in such a hurry.

The prince pushed him aside and said, "Is it any of your business where I am going? Don't bother me!" And he ran on down the path.

The dwarf decided to punish the king's son. He made the path twist and turn and hide among tangled vines and ferns and thick trees. Finally, the prince could no longer stand on his feet, and he fell headlong into a mass of vines that twined themselves about him and tied him so fast that he lay helpless on the ground.

When he did not return home, the second son said that he would go and find the water of life for his father. But the same fate befell him, for he too, held the same selfish thought.

When the two older brothers did not return, the youngest son took his calabash and started out, thinking that he might find his brothers as well as get the water of life for his father. On the path, he met the same little dwarf, who asked him where he was going.

The prince answered the dwarf kindly, and then asked, "Oh, could you help me in any way? My father will soon die if I do not find the living water of Kane, and I do not know the way to go."

The little dwarf smiled. "You have been kind — not like your brothers, who were rough and unmannered

— and I will gladly help you. Here, take this strong staff! The path will open before you at its bidding. Walk until you come to the palace of a king who is a sorcerer. Within the king's palace is the fountain of the water of life."

Then the dwarf put three packages containing food in the prince's hand. "You cannot get into the palace without these bundles of food," he said. "When you come to the door of the palace, strike it three times with your staff and it will open. But don't be frightened by the two dragons you will then see. When they open their mouths to devour you, toss the food to them, and they will turn away. Then hurry into the courtyard and fill your calabash with the living water. But you must hurry, because at midnight the doors are bolted fast, and you cannot escape."

The prince thanked the ugly little dwarf and went on his way. After many miles of traveling in the beautiful forest, he found the sorcerer's palace. He knocked on the door with his staff as the dwarf had told him to do. When it had opened, he saw the dragons and threw the food into their mouths. Across the courtyard, he saw a large doorway. Some invisible force urged him to cross the courtyard and step into the room. There he found the most beautiful young maiden he had ever seen. He fell in love that very moment.

She showed him where to fill his calabash with the water of life, and warned him that he must hurry, for it was nearing the midnight hour. He dipped his calabash into the fountain and ran out the door just in time.

On his way home, he kept thinking of the little dwarf, of the a'a, and wished he might see him again to thank him for his help. Suddenly his wish came true. There before him stood the smiling dwarf.

"How did you fare on your journey?" he asked the king's son.

And the prince told him of his good fortune and offered to pay the a'a for his help. But the little man would not hear of it and said, "Since you treated me with kindness, and appreciate my help, I will give you one more wish."

"I wish that I might find my brothers," the prince said. "Can you help me?"

"They are dead in the forest," the dwarf told him. "Let them stay where they are. They have evil hearts."

But as the prince insisted that he must find them, the dwarf showed him the tangled path in the forest. With his staff, the prince opened the way to where his brothers lay. Then he sprinkled a little of the water of life over them and they came back to life, as strong and healthy as before.

The youngest brother then told them about his success in finding the living water of Kane and how he had been promised a beautiful bride. The brothers became angry and jealous of the young prince. When their youngest brother had fallen asleep, they decided to kill him. But the magic war club the chief had given him seemed to defend him.

Then the brothers took his calabash with the water of life, poured the precious fluid into their own jars, and filled his calabash again with sea water.

When they reached home the next morning, the unsuspecting young prince ran to his father and told him to drink deeply from his calabash. Immediately the old king grew sicker than ever.

Then the two evil brothers rushed forward, saying the young prince had tried to poison their father.

8

They gave the king the real water of life and he became strong and well right away.

The angry king banished his youngest son. He lived alone in the forest a long time, until three kings he had helped on his travels came to his father bringing gifts and proclaiming the courage and kindness of the young prince who had aided them with his magic war club. Then the father sent messengers out to find the prince and return him to his own home.

Soon after, a beautiful princess sent word everywhere that any prince who could walk straight to her along a line drawn in the air by her sorcerers, without turning to left or right, should become her husband.

Quickly the young price hurried to the land of the beautiful maiden. There before him stood the beautiful princess of the palace of the land of Kane. She ran into his outstretched arms and then sent her servants out to proclaim that her future husband had been found.

The brothers dared not return home; they departed to faraway islands and never came back. But the prince and princess were married and later became king and queen, living in peace and happiness and administering the affairs of their kingdom with wisdom and kindness.

Little Yellow Shark

KAEHU was a little yellow shark whose home was in the clear and gentle waters of the bay of Puuloa, known today as Pearl Harbor. The bay was a quiet, peaceful spot in those faraway days when only outrigger canoes were seen, where gay, happy Hawaiians played or swam along the shores.

Now, although everyone always spoke of Kaehu as the little yellow shark, he was not so small. But he was called little because he was young in years. Yes, Kaehu was young and strong, but he was also old with wisdom, for one of his forebears, called Kamailiili, the shark god, had given him wonderful magic powers and had made him very wise.

Kaehu had been born off the coast of Puna on the southern end of the big island of Hawaii. There he lived contentedly with his parents, who guarded the great cliffs overlooking the sea, until he grew big enough to take care of himself. Then he had said good-by to his family and had started out on a life of adventure.

He came at last to Puuloa, or Pearl Harbor. There he decided to make his home.

Kaehu loved his new home in the big bay, and he found many other sharks living there, who became his friends and playmates.

But sometimes he was filled with longing for his childhood home on the Puna coast, and one day he grew so homesick that he called his shark friends together and told them he was going back to his old home. They decided to go with him, and so began the journey from Pearl Harbor along the Oahu shores to the open sea.

While swimming along outside the reef at Waikiki, Kaehu and his friends met a shark visitor from Maui. His name was Pehu, and he was a very different sort of shark from Kaehu and his friends, for he was a Man-Eater!

When Kaehu and his friends came upon him, he was swimming back and forth, back and forth at Kalehuawike, which is the name they called the surf along the reef outside the present site of the Moana Hotel.

"Why do you swim in just one spot?" asked Kaehu, although he knew the answer because he was so very wise. He knew that Pehu was eagerly waiting for some unsuspecting surfrider to come out far enough so that he might catch him and have a fine meal for himself.

"I am looking for a crab for my breakfast," Pehu replied. Of course Kaehu knew that the evil shark was not telling the truth, but he answered in a friendly way. "We will help you catch your breakfast. You go out a bit further, near the coral reef. My friends and I will go even further out, into the open sea. When a number of surfriders come, we will drive them toward the shore in a great rush, and then you can easily catch what you call your crab." This greatly pleased the Maui shark; he went close to the reef and hid himself in its deep shadows.

Then Kaehu went back to his friends and said, "We must kill this maneater who is destroying our good people. We will all go and push Pehu into the shallow water." Then he outlined his plan of action.

A number of surfriders were playing and laughing in the waves. Pehu called for the other sharks to come and help him capture his prize, but Kaehu called back, "Not yet! Not yet! We must wait for a better chance!" Kaehu had his eyes on two men cavorting in the surf. Finally they started in toward the shore on a great wave, from out where the high surf begins.

Kaehu called, "Now!" as he signaled for an attack. Kahu had planned that he and his shark friends would rush in under the great wave as it passed over Pehu and crowd the men and their surfboards to one side, so that when the evil shark leaped to catch one of them, they

11

would both be out of range. And this is just what they did! As Pehu floundered in the boiling surf, the sharks hurled him over the reef! How they tossed him! Over and over until he finally plunged head-first into a deep hole in the coral. Pehu thrashed about with his great tail and the waters were disturbed as though there was a bad storm. But his thrashing was all in vain, for he only forced himself further and further into the hole, and he could not escape.

The surfriders hurried to shore and told their friends what had happened. Then they all swam out with their sharp knives and killed the wicked Pehu. When they cut open his body, they found human hair and bones inside the maneater. Proof enough that this was the shark who had been destroying some of their people.

There was great rejoicing that the evil one was finally dead. And the two men who had been surfing, and had seen the great company of sharks near the reef, now understood that the leader of them all was in reality, the little yellow shark from Puuloa; Kaehu, whose ancestors were wise and kind and powerful; Kaehu, who loved the people of Oahu and hated all evil things that harmed them. They knew then how he had banded together the other good sharks and had used his powers and wisdom given him by Kamailiili, the shark god, to save them.

When the body of Pehu had been brought ashore, they cut it into hundreds of pieces and put them into baskets. They carried the baskets from Waikiki to Peleula, an ancient ceremonial spot, known today as the intersection of Nuuanu and Beretania Streets in downtown Honolulu.

They cleared a large area and set about building an immense imu, or oven. The chiefs and their counselors, the warriors, wrestlers, the women, young girls and the keikis (which is the Hawaiian name for little children), gathered about the imu. When the fire was an angry red, in went the remains of the wicked Pehu. Then around the fire they sang and danced and chanted old meles appropriate to the great occasion. No longer need they fear the terrible maneater, and they chanted over and over again their gratitude to Kaehu for his good deed. The celebration lasted until the last piece of the once fierce shark had been reduced to ashes.

All those who saw or heard of Pehu, the man-eating shark that was killed because of Kaehu's cleverness, never forgot the little yellow shark who lived in the blue waters of Puuloa, or Pearl Harbor—never forgot how he had saved them! And the hole in the coral reef off Waikiki where Pehu was caught and killed is still known to many of the old-time Hawaiian fishermen.

The Heiau of Polihale

THE priests of the old Hawaiians were a clever lot. They chose a perfect place for a temple dedicated to the dead. The land of the dead, or Po as the Hawaiians called it, lay a mile or two out in the ocean, beneath the waves in the long sweeping bight that lies between Nohili, the Barking Sands, and the point of Nualolo on Kauai.

As you approach the temple, you find the ocean waves crowding you on one side and, on the other, rugged cliffs that rise higher and higher. The last valley— Haeleele—is passed and a straight cliff more than one thousand feet high towers over your head. When the great typhoon swells come roaring in, they wash up the slope of the cliff and cut off all travel toward Napali. And just where the sand beach ends and the rocky shore begins is a well of bubbling water, a sacred spring. Only the priests could drink its waters. At night the sea birds scream and cry as they roost high up in the cliffs, and when the surf is high, the ehu kai, or sea spray, rises like smoke along the shore, giving the place a weird look.

Here on the talus slopes of the thousand-foot cliff, almost one hundred yards east of the sacred spring, the priests built their heiau of Polihale. The first terrace is faced with large rocks and is quite large. And so the temple climbs up the hill, terrace upon terrace, five in all. When it was built no one remembers, but the stonework today is as good as when it was first constructed, maybe a thousand years ago.

The priests were tabu, or sacred, and were held in great fear by the common people, for this was the temple of the dead and the soul of everyone who died had to go to Polihale Temple to be purified before it could enter the land of Po. Those who were accepted climbed to a big black rock some eight hundred feet above the temple, and from there they dived into Po. Here human sacrifices were offered. Here came Hawaii's last king — King Kalakaua — about 1886 to pray to the ancient Hawaiian gods to cure him of a sickness the white doctors had pronounced fatal. He sacrificed a black pig and a white rooster, but the god Miru of the land of Po refused to help, and Kalakaua did not get the few extra years to enjoy the life he loved so dearly.

The terraces still stand, though gone are the priests and all their glory. But though the temple is abandoned and neglected, it is still venerated and people go and place little altars upon the terraces.

Near the temple lived a family who later moved to Mana. The son became my father's head luna, or overseer, and he told me about the temple and showed me how to build an altar of my own and how to pray. The old religion was gone soon after Captain Cook landed on Kauai, but the old superstitions still lived on, for who isn't a bit superstitious, really?

As time went on, I became manager of the ranch in which this famous heiau lies. Still later I was elected to the Hawaiian Legislature. It was the session of 1905, and a long one. I was Speaker of the House. My friend, Billy Harris, was floor leader.

The regular session ran its course. So did an extra session called to pass financial bills. But the last one was hopeless. It seemed that everyone had to put something into the appropriation bills, until almost three times the amount of revenue in sight was given away. And then we adjourned.

I had been away from home almost five months. It was grand to be back on the ranch — away from the noise and bustle of Honolulu and out on the range again. But barely a month had passed when early one morning, as I was walking down to the stables, a carriage drove into the yard and out stepped my friend of the legislature, Billy Harris. He looked sick.

"What's the trouble?" I asked, "What's happened?"

He moaned and sighed. "Haven't you heard the news? The governor called a special session of the legislature to straighten out the appropriation bills, and we meet next week. I jumped the first boat to

15

Kauai. I wanted to talk it over with you."

I saddled another horse and Billy and I rode away toward Mana as we discussed the situation. The more we talked the worse it seemed. In the legislature there were the old awa-drinking, watery-eyed hack driver who sat next to Harris; the so-called Cannon Ball of Kohala; and a bunch of other legislators who didn't care a rap if the bills were overloaded, just so long as their own favorite items were there. We laughed as we remembered the emergency bill the governor sent down during the session. It had called for $25,000, but when it finally got out of the House it called for almost half a million!

By the time my work was done we had ridden far away along the land and were quite near the temple of Polihale, so I suggested to my companion that we go take a look at it. We tied our horses to some nearby bushes and climbed up onto the old terraces. And it was then that I had an inspiration! "Billy," I said, "let's try some kahuna business. Let's pray to the god Miru for help."

He laughed at me and said I was crazy, but I started to build an altar. He watched me a few moments, then he began to build one also. Up on the cliff I saw a white flower, the pua ahiahi or night flower, that the sun had not yet touched. I clambered up and picked it and placed it upon my altar. Billy, finding nothing better, placed a lantana flower on his. Then, standing beside our altars and facing the land of Po, I prayed to Miru in the best Hawaiian I knew. I told him the session could be over in fifteen days if no one tried any monkey business. "Pepehe — strike dead," I cried, "anyone who starts to filibuster. They only bring shame to Hawaii." I finished my prayer and bowed low over our altars. At that very moment a small cloud shut out the sun. "The god Miru has answered our prayer," I cried out. "Mahalo, thank you!"

Of course Billy Harris and I went to Honolulu to attend the special session. All the old gang was there. The old officers were re-elected. In a few minutes the governor's message was in our hands. We took a recess. I stepped down from the Speaker's platform and met the old hack driver face to face.

"Hello, Mr. Speaker," he said. "How long you think this session will last?"

"Oh," I replied, "it won't take long to straighten out those bills. It can be done in fifteen days."

"What!" he exclaimed. "Impossible! It will take all of sixty days and then nothing will be accomplished, only hopapa, hopapa, hopapa — wrangling all the time."

"Well," I said, "it's up to you and your gang, but I will tell you a little story. Do you know about the heiau of Polihale?" I asked him.

"Of course," he said. So then I told him all that Billy Harris and I had done at the temple the week before. He looked at me in amazement, his eyes watering, and finally gasped out, "But, Mr. Speaker, you surely don't believe in those things?"

"Well," I said, "I don't know. I was born on Kauai not far from the temple of Polihale and I knew some of the old kahunas who lived and sacrificed there. The Greeks and Romans had Jupiter and Mars. The Japanese worship Buddha — the Chinese, Confucius. I recognize Jehovah, but I am not so sure that the old Hawaiian gods have no power. Anyway, I am not going to take any chances. I will get through in fifteen days if I can."

17

I left him and went out to lunch. Returning later, I was entering the hall by a back door when I saw the old hack driver sitting near it surrounded by his cronies, and he was talking in Hawaiian. I caught the word "Polihale." I slipped away and entered through the front door.

The session went on. A hundred thousand dollars was cut out of the Cannon Ball's favorite items. I glanced at him but he sat with glassy eyes gazing into space. One of the other leader's pet bills was smothered. He sat and squirmed and kept wiping his eyes. He looked at me but never uttered a word. The top-heavy bills were slashed and cut to pieces, but never a peep did we hear from the old gang. The days were full of work, the bills were ready and finished, the last vote recorded, and the new bills went to the governor. Our work was pau—finished. And it was the night of the fifteenth day.

Billy Harris rose from his desk. "Mr. Speaker," he said. "I move we adjourn, sine die." The session was over.

I stepped down to the floor and he and I shook hands.

"It worked," he said, in a triumphant voice.

"Sure," I answered. "Great is the Heiau of Polihale."

Maui, the Demi-god

MAUI was the youngest member of his family. He was a very clever fellow. He was also full of mischief and liked to rollick with his many playmates. Now, Maui, although very human indeed, was gifted with

18

supernatural powers which surprised even himself sometimes. He could become invisible, or he could change his human form into any kind of animal. Not only that, but he could perform feats of daring and strength that far outdid the efforts of all his brothers and friends combined. The only trouble was, Maui loved to do tricks.

Sometimes his pranks made his parents scold him severely. But Maui didn't mind. He was having fun.

Not always, though, did Maui use his talents to play tricks. When anyone was in trouble, he was the first to help. And, after these wonderful deeds, Maui would be welcomed back into the family fold. In fact, he enjoyed his new position so very much that sometimes he would almost decide not to be bad again. Almost, but not quite.

But there was one deed of Maui's that was so wonderful it has lived forever in the legends of Hawaii. That was the time he lifted the sky and made the earth bright with sunshine all day long.

For long, long years, the people had lived in darkness. Sometimes this condition annoyed Maui because it interfered with his fun. It not only annoyed him, but trouble him, too, because nobody had done anything about it. You see, the heavens had fallen down and the clouds couldn't be separated from the earth. No one had ever been strong enough to lift them. The plants in the forest had tried to help, but they had only succeeded in lifting the sky a few inches. And Maui and all his friends had to crawl around on their hands and knees. Only in certain places had the trees forced the sky high enough for men to stand. Everybody lived in caves or low grass huts, which were sorry places at best. There weren't any windows or doors, just low openings to crawl through. The thatch on the huts kept rotting from the dampness, for there was no warm sunshine to dry it.

Now, the cave where Maui lived was right at the foot of a great extinct crater. He decided one day to explore this crater and some of the caves around his home. He set out, crawling on his hands and knees. Once in a while he bumped his head against the dark, low clouds. And sometimes he cut his hands on the rough lava. But Maui kept on until he finally came to a forest. Here the sky was a little higher and he could stand upright. But it was still dark. He walked on a ways until he arrived at a small open space. It was very, very quiet in the little clearing. A disturbing quiet. Strange . . . and weird. No breeze touched the leaves of the plants, and the air was close.

Maui had never known fear, and he really didn't now, yet he had never seen such a place. He turned and looked around him. His eye caught the outlines of a small hut set at the far edge of the clearing. In the dusky light, he thought he even saw a figure huddled in front of it. He hoped it was someone, because he was tired of being alone.

"Hello!" he called. There was no answer. All was quiet. Maui paused a moment and then sauntered slowly across the clearing. He could see quite well now and sure enough, there was a figure by the hut. It was an old, old woman, bent with age, sitting hunched over a gnarled staff. Her face was very wrinkled, but her black eyes, that looked intently at Maui, were bright and piercing. Beside her on a tree stump was a gourd calabash filled with water, and a coconut shell brimming with wild berries. Maui was thirsty, and a little hungry.

20

"Give me a drink from your gourd!" he demanded of the old woman. To his surprise, she remained still. Again Maui spoke — this time somewhat fretfully, for he was tired as well as thirsty. "Give me a drink from your gourd." Saying this, he stepped a little closer. Silently the woman handed him the calabash, watching him closely all the while.

When Maui had finished, he placed the gourd back on the stump and sat down on a nearby log.

"My name is Maui," he announced. "I come from the other side of the crater. The sky is so low all the people have to crawl around. It is much nicer here."

With this, the old woman moved again, this time to offer him some of the wild berries.

Maui was hungry and ate the berries greedily. He looked up to thank the old woman — but she had disappeared. He was worried. There were a number of things he wanted to ask her. Presently she appeared again, holding in both hands a large shell filled with more of the wild fruit. This too, she offered to Maui. He wished she would say something. Finally, in exasperation, he asked, "Who are you, old woman, and why do you live here alone?"

Then, out of the silence, she spoke, softly, "I am Nani, your friend."

Maui waited for the old woman to say more, but she remained quiet. Finally he rose to go, but suddenly realized that daylight had faded into darkness. He knew he would be hopelessly lost if he ventured out into the forest now. As if reading his thoughts, Nani, too, rose and went to him. Placing her withered hand on his arm, she said in her soft voice, "You may stay here tonight if you wish."

The next morning, as Maui was getting ready to

leave, he said to the old woman, "You have been very kind to me. Is there anything I can do for you? What do you want more than anything else in the world?"

Her bright black eyes looked intently at Maui. Then she replied, "I am an old, old woman, and I do not have much more time on this earth. You have in you the power and strength to bring light." With that the bent form turned and entered the thatch hut. Maui was alone.

He started on his wearisome journey back to his home, thinking all the while how he was to accomplish such a task. As he was crawling along, he accidentally bumped himself on a low cloud. It gave way a little. Noticing this, he thought that perhaps he could lift the whole sky if he really tried.

He braced his feet on the ground and his shoulders solidly against the sky. He struggled mightily — pushing and pushing and pushing. The clouds gradually were lifted higher and higher until they were at the very tops of the trees. Then Maui climbed upon a low hill and pushed the sky still higher. At this point, Maui called upon his supernatural powers to make him grow taller and even stronger. He grew until he was taller than the highest mountain and stronger than the mightiest of the gods. Once again he braced himself, took a long deep breath and with one powerful heave, the great strength of Maui thrust the sky upwards to the heights where it has remained to this day.

Maui returned home and found all his friends rejoicing in the newly found sunlight. They worshipped him for his wonderful feat. Now, indeed, was Maui a true god.

The Ghost of Puukapele

I SHALL never forget a night many years ago as we sat around the fire at Kokee. Kahuna Nui was our host. There were Jack Brodie, Kauka, and several other good friends, and as the fire sank into the coals and the night took on that mysterious silence, Kahuna Nui began to speak.

It was in the late 1800's, he began. I was camping in the hills around Halemanu with a gang of workmen. One night I was returning to the hills from the lowlands. I was alone with my horse and three dogs. I was jogging along the lonely trail on the broad back of Lehulu with my three dogs trotting silently at my side. We swung around the bend of Puu Moi and I noticed a waning moon hanging over the canyon. It must have been between ten and eleven o'clock and there was just enough light to see the indistinct outlines of all sorts of objects.

Suddenly and for no apparent reason the dogs began to growl; their hair stood on end, their tails went between their legs, and they slunk away into the brush. I was at a loss to understand their action but felt confident that they would rejoin me shortly. Lehulu kept jogging along up the winding trail. Just as we reached the top of the hill, he gave a loud snort, trembled all over, and dashed madly down the other side. It was quite a while before he quieted down and the three dogs rejoined me.

Next day an old Hawaiian from Waimea brought poi to camp, and after much urging on my part he

23

consented to tell me a story of the hills.

"To you skeptical haoles," he began, "this tale may seem untrue, but we Hawaiians know it is true, and that it really happened just as I will tell it to you." And this is the story he told:

Many hundreds of years ago, an old Hawaiian named Papu went from Pokii to Kalalau to visit friends, and after a long stay he made a large pack of dried fish and, climbing the cliffs, started home again to Pokii.

A few days later some young men arriving in Kalalau inquired for Papu. "Why, he went some days ago," said his friend.

Since the old man had not returned to his home, they suspected trouble and at once started back in search of him. Finally they found his body lying in the brush, his head crushed and his pack gone. Sadly they buried him where he had been killed, and returned to Pokii.

Now every year the spirit of the old man comes back to the spot where he was murdered, and sits by the side of the road, with a pack of dried fish on his back, and in revenge he kills the first man who passes that night.

"And when does old Papu come back?" asked Kahuna Nui. "This is the month of August."

"I cannot tell," said the old poi man, "until I figure it out in the old Hawaiian calendar." He began to mumble and count. Finally he said, "Either last night or tonight he should be there."

"Where, pray, did the murder occur?" asked Kahuna Nui.

"Oh," replied the poi man, "Kapuwahiaola is the place, and he sits on the left side of the trail."

24

Kahuna Nui then related what had happened the night before.

"That is easily explained," said the old poi man. "The dogs and the horse, being more sensitive than man, sensed the presence of the spirit when you could not. He didn't kill you for the simple reason that you did not belong to the clan that had killed him."

As Kahuna Nui finished his story, my dog Pax crept up and put his cold, wet muzzle into Kauka's hand. Kauka gave a yell and sprang to his feet. He thought Papu's ghost was trying to shake hands with him. Other stories were told around the dying fire that night in Kokee when Kahuna Nui was our host, but this one I was to remember long years afterward.

One night it so happened that I was going up that same long, lonely road with a load of provisions. I was late and was anxious to get to camp in a hurry. Jogging along the road, as I turned the edge of the canyon, there I saw the moon hanging over the canyon and giving a dim light just as Kahuna Nui had described it so many years before. The story he had told that night, the camp scene at Kokee, came back in a rush.

I had no dogs, but I was riding a gentle little mare. As we came near the spot where the old Hawaiian, Papu, was supposed to sit, I peered into the gloom trying to see, when suddenly and without warning my mare let out a frightened snort, plunged madly into the air, and was flying full speed into the valley beyond. As we swept around the bend, a dark shadow passed in front of us and the air was full of that musty smell that old dried fish gives off.

I turned in my saddle and called out in Hawaiian, "Owai kela?" (Who's there?) But all I got was a cold chill that ran up and down my spine.

On rushed the mare at breakneck speed. I seemed unable to stop her, though it may be that I didn't try too hard. Anyway, she didn't stop running until we got up near the open ridges around Puukapele, where she quieted down, and we got to camp without further adventures.

No Hawaiian I ever hunted with would travel that road at night. I have not since. And if anyone of you do not believe this story, ride up there yourself, alone, at night, and see what happens!

Pueo, King of the Owls

HIGH up among the rainbows of Manoa there once lived the king of the owls. His name was Pueo — and Pueo was a wise old owl. The Hawaiian people had built a temple for him, and here it was that he watched over them and protected them from all harm. Just to show you how fair and honest he was, let me tell you a story about him.

Pueo was sitting in his temple one day when suddenly he heard a loud commotion in the valley below him. This was so unusual that he looked down to see what was the trouble. There in the valley two natives were fighting. Crowded around them were hundreds of people, shouting and growing more excited every minute.

Pueo was angry. He immediately sent for a priest and demanded the tumult be stopped. He declared, moreover, that the culprits be captured at once and sentenced to die.

"Oh, please, good Pueo, listen to me! I am innocent." But the owl king replied, "You have dared to disobey me. You must die!"

The native begged and pleaded. Finally Pueo allowed him to speak. "Let me hear what you have to say." The prisoner told his story and when he had finished Pueo decided the man had been accused unjustly, and set him free. The owl king himself was so impressed by this episode that he made it a custom thereafter to allow every accused person to speak for himself before the final punishment was settled upon him.

It was not long after this that Pueo led the great battle of the owls against a chief at Waikiki. I will tell you how it happened.

Not far from the upper end of Fort Street there lived a man named Kapoi. He was a fisherman. And when he wasn't fishing he was mending his tiny thatched hut, which was always falling to pieces. The storms would sweep down and carry bits of it away, and Kapoi would patiently put it back together again. One day he went down to the Kewalo marsh, where the tall, strong pili grass grew. "Now," thought Kapoi to himself, "the winds will have to blow hard to tear this away."

As he slogged through the marsh gathering the grass, he discovered a nest of owl's eggs. "Oh!" he whistled softly. "A fine dinner I will have tonight." Joyfully, he picked up the eggs and carefully put them in his sack. That evening after he had finished working on his hut, he built himself a fire. He was wrapping the eggs in ti leaves and thinking all the while how good they were going to taste. Just as he was about to put them on the hot stove, an owl flew down beside him.

"Oh, Kapoi, give me back my eggs!" Startled, Kapoi looked up.

"Are these yours?" he asked.

"Yes, don't eat them," begged the owl. "Please give them back to me."

Kapoi was disappointed. "But then I won't have any dinner." The owl begged and begged. Finally Kapoi, being a kindhearted man, was touched by the entreaties. "All right," he said at last, "you may have them."

The grateful own gathered up her eggs and flew with them to a safe spot in a tree. Soon she was back. "You shall be rewarded for your kindness. I will be your own god and will protect you and your household from all harm."

Well, Kapoi was so happy that the following day he set out to Manoa Valley and there built a temple for his owl-god. He brought some bananas and a sacrifice for the altar. And as a final tribute, he declared a day for the customary tabu to begin and also the day when that tabu should be lifted. Kapoi then went happily to his fishing, thinking that all his trouble was over. But it wasn't.

Over at Waikiki there lived a chief named Oahu a Kakuhihewa. He was the king after whom the island was named. This king was strong and powerful and rich. Now it so happened that Kakuhihewa was also building a temple. And he declared his tabu over all the people and made an additional decree. If any person should build a temple with a tabu on it and should lift that tabu before his was lifted, that man should pay the penalty of death. Poor Kapoi knew nothing at all about this. The king was a kind man, but he thought that Kapoi had committed a serious offense in the eyes of the people and should be punished.

Kapoi was taken a prisoner and placed in the temple to await the execution. The time was set for sunrise the following day. But all was not over for Kapoi yet. His own little owl-god had watched the whole thing from the treetops and had followed him to his cell. Kapoi heard a whisper outside the high window. "Don't be discouraged. I will help you." And off she flew. Over the beach — and the marsh where Kapoi had found her eggs — over the little thatched hut. She flew until she came to the beautiful temple of the King of Owls. There she knew she would find justice.

Pueo listened patiently and quietly while Kapoi's owl-god told his story. The good Pueo decided to help. He sent his priests to gather together all the owls of all the islands. And by evening they had arrived — from Hawaii, Maui, Kauai, Molokai, Lanai, and the rest of the islands. Pueo then told them they were going to battle the great king of Waikiki.

Just before daybreak the next morning, the owls flew down to the temple where Kapoi was a prisoner. As the sun came up, the owls rose in a solid mass and spread wide their wings. They looked like one great black cloud in the heavens, and they did not let a single ray of the sun strike the ground. Below them, the warriors were thrown into utter confusion. They tried to drive the birds away, but the owls flew down and attacked them. They threw dirt on them and tore their clothes, until finally the warriors scattered and fled in pain and fear.

Thus was Kapoi saved by the cunning and wisdom of Pueo, King of the Owls.

Pikoi Was Good at Shooting Arrows

NOW Pikoi was a curious young fellow, and was always asking his father questions. His father, who was known as Alala, the Raven, was a patient man and answered his son to the very best of his ability.

One day Pikoi heard a great commotion far below his home and near the beach. "Why are they shouting down there?" he asked his father.

"They are playing a game called ko ieie," his father replied.

"But tell me — how is the game played?" curious Pikoi inquired. Then his father explained how each contestant found a smooth board and threw it into the river at a spot near the rapids. The board had to float steadily in one place without going down the rapids. And the one whose board floated the steadiest without being carried down over the rapids won the game.

"Oh, that sounds like fun," said Pikoi. "May I go down and watch them?"

"You may not only watch, but you may join in the game if you wish," his father told him.

And because Alala was a kind parent and because he wanted his son to win the game, he himself smoothed a board for Pikoi and gave it to him. Pikoi ran off happily with the smooth board tucked under his arm. It was the first time he had ever been with a crowd, and all by himself, but he didn't mind.

Now Pikoi was an odd-looking young fellow that attracted everyone's attention. He had a sharp face with a long, rather pointed nose, and he had little bones, and hair that was just like a rat's hair.

When the crowd saw him, they began to call him Rat and they would shout, "See the Rat! Look at the Rat! What is a Rat doing here with us?" But Pikoi didn't care what they said. He just stood by and watched them cast their boards into the river. Then quietly he stepped up and placed into the current the board his father had smoothed out for him. It floated the steadiest of all the boards. Soon the crowd was calling for him — acclaiming him as the winner.

Of course, some of the boys got jealous of him. They grabbed his board away from him and threw it far out over the rapids. Pikoi never stopped to think — he just jumped after his board, a great big jump that carried him over the rapids and down to the sea.

"Aha, we got rid of him all right," the boys said to each other. "He won't bother us any more. What right has a Rat to come with us anyway?"

For two days and two nights, poor Pikoi floated on the ocean currents, and then he was washed up on the beach of another island. There he lay, cold and wet, hungry and exhausted.

But then a strange thing happened. Along came a man called Kaua. "Where did you come from?" he asked Pikoi.

"From the sea," whispered tired Pikoi. Then Kaua, who was a servant, took Pikoi with him to the house of his two young mistresses.

The servant explained how he had found him lying on the sand. Then the two young women, who were sisters, asked Pikoi, "But where did you come from? Where were you born and have you no family?" Then Pikoi told them that he was from Wailua on the island of Kauai. "Alala, the Raven, is my father," he said. "And Koukou is my mother."

31

When he said this, the young sisters ran to him and cried over him, because they knew he was their own brother. They had left Kauai sometime before to marry and live on this island. And when their husbands came home, a great luau, or feast, was prepared to honor Pikoi. A pig was killed, yams were made ready, fish were caught, and a great imu, or underground oven, was dug in the ground.

Now while the preparations for the great luau were being made, Pikoi wandered away from the house to where there was a big crowd of people. All kinds of ancient games were being played, and everyone was having a glorious time.

The king and queen were on hand to watch the games. As Pikoi stepped up, he heard the king and queen make a wager on a man's shooting. He was shooting arrows at rats. Yes, and the man was none other than a prince: Prince Mainele.

Now the king was winning from the queen, for he was laying wagers all the time on Mainele's shooting. Pikoi stood nearby and watched the game for awhile. But finally he could keep quiet no longer!

"Why, anyone could shoot as well as that!" he boasted aloud.

When the queen heard him and then saw that he was a stranger, she said laughingly, "So you think you could shoot as well as that? If you can, then I will wager my property on your ability." Of course Pikoi felt proud and happy, and he was determined that he would win for the queen.

The prince and Pikoi took their places. Whichever one struck ten rats with one arrow would be the winner. Prince Mainele shot first. His arrow sped straight and true through the air and right through ten rats.

They cried, "Mainele has won! Mainele has won! No one can do better than that!"

"Humph!" said Pikoi. "He must be left-handed. I thought he was going to shoot the rats through their whiskers!"

The prince heard what Pikoi said, and he was angry, indeed! "Who ever heard of such a silly thing!" he cried, excitedly. "No one has ever been able to shoot rats through their whiskers."

With confidence and a smile, Pikoi stepped forward. "Look then — for you will see someone now," he said.

So new bets were made as to whether or not one could shoot rats through their whiskers with an arrow. But when Pikoi drew back his bow and was all ready to shoot, the rats suddenly disappeared. Not a one was in sight! Then Pikoi said a charm that he knew would bring them back. And this is the way it went:

> I, Pikoi,
> The offspring of Alala the Raven,
> The offspring of Koukou:
> Where are you, my brothers?
> Where are you, O rats?
> There they are,
> There they are!
> The rats are in the pili grass:
> They sleep, the rats are asleep!
> Let them awaken:
> Let them return!

And while he spoke, back came all the rats. Pikoi then took careful aim and let his arrow fly. Sure enough, it struck ten rats right through the whiskers at one time, and the point of it held not a rat, but a bat that had gotten into the way of the fast-flying arrow. Not only had he caught ten rats by their whiskers, but a bat as well.

Now Prince Mainele saw what had happened. He said, "It is a draw, I shot ten rats and he shot ten rats. What does it matter about the whiskers?"

At first the people all agreed with Mainele. But not Pikoi — no! "The bat counts as a rat," he insisted. "No, no!" shouted the crowd. "That is not so! That is not so!" "But it is true," Pikoi kept repeating. "Remember the old words of the old days." And again he started chanting the old words that everyone knew:

> The bat is in the stormless season.
> He is your younger brother, O rat:
> Squeak to him.

Then, of course, everyone agreed that the bat must be counted as one more rat, so Pikoi had killed eleven rats with his one arrow — and had won the contest against Prince Mainele.

While the king and queen settled bets, Pikoi ran back to his sisters' house. And he was just in time, for the food was being taken from the great imu. He sat down all by himself and would not say a word to anyone while he ate all the good things before him — pig and poi, yams, opihi, seaweed, bananas, and all the other delicious foods. When he had finished eating, he was a changed person. Gone were the sharp features and the small bones. Only his hair looked the same. Otherwise he was a fine-looking young fellow. Pikoi became a great favorite of the king and queen, and several years later they gave him their lovely daughter in marriage. Pikoi remained on the island with his sisters, the king and queen, and his beautiful bride all the rest of his days.

The Disappointed Hunter

THE road leading to the top of Mount Waialeale is a long and difficult one, generally a slippery and rutted one as well. It begins at Waimea and winds up and up until you reach the four-thousand-foot level, but from there on it heads up against the northeast trade winds and rises gradually until the five-thousand-foot summit is reached.

One day, I decided to ride up to visit my cousin, Francis Gay, who was staying at his summer camp far up the road to Waialeale. When I arrived, I discovered he had company; his brother-in-law, Charley, was staying with him. After my arrival, we spent a lot of time hunting wild cattle and had a great time.

When I had been there several days, Charley suggested one fine morning that we make the trip to the top of Mount Waialeale. I was enthusiastic and anxious to start as soon as possible. Only my cousin seemed lacking in enthusiasm. Finally he said he guessed he wouldn't go, for he had been to the summit about ten years before, and once was enough for him. However, he did not dampen our spirits and we decided to make the trip anyway, taking two of the native boys along as guides. Their names were Kualo and Malamaiki. These fine Hawaiian fellows had made the trip with my cousin before and knew the hazards along the way. We took our blankets and supplies needed for a three-day trip and started off.

As we were mounting our horses, Charley and I, my cousin called to me, "Have you got your rifle with you? Better take it along and be on the lookout for bog bulls."

"What's a bog bull?" I asked, as I strapped on my rifle.

"You'll find out!" Francis laughed, as we rode out of the yard.

Two hours' ride from camp and we were in a dreary belt of forest. On one side of the trail was the deep gorge of Kahana; on the other, shallow gulches and dying trees and logs, and swamps full of long, coarse grass and ferns. So this was where the big wild bulls came when they were old and had been driven from the herd by younger and stronger rivals! I had heard of this spot, but had never seen it before, this strange place where they wandered about, day in and day out, leading a lonely and savage life. These old bulls feared no one. And why should they? Human beings — the few who came — were only another species of animal, and perhaps an enemy with whom to do battle. Instead of running away and hiding from hunters, they came boldly out and attacked with great fury. They were dangerous, and hunters had to be on the lookout all the time or they might be ambushed.

We passed through the place safely with Kualo in the lead, and soon found the trail toward Waialeale. There had been no sign of cattle. It was peaceful, but gray and drear. The ridge we traveled was narrow and we moved slowly. On one side was the deep valley dropping away several thousand feet to the river that flowed through it. On the left was swampy, undulating country full of large trees, dead logs, and tall grass.

My dog Jingo trotted behind me. Suddenly he darted past me and Kualo, racing ahead and barking wildly. Kualo drew up beside me and said, "Take your rifle and go ahead. It may be only a pig. If so, all right, but if it is a bull — look out!"

I grabbed my rifle and ran ahead up the trail. It was a

36

single trail, and a rough one, up and down over little hummocks of rock and dirt. I was soon a hundred yards or so ahead of the rest of the party, and as I came out on the top of a small rise, there before me I saw a great bog bull! He came trotting out of the jungle and stood facing me. He was huge, and bright against the landscape, for he was red. He held his great head high, sniffed the air angrily, and started down toward me with hatred in his eye. I waited, my rifle was cocked and loaded. Down the trail he came — out of sight one moment, in view the next. I could hear his heavy footsteps come nearer and nearer. Suddenly, there he was not fifty yards away!" "What a beauty he is," I thought. Then, remembering that he was on his way to do battle and to kill us if he could, I aimed and fired.

The shot stunned him for a moment, but on he came, faster than before. Then Jingo rushed behind him and bit him in the leg. He turned and tried to hook the dog, but Jingo was too quick for him. I shot again. The great bull staggered and sank to his knees. I sent another shot into his huge body to end his misery. He rolled over into one of the small bogs. In the distance I could hear Kualo shouting, "Good boy! Maikai! That's good! You got him!"

In a moment, he came running up the trail after me. He looked again at the fallen monster. "I know that bull," he said. "He almost got me a year ago up in this same country. He was a wicked fighter." I felt proud, indeed, that I had killed so ferocious an animal. And that was how I learned about bog bulls.

But now I want to tell you a little sequel to this story — something that happened twenty years later to be exact, and twenty years is a long time — but there are still almost as many bog bulls high on the slopes of

Mount Waialeale as there were when I shot my big red one.

I was sitting on my lanai at Hoea, smoking my pipe and taking life easy, when up drove a car I did not recognize, and out stepped a big, rugged man. He took a rifle from the car and came up the steps.

"My name is O'Hara," he said, introducing himself. He handed me his gun. "This is your brother's gun. I borrowed it from him before he left, and he asked me to return it to you." He also took off a belt of cartridges and handed it to me. "I bought these shells, but I have no use for them. He is welcome to them. Tell him thanks," he went on, "but tell him also that I am a most disappointed hunter."

"How so?" I inquired.

"Well," he said, "I had to make a trip to Waialeale, and I was told that away up in the swamp country one is liable to meet the big bog bulls, who are very fierce and who attack the traveler on the narrow ridges. Oh, how I wanted to meet one! That is why I borrowed the gun. But it was just my hard luck not to even catch sight of one of those brutes, all the way up and all the way back."

I then had the fun of telling him of my experience with the big red bull. How his eyes glistened as I talked. "You lucky man," he said. "I would have given a thousand dollars for such a chance!"

With that he left. I put the gun and belt away and thought to myself he was not the only one who had told me a hard-luck story about hunting the bog bulls. I had made several trips and had only seen one — the big red one I had killed so long ago.

A few days later, a young man from Honolulu came to visit me. He had a few days' vacation and

38

begged me to go hunting with him and also to lend him a gun. I gave him his choice of my gun or my brother's .32 that O'Hara had recently returned. He took mine.

As we rode along the rim of Waimea canyon looking for game, I suggested that we try our guns to get the feel of them, remembering that this gun of my brother's was new to me also.

I found the magazine full of shells, so I pumped one up into the chamber and closed the breach. The cartridge slipped in easily enough until the last one-eighth of an inch, and there it stuck. I worked it out and tried another. The same thing happened. Then I examined the shells to see what was wrong. All were .32 special — but the rifle was a .30-40!

Suddenly I burst into laughter, remembering the long face of O'Hara, the disappointed hunter. He would never know how lucky he had been not to have met a fighting bog bull! Better be disappointed than dead!

Ka Awa Ko

WELL, the big red bog bull lay dead. So Kualo, our guide, led on. We rode a mile or so further into the mountains and then had to tie the horses, as the ground became too soft and boggy for them. We found a little dry rise and there we left them, after we had gathered armfuls of grass for them to eat and given each one an affectionate pat or two. Shouldering our packs, we entered a dismal, swampy area. The trail that had been blazed by my cousin and the Hawaiian boys ten years before was almost overgrown with moss. Kualo had great difficulty in following it. Every few minutes we would lose it. Then I would stand by the last blaze and send the men ahead to find the next one. The trail would then have to be cut open before we could proceed.

It took a long time, but at last we came into a little valley. The bottom of the valley was open, but was lined on both sides with tall lehua and lapalapa trees that shut out the light. The day was overcast and, although it was not raining, the place was gloomy and dismal, and I began to think we were in the wrong valley. It was most depressing. My pack was beginning to feel heavy and we had had four long hours of tramping and cutting. It seemed as if we were getting nowhere.

Kualo, however, kept slashing away through the tall ferns and suddenly Malamaiki shouted, "There it is!" And sure enough, up on a slope to our left, cut into a cliff, we spied the cave.

Everything was all right again. We had reached our camp site. We could sleep in a dry cave, thank goodness! And cook our meals in comfort. We dashed through the ferns, climbed the slope, and threw down our packs. Our troubles for that day were over at last!

The next morning, after a hearty breakfast, we were off for the top of Waialeale. The day was clear. However, Malamaiki rolled up his big raincoat and put it on his shoulder. Kualo said, "What for you take that heavy pack? No more rain today. Two hours up, one and a half hours back, more better leave it in the cave."

But Malamaiki replied, "That's all right, Kualo, but everyone say Waialeale number one wet place. I no like get wet."

We followed the river to a waterfall, climbed up, and

were soon on the slope leading to the top. The trail was more open and required little cutting, and after a while we came out into open country and could see the top of the range above. About half-way up the trail, we passed two odd-looking columns of bright red clay. They were about eight feet tall and looked as if they did not belong there, but as though someone had built them. How had they come there? I pondered the question as we passed them. They were a strange sight in that isolated spot! On we went, down into a small valley, on to its end, and then we were right at the brink of the five-thousand-foot cliff. Around one small hill, and there lay the little lake that is always rippling with the wind, Waialeale. It looked cold and lonely. Now we were on top of the famed rain mountain. It was clear on top, but to the east we could see nothing below but dense clouds.

I had had enough. I was ready to start back, but Kualo said, "Come, you haven't seen all. You must see Ka Awa Ko."

He led me to the end of the lake, and there, cut into a small lava mound, he pointed out a perfect little altar. "This altar is dedicated to Ku, the God of War," he said. "Those who come here must lay a sacrifice or offering to Ku to keep him in a good humor, for if he gets angry with you, he can make things very bad."

I stood looking at this ancient altar, built by whom and how long ago who could tell? How many people had placed offerings on it, I could only guess. That it was dedicated to Ku, the god of war, was most appropriate. It certainly was a battle to reach the place, and in the olden days when the natives traveled wearing only a malo, it must have been an ordeal to face the rain and cold of that dreary spot. Kualo passed his hand over the altar. "There is nothing on it," he said. "Sometimes visitors leave coins as offerings."

"I am sorry," I said. "But I have no coins with me; in fact, nothing that I could leave as an offering."

"Then let's get going," Kualo answered. "It looks black."

And calling to the others, we started back. And that remark must have made Ku, the god of war, mad. Suddenly clouds began pouring in from every side, swirling and spinning around us. Everything was blotted out; we could hardly see ten feet in any direction, and we drifted before the roaring wind. "You are going too far to the right," I yelled at my guides. "Go to the left!"

But they insisted they were right. I stopped. Charley waited with me in a little hollow. And then the rains came! Malamaiki opened his big raincoat, and he and I took shelter together. Charley refused to join us. "I like it," he called, laughing.

But harder and harder came the rain. It was a real cloudburst, and soon I saw Charley begin to shake. We pulled him in with us and warmed him. I kept looking off to the left. Suddenly a rift came in the fog and, for a moment, I saw the small valley and the ridge on the opposite side, and the two red clay pillars. I pointed my hand at them, and they vanished. "Hold your hand like I did," I told one of the boys. "And answer me when I yell."

And I ran into the fog and rain. It was like trying to run in a blacked-out room. But I finally found the clay columns and our footprints in the soft earth full of water. I yelled, and was answered. Soon all of us were together once more, with the exception of Kualo. I called again. A faint answer came, then Kualo's voice in the distance, saying, "What's the trouble?"

"No trouble," we replied. "Come. This is the way out."

"Impossible," came the answer. "The road is some-where over here."

"All right," I yelled back, "but we are by the two red clay pillars, and here are our tracks. We are going back to the cave. If you want to stay up here all day, that's up to you. We are off. I will wait three minutes and then go."

"Wait! Wait!" answered Kualo. "Perhaps you are right." I waited, and soon he appeared like an apparition through the fog.

"Ta hu hu?" he asked. "How did you find it? Let's run!" We ran down the ridge and through the woods. The stream was a roaring torrent. We jumped into the basin below the waterfall, scrambled out, and didn't stop running until we were safely back in the cave.

The return to camp was easy the next day. I thought I would never try Waialeale again. Now I understood why my cousin had refused to go with us. But how often we change our minds. Some years later, a young man named Pickup asked me to go with him, as he had been sent to read the rainfall in the new rain gauge that had recently been placed atop Mount Waialeale. He was such a pleasant fellow that I consented, and the two of us went up. Remembering about Ku, the god of war, and his altar named Ka Awa Ko, I selected an offering I thought might please the god. Never having bought a gift for a war god before, I was a bit uncertain, but as I bought some smoking tobacco, I seemed to know at once what would please him — a little red tin of Prince Albert. Just the thing! I picked it up and put it in my pack.

When we reached the top of the mountain, thick fog was blowing over it. We had a little difficulty locating the rain gauge, but eventually found it.

"Over five hundred inches," said Pickup. "Not bad for eight months." Then I showed him the little lake and introduced him to Ka Awa Ko, the little altar dedicated to Ku.

"Ku," I said, "great god of war, I am Elika, son of Kanuka. Accept this little tin; it contains a very delicious smoking tobacco. I know you will enjoy it. Mai hu hu oe iao."

"What are you saying?" Pickup asked.

"Silence," I whispered. "I am asking Ku to be good to me the next time I come here, and not to be angry with me!"

Pickup laughed. "You heathen," he said, and we left the spot and ran back to our camp in the cave.

A few years later, I made the hazardous trip again with a party. The weather was beautiful. Not a cloud in the sky; the air was soft and cool. On the open ridges we got a wonderful view — huge white rocks I had never seen before sparkled on the ridge. It was glorious. I took them to visit Ka Awa Ko. There was the altar, but my tin of tobacco was gone. Ku had come and taken it away. I told my story of the offering, then stood by the altar and thanked Ku for his favors. It was clear and beautiful in all directions. We could see the rim of Waimea Canyon and the old volcanic cone of Puka Pele, while out in the ocean, far, far below, like sparkling gems lay the three islands: Niihau, Lehua, and Kauai.

Ku was good to me. So, my friends, if you decided to take a trip some day to the top of Waialeale, carry a small offering with you, and place it reverently on the ancient altar of Ka Awa Ko, sacred to Ku, the ancient Hawaiian god of war.

44

The Ghost Dance on Punchbowl

NO OLD TIMER walks around Punchbowl any more at night. Who doesn't shiver a bit when waning moonlight casts eerie shadows? I don't suppose you believe in ghosts — well, who does? — and yet, sometimes I wonder.

Keoki and I had gone fishing one night, many, many years ago. Always before, we had gotten our nets filled early, but on this evening, the fish wouldn't come near us. It was so late when we got back that Keoki suggested we walk over to his house, which was at the foot of Punchbowl. I could stay the night there.

It had been a beautiful evening. Out on the coral reefs the breezes cooled the soft air, and a full moon tipped the waves with sparkling silver. But as we approached town, I sensed a difference in the atmosphere. The evening was still beautiful, and the moon patterned lovely silhouettes with the shadows of the trees. But everything was so still — almost a hushed, expectant silence. I felt as if I were looking at a painted picture, only I was a part of it.

I turned to my companion. "Keoki," I said, "for goodness sake, say something." Keoki wasn't talking. He was staring. I followed his gaze to the brow of Punchbowl.

"Keoki, what's the matter? I can see only a wisp of smoke. Probably someone living up there has just built a fire. That's nothing."

"Maybe you're right, but I'm remembering what my father told me about smoke over Punchbowl. And it wasn't smoke — it was ghosts! You know about aumakuas, don't you?" I nodded my head. "They are the spirits of dead people — your ancestors and mine — and they're more powerful than you or me or anybody. If somebody does something to hurt you or any of your family, the aumakuas will come and punish that person. They will even kill. They will live in the bodies of those they wish to harm, or they can live inside animals. Did you know that over in Hilo the grandfather of a friend of mine was saved one day by a spirit living in a shark? His canoe upset and this shark brought him safely back to shore. That spirit inside him was the aumakua of his family and protected him from danger."

I glanced again at the shadows on Punchbowl, but there was no trace of smoke now. I felt a little troubled, and also a little annoyed because Keoki had succeeded in disturbing me; but I had to know the story about those wisps of smoke, and Keoki was willing to tell me. This is the strange tale he told me on that night so long ago:

Once upon a time there lived a young ruling chief of Oahu named Kakei. He was strong, daring, and active in all kinds of sports. He could use a spear, a war club, and sling stone better than anyone else. His rough-and-tumble court was filled with restless young men like himself who would fight at a glance. They gambled heavily, winning one day, losing the next. Yet they took all that came along as a matter of course.

Then one day, bored with gambling, Kakei gathered all his young chiefs together and told them to go to their homes and make preparations for a voyage and a battle. The young men were eager for a good fight. Off they went to get ready for it. It was impossible to keep the people from knowing what was going on, and excitement spread all over the island. The best of the old canoes were repaired and repolished. New and stronger canoes were built. The bravest and sturdiest men were selected to fight. Even the women were set to work making tight, strong mat sails for all the canoes. They gathered together all kinds of food and provisions, enough to last for a long, long journey.

Night after night the people talked of nothing but the coming battle. The men wagered heavily as to which of the chief's enemies they were going to fight and how much booty they would take. They speculated on the new lands and the new wealth. Oh, it was going to be a wonderful battle. The days passed swiftly . . . weeks . . . months . . . and finally the chiefs declared they were ready.

The day was set, and every person on the island came to see the gay and joyous departure. It was a splendid sight. The warriors, brilliant in their bright yellow and red war capes, wore proudly their hideous war masks. Waving good-by to their friends, they leaped into the canoes and raised their sails. The great moment had come. The people on shore waved and shouted until the great fleet sailed out of sight.

As soon as the canoes left, they headed north — the destination, Kauai! The night was clear and the wind strong. It was just at dawn, as the first rays of the sun were breaking over the horizon, that Kakei and his army of warriors landed and raised their war cry.

The sleepy village of Waimea was stunned by the unexpected attack. The men, half awake and dazed, tried to stop the invaders, but it was impossible. The battle was short and decisive, and in a very little while many people were killed. The thatched houses were afire, and soon the village was in ruins. Kakei's warriors seized all the plunder they could lay their hands on and pushed the women and children into the canoes. After the captured boats and their own great fleet were filled, they set sail again.

When the victorious band returned home, they spread the booty all over the beach for everyone to admire. Kakei ordered a great feast to be prepared on the slopes of Punchbowl to celebrate the wonderful victory. Everyone was rejoicing and excitement was high. But the women and children who had been taken captives were not happy. They wept quietly among themselves for their lost husbands and homes.

That night, all the people assembled and Kakei and his victorious warriors gathered around the poi bowl, while hula girls danced happily before them.

Suddenly, without warning, the earth shook beneath the crowd. The poi bowls rocked as if tossed on the waters of the sea. The feast was thrown in all directions, and everything danced as if alive. The earth shook again and again, each time more violently. The great rocks on Punchbowl were torn apart and came crashing down the hillside in heavy masses. The people fled screaming in horror.

Then came a mighty earthquake and a roaring blast as the whole side of Punchbowl split wide open. Hot lava poured and and bubbled down the slopes. Masses of steam and foul gases belched through the deep wide cracks of the mountain.

Then a wonderful thing happened. Above the flowing lava, among the settling clouds over the crater, the aumakuas of Kauai moved in a solemn and stately dance. Back and forth — back and forth — keeping rhythm with the bursting gases. This was the ceremonial, sacred dance of the spirits — the family spirits

48

of the captured people. When they finished, they would bring swift punishment to Kakei and his men.

But while the ghosts continued their awful dance, the terrified king hastily collected the stolen plunder and threw it into the captured canoes. Then he brought back the prisoners and put them, too, in the boats, and set sail quickly for the island of Kauai.

And then another miracle happened. As soon as the canoes passed out of sight, the earthquakes stopped. The fires died away, and the flood of lava cooled. The aumakuas had accepted the peace offering of the king.

Keoki and I were close to his home by now. I looked up once more to the brow of Punchbowl. It was there again . . . the wisps of smoke. I shuddered and ran into the house. Those weren't wisps of smoke . . . those were ghosts dancing again!

Sweet Leilehua

ONE day, over a hundred years ago, a young and handsome Hawaiian stood on the crest of the hill at Leahi. He was strong and erect, with the martial bearing of a chief. Upon his head was a helmet of yellow feathers. His clothing was of brown kapa cloth, and on his shoulders lay a small feather cloak. Around his throat was a necklace of shells and shark's teeth, and in his hand a spear of kauila wood. He was Hakuole, one of the bravest of King Kalanikupule's warriors.

Below him lay a dense thicket of hau trees and, a few yards beyond, the white beach of Waikiki. In the blue-green waters which stretched out to the horizon there was only the break of the white reef, on which the waves rolled with the sound of thunder, and here and there a fishing boat.

Hakuole was watching for the first sight of the canoes, for word had come that the great Kamehameha was on his way to attempt the conquest of Oahu, and so complete the subjugation of the eight islands. He had embarked with the veterans of his army, and his fleet of war canoes was speeding him, that very moment, to meet his last, great rival, Kalanikupule.

But Kalanikupule was not caught napping. Watchmen were stationed on Makapuu, Koko Head, and Leahi, and for two nights the shores had been constantly illuminated by the burning of papala sticks. As yet, there was no sign of the great one, but they knew he was on his way, and keen was the anxiety of the people of Oahu.

Hakuole at his lonely post wished they would come. Anything was better than the suspense of waiting. With eyes still turned seaward, he flung himself down wearily under a milo tree, whose quivering leaves seemed like his own heart.

He not only wished to get the battle over to end this tension but also for another, more pressing reason. Hakuole was in love. He longed to declare his love, and — if it was accepted — to marry and take his bride to the house he had built for her. But what could he do? This horrible conflict was impending and who could say what would be the outcome? Who was even sure of surviving?

He lay thinking these unhappy thoughts when suddenly the bushes parted and a face peered through, with large soft brown eyes, olive skin, and wavy black hair. It was Leilehua! Sweet Leilehua — most beautiful of all the maidens of Oahu, daughter of the great kahuna, priest of Lono.

Raising himself and stretching out his arms, he cried, "Leilehua, my Leilehua, my beautiful scarlet flower!" But even as he spoke, she vanished, dropping at his feet a wreath of brilliant lehua. He was perplexed. Had he frightened her away? Had she dropped the lei in her haste, or had she left it for him? He did not know, but he was no longer worried, for he had seen the light in her eyes and knew she loved him. Placing her lei around his neck, he felt as strong as Kamehameha, and vowed aloud, "I will conquer now and live for Sweet Leilehua!"

At that moment a shrill cry pierced the air, "E ala, e ala, e ala-a-a-a—." It was the voice of the lonely watcher far to his left. Then shriller still, like harsh shrieks of sea-birds, followed the blasts from the shell trumpets, waking all the echoes of the dead crater. The startled gulls in the marshes took wing, their cries breaking the peace which had reigned all morning. The horizon and the sea were at once alive with the flash of paddles and swiftly moving outriggers filled with innumerable warriors in feather cloaks and helmets. The sun striking the tips of their spears gave forth darting streaks of light that blinded the anxious watchers. Leading them all was the famous double war canoe *Peleleu*, carrying the mighty chief who was destined to make Hawaii a nation.

Hakuole saw the Hawaiian troops landing unopposed, but he knew Kalanikupule was waiting with his finest warriors on the southern side of the island. It was there that he had chosen to meet his rival among the palis, rather than on level ground. Hakuole hastened to his designated post.

The clash of invader and defender came about as you have heard. Kamehameha finally pushed the defenders of Oahu to their deaths while the sorrow and anguish of the women was voiced in that mournful wail, "Auwe! Auwe!"

But those who were left knew they must make the best of their fate. They said to one another, "Come, let us hasten to take gifts to the new king and pay our homage. Perhaps by so doing he will deal kindly with us and no more wars shall come to our people."

Kamehameha presided over his court with royal splendor, surrounded by all his attendants, when his new subjects came bearing their tributes. After many wonderful presents had been placed before him, Kamakahou, the kahuna, approached the royal couch. He was the father of Leilehua and had been among the advisers of the fallen chiefs, and his reputation was great. He hoped by pleasing the new king to obtain favor for himself. Therefore, he came leading his daughter Leilehua and offered her with these words, "O king, behold the kaikamahine; take her, the light of my eyes, and let there be peace between us."

The beautiful maiden wore a wreath on her head of the lehua flowers from which she had taken her name. She stood for a moment and then fell weeping to her knees and looked at the king with pleading eyes. Kamehameha advanced toward her and the shout began: "Nani loa! Maikai loa! e—" but it ended there, for into the circle strode a young man.

He was covered with blood and dust from the battlefield but stood erect. Around his neck hung a torn garland of flowers—of lehua blossoms. He did not flinch before the gaze of the king, but caught the hand of Leilehua. He lifted her up and, without a word or sign, quickly bore her away.

Silence fell upon the people. Was Hakuole mad? Had he become bewitched? They saw the thunder-cloud on the face of the king. What awful fate had the young warrior brought upon himself? Would he be offered as a sacrificed, clubbed to death, burned, or buried alive?

Guards seized the youth and the maiden and brought them back before the king.

"E Hakuole, so you are tired of life, tired of fighting. You dream already of maiden's eyes and a life among the nala. You would let the prows rot on the beach, seeking no more for the glory a man ought to love. Well, as you mean to stay among the wahine, and love a maiden here more than you fear me, I suspend you from a soldier's duty till the moon, Ikiiki, returns. Away! And for the girl Leilehua, the faithful in love, all the lands which were her father's are hers from henceforth. Take the kaikamahine—beautiful she is as the morning breaking the shadows—and may the loves of Leilehua and Hakuole be as glorious to Hawaii as the wars of Kamehameha."

As he spoke these words, Kamehameha the Great won not only obedience from his people but won their hearts, forever.

The Poison Goddess of Molokai

KANEAKAMA was as handsome a young fellow as could be found on the eight islands. He was skilled in the arts of war and the learning of the priests. However, he had one bad habit—he was a gambler.

One day, long ago, he was lying in his grass hut on the slopes of Olukui. A deep frown creased his forehead and occasionally he sighed. Kaneakama was sad. He had been playing maika all day long and luck had been against him. Throw the smooth black stones as he might, they would not go straight. "Surely the devil himself is inside them," he thought. He had tried and tried but today he had lost everything he owned. Everything but his pig—a miserable little scrawny black pig.

"Why didn't he stake the pig?" Ah! Kaneakama had been asking himself the same question. Each time the thought came to him, he repelled it, saying, "I will not be tempted by the evil ones. Begone from my head, O wicked thought!" You see, he had dedicated this pig to his aumakua or guardian goddess. Kaneakama was a bit of a rascal, as I've told you, but though the fellow had his faults he was too pious to break a vow to the gods.

As he lay feeling sorry for himself, his eyes closed and, without really intending to, he fell asleep.

As he slept, he had a wonderful vision. In the midst of an aura of light stood the loveliest maiden he had ever seen.

While he gazed, spellbound, the goddess spoke. "I command you, Kaneakama! Take your pig and stake it

54

in the maika game."

The glorious vision vanished. Kaneakama lay dazed for a long time.

The very next day he did as he had been told. Certainly the command of a goddess took precedent over a mortal conscience.

Well, he played maika all that day and if he had had the worst of luck the day before, this day he had the best. When darkness came he returned to his hut a very rich man indeed, and he knew that he owed his good fortune to the goddess of his dream. So he said to himself, "I will dedicate one-half of my newly gained riches to the service of the goddess and build a temple where she may dwell and receive my worship."

When the temple was finished except for its central idol, the vision of the aumakua came to him again. She addressed him in a wonderfully sweet voice, saying, "Tell the king that the akua wish to dwell in the temple of his court. He shall have great power for sheltering them. Let him send warriors to the top of Maunaloa to hew an image out of the tree they find there. This shall be my shrine in the heiau you have built. There you shall be my high priest—the worshipper and lover of Kalaipahoa the terrible, who is dreaded by all mortals."

When Kaneakama had told the king, the king was so pleased that he chose three hundred of his bravest men and armed them with axes, knives, and many folds of kapa cloth. Commanded by Kaneakama, they set out to find the spot designated in his dream.

No man walked with quiet in his heart. Had they not heard of Kalaipahoa? She it was who had come to Molokai long ago and made her home on Maunaloa. There the earth was burnt and blackened. There also was the dwelling place of Laamaomao, god of all the winds.

55

Some of the winds often broke loose from the god's calabash and hurled intruders far off into the Paiolo Channel.

Still the men went onward, and each step tightened the icy wall about their hearts. After hours of climbing, they came to the forest belt, and there the silver kukui leaves seemed to quiver sympathetically. They traveled on to the black lava slopes and at last before them, half hidden by mist, lay the huge extinct crater. The mist parted as they went downward until they saw a great black blotch of ground. The only whiteness was that of the bleached and glistening bones of the victims of the evil power found here. In the very center of this place of death strangely enough there grew a tree, erect and verdantly green, with thick foliage. As they gazed in wonder, several birds flew toward this inviting resting place, but alas, as each one reached the edge of the black circle, it fell to earth and died instantly.

The men watched with horror and said to one another, "It is true; her very breath is death to any living thing!"

One hundred men turned from the sight and ran blindly down the mountainside, stumbling and screaming in their terror. Kaneakama commanded twenty of the remaining warriors to take their axes and advance toward the tree. But when they had gone but twenty yards, they fell lifeless. Five times he sent fresh detachments forward, moving in a circle. Five times they perished, until their bodies formed five circles about the tree.

Then Kaneakama forced half of the remaining hundred to swathe themselves in the kapa cloth, and with this protection they were able to reach the tree. But as each man struck his first blow, he toppled over and died. However, as the last ax cut into the wood, the tree fell with a deafening roar. The remaining warriors (still wrapped in kapa) cut away the branches, working feverishly, as men continued to faint constantly all around them. Soon the rough shape of an idol was ready to be carried back to the heiau.

There was great rejoicing at court when the idol was placed in the shrine, which was then dedicated with many human sacrifices. The rejoicing and excitement of all the people combined was small indeed compared to the unearthly joy of Kaneakama as he assumed his duties as high priest and lover of the goddess.

For as he ministered before the shrine he did not see the horrible idol and its distended mouth with hideous rows of shark's teeth. He saw instead the celestial beauty of the maiden of his visions. To others she was terrible and worshipped with fear, but to him she was always gracious and breathtakingly beautiful.

For a long time Kaneakama asked no more than to be allowed to wait upon the shrine and perform all the accustomed rites. Finally, however, he longed for a sign. Pele, the volcano goddess, had had a mortal lover and had come down to earth to dwell. Why shouldn't *his* goddess give him at least a sign? He began to envy rather than pity all those who had died for her.

But one day the sign came! He had a dream in which he seemed to be in Paliuli, the elysian land. He saw Kalaipahoa in all her radiance, surrounded by the men who had perished shaping the idol.

"O Kalaipahoa," he cried, "why do these serfs who died at Maunaloa stand in thy presence and see thy face, while I who toil always in thy service have no reward?"

"Foolish mortal!" she said, smiling upon him.

"The great chiefs have their 'companions in death,' but *your* household has gone before you. You shall have your reward tonight."

She bade him bring the puhenehene board and play the gambling game. Alas! such was his confusion that he lost every game and soon had nothing left to stake. "Stake yourself!" cried Kalaipahoa. Once more the stones were thrown and once more he lost. The vision vanished—still smiling at poor, confused Kaneakama.

"What does it matter?" said Kaneakama sadly. "I am the lover of the goddess; I will die. I will prepare an offering for her, place bananas in her hands and then *share* her feast. It may be she will at last bid me to come and sit at her feet."

He prepared his offering and dared to eat the food he had presented to the goddess. From her hands he must have received the gift of death, for when the temple slaves came next morning to the heiau, there before the shrine lay the lover of the goddess —dead, but with a look in his eyes of celestial joy!

My First Encounter with a Wild Bull

THE fire was beginning to crackle in the old fireplace, and the candles were being lit as we rose from the dinner table and wandered into the big living room.

That day, we had been for a long ride away over into the Kumewela woods, and in a little grassy glade had found tracks of wild cattle and a place where a big bull had been pawing the ground, exercising his fighting muscles.

58

The little children had become very excited. There were not a great many of the big bulls left in the mountains. They had been hunted for many years, and it was only a matter of time before the wild cattle would be exterminated.

As we sat down around the fire, Val, my little boy of eight, said, "Papa, when you were a little boy, did you ever see a wild bull?"

"Yes, I did," I replied, "and I was about your age at the time when I went to hunt a bull. I will tell you about the big red bull that lived near the lime trees."

Val sat on the floor at my feet and listened intently while I told him this story:

Over on the western side of the high divide of Kauai, some unknown man had planted lime trees many long years ago. One day we went for a walk to gather limes, and as we descended the slopes of the hills we came upon fresh cattle tracks that looked as if some big bull had made his home there under the big koa trees.

"A big bull," I thought to myself, "living alone in the deep woods! How I would love to see him!" So I kept my eyes wide open, hoping to get a glimpse of him, but no bull was near and we finally returned home. As I walked along farther, I noted the trail well, and for days I kept thinking of the bull.

One day I sneaked out of camp alone and headed for the lime trees. I just had to find that bull!

After an hour's walk, I was at the top of the divide. I left the main trail and headed down the western slope through the old forest. The koa trees were enormous and a deep shade covered the woods, but I knew my way and kept sliding as noiselessly as I could, on the alert all the time, expecting every minute to see the bull. But the woods were empty. Finally, I came near

the lime trees, and just as I was despairing of ever seeing anything, I spied a big red bull standing in the shade
of the trees. He was a huge old fellow, and as I lay on
the ferns and watched him, I noticed that his eyes were
closed. He seemed to be sound asleep. I had a mad desire to get nearer to him. I dropped to the ground and
crawled on my stomach until I was within a hundred
feet of him, when I saw a big log lying next to him.
Carefully, quietly, I slid along and finally got behind
the log. I peeked over and there he was, standing not
twenty feet away. He was a beautiful bull. He had once,
no doubt, been king of the herd, but had been driven
out and was spending the last years of his life in this
quiet spot. I lay and watched him, his huge neck and
shoulders and his big sharp horns—still a grand old
fighter.

Suddenly, he opened his big red eyes and looked right
at me. He saw me, I know, for his face took on a queer
look and a slight quiver went through him.

A queer feeling went through me also, as I realized
that I was only a very little boy lying behind an old rot-
ten log, and I knew it was useless to try and run; he was
too close. I lay and trembled, and then I remembered
that I had heard my father say that wild animals are terribly frightened of the human voice. I would test that
remark. I let out a bloodcurdling yell.

The effect was wonderful. The huge bull made one
mighty jump right up into the air, and instead of coming for me, he headed the other way with his tail in the
air. Away he went—full speed—into the jungle below!
My, what speed he had! He simply tore along the
ground; in and out of the big trees he flashed, breaking
the dead branches underfoot with the sound of thunder.

In a few minutes he was out of sight, and I was left

alone, a little boy lying by a log in the deep forest. I had scared the big bull out of his wits. My, I felt proud! I jumped up and hastened back to camp. I had seen a bull and beaten him. I was a hero!

Mrs. Naumu Goes to the King's Birthday Party

MRS. NAUMU lived in Waimea, the town made famous by Captain Cook, discoverer of the Sandwich Isles that later became known as the Hawaiian Islands. She was a prosperous old lady, quite high in native society, and proudly claimed descent from some old chief's family, though we children thought her only claim to fame lay in the fact that at fifty years of age she was enormously fat, weighing at least three hundred pounds.

One day my sister Ida had a toothache, and my father decided to take her to the dentist in Honolulu. They rode horseback the thirty-five miles to Nawiliwili, where they were to board the old steamer, *Kilauea.*

Out at anchorage in the bay lay the steamer, rolling in the great swells that were striking the shore. At five o'clock the captain called, "All aboard!" And the passengers were helped into the ship's big rowboat and rowed out to the steamer.

In the boat sat Mrs. Naumu. She was in high spirits, for she had received an invitation to attend the big luau that King Kalakaua was giving to celebrate his birthday.

The small boat drew alongside the steamer, and

the passengers, one by one, climbed up the steep little ladder. It came Mrs. Naumu's turn. Two big boatmen helped her onto the ladder. She grasped the ropes, and the steamer rolled up, the rowboat moved out. There she hung for a moment; then, letting out a scream, she fell like a stone into the ocean, between the steamer and the rowboat.

When she came to the surface, they managed to haul her into the boat. And when the rowboat was hoisted up on the davits, they hoisted the old lady with it.

Mrs. Naumu then opened her bag, took out a large plush holoku and a pair of fancy buttoned boots, and was soon quite happy again in these dry clothes. The steamer pulled up anchor and hauled away for Honolulu, plunging and tossing in a lively sea as night came on. The crossing was very rough.

Ida had a cabin opening on the deck, whereas all the Hawaiians slept on deck. About midnight a great shout went up. Mrs. Naumu had fallen overboard!

Ida called father, and there was great excitement. The steamer stopped and a boat was lowered and rowed away into the black night, looking for the passenger. An hour went by. People were getting anxious, when the click of oars was heard. Up came the rowboat, and calmly sitting in it was our friend Mrs. Naumu. The boat was hoisted again on the davits, and soon she was back again on deck among her friends.

When the boat found her, Mrs. Naumu was swimming along towards the steamer lights. In her hand she held a large bundle. She had taken off the silk stockings, her fancy buttoned boots, and her plush holoku, and had rolled them into a neat bundle.

"Weren't you terribly frightened, and are you hurt?" asked my sister. "Oh, no," she replied. "That was nothing. The only pilikia is that I have ruined my lovely plush holoku and will have nothing to wear tomorrow to the king's birthday party! Auwe!"

Lepe, the Bird Maiden

THIS is the story they told long ago about Lepe, who changed from a little bird into a beautiful maiden, and of Kauilani, her brother, who had a magic girdle and a magic spear.

Now Lepe was born in the form of an egg, and when her father, Chief Keahua of Kauai, knew what had happened, he cried, "Throw the egg into the sea . . . offer it to the sea-monster . . . get rid of it . . . throw it away!" But the mother begged to save it. And while they argued about what should be done with it, Palama, the grandmother, arrived in a canoe from another island. She said, "Give the egg to me. If I have it, then you both should be pleased. Keahua will not have to see it, yet my daughter will know that it is safe in my hands. Let me keep it, and we shall see what becomes of it." She took the egg in the great canoe with her and returned to the island of Oahu.

When she returned home, she told her husband what had happened, and together they decided there must be something very strange and unusual about the egg.

"Let us build a house of the finest grasses and forbid

anyone to enter it. There we will leave the egg and see what happens," the husband suggested.

They gathered the finest grasses and built a little house. Inside they placed beautiful tapa cloth for a bed, and put garlands of vines about the walls. Then they wrapped the egg in the softest tapa and left it there.

Day after day, Palama went to the little house and peered inside. For a long, long time, nothing happened; but one day when she raised the mat at the door and looked within, what do you think she saw? A wonderful bird, and the most beautiful one you can imagine, had been hatched from the precious egg. Every kind of feather she had ever seen on any bird was upon this one. All the colors of the rainbow, and many other shades as well.

Palama called excitedly to her husband to come and see. Then, moving gently, so as not to frighten the bird, they fed it cooked sweet potato. "What shall we name it?" Palama whispered. "Let us call it Lepe," replied her husband. After the bird had eaten, it went to sleep, tucking its head under its beautiful little wing.

Now, there was a sorceress of the sky known as Keaolewa,* or Moving Cloud. She came to Palama and her husband in the form of a woman, and told them that she was going to make a bathing pool for Lepe. And she did.

It was a nice pool, and near the seashore. The bird enjoyed the pool and would go to the edge, ruffle its gorgeous feathers, drink of the clear water, and then go in and really swim and dive and splash about, just as you probably have many times. When it was tired of playing in the pool, it would fly into a nearby tree and sit in the sun to dry its bright feathers. When the sun had warmed and dried it thoroughly, the bird would fly into the little grass house Palama and her husband had made, cover itself with the soft tapa, and go to sleep.

Now, one day the bird flew to the pool as usual, but when the water touched its feathers a startling thing happened. The beautiful bird with the wonderful plumage became a young girl, a lovely young girl. For a moment or two, she stood by the bathing pool and looked at herself reflected in the water, and then she hurried into her own little house and stretched herself out on the tapa, with her face buried to the ground, and cried out to Palama.

Palama and her husband were in their own house, but they heard the voice that sounded like a small child's voice, and they said to each other: "Who can that be? What does she say?" They listened intently and again came the cry, "Oh, where are you? Won't you please come to me?"

Palama jumped up with surprise. "Why, that voice comes from the house we made for Lepe. Let us hurry!" When they lifted the mat and looked within, there lay the beautiful young girl on the soft tapa cloth. "Can it be that Lepe has become a girl?" they cried.

How glad they were that they had kept the fragile egg and cherished the beautiful bird. Palama brought the girl her choicest tapa for a skirt, and the sorceress of the sky gave her a wreath of green feathers that she always wore.

And now Lepe, the bird maiden, had two bodies. In one of them she was a bright feathered bird, and in the other she was such a beautiful girl that a radiance surrounded her, bringing joy and happiness to Palama and her husband.

Now, during all this time, another child had been born to Lepe's parents—a little boy who was not very strong. Finally they decided to take him to Waiui, the Wondrous Water, and they bathed him in it. Immediately the little fellow began to grow, and soon he had both the strength and the size of a man, although he was still just a boy in years. Kauilani was his name.

One day his proud father looked at him and said, "My son, you have now become a man. Soon you will be able to help me against the monster who killed my people and drove me from my lands." Kauilani was pleased with what his father had said and straightway went forth to do battle with the enemy.

His father had given him a magic girdle and a magic spear to aid him in the fierce battle. The girdle added strength to Kauilani's own great strength and the spear had belonged to his famed ancestors. When his father gave him the magic spear, he said, "Koawi koawa is its name. I will tell you how to use it."

Then with the magic girdle about his waist and with the magic spear in his hand, Kauilani went down to the seashore. The great monster came out of the sea and after him. Kauilani twirled his spear in his hand and chanted, "O Koawi koawa, strike! Strike for the lives of us two!"

Again and again the magic spear struck at Akuapehuale, the monster, until he finally fell dead. Then Kauilani made a great fire and burned his body. The smoke rose and drifted along the precipice, and Keahua saw it and knew his enemy had been killed. With great joy he returned to his home and prepared a feast for his victorious son.

As a reward, his parents gave Kauilani a fine feather cape to wear with his magic girdle, and then the boy decided he would go in search of the sister whom he had never seen. He took his magic spear and started toward the sea. With great care, he laid his spear upon the water, and then he stood upon it and the spear carried him over the waves like a flying fish and across the sea, speeding from Kauai to Oahu in no time!

When he reached the beach, he flung the spear from him, not realizing how strong he was, and it sped through the air and went flying along until it came near two women. And there it plummeted to earth.

When the women had examined the wonderful weapon with the polished shaft and head, they decided to hide it for safekeeping. Then they went about their work as usual.

It wasn't long before Kauilani came along their way and asked if they had seen his companion. "No traveler has passed this road," they answered.

Then he asked them if they had seen a spear traveling by itself. Again they told him "No," but Kauilani was suspicous and he asked them, "Have you hidden my spear?"

"What are you talking about?" they said.

Then Kauilani called out in a loud voice, "Koawikoawa, Koawikoawa" and a sharp voice answered, "Here I am! Here I am!" From its hiding place it came, and once more Kauilani took it up.

Kauilani threatened the spear. "If you leave me again or get lost, when I find you, I will break you."

"You must not injure me," the spear replied. "If you do, your travels will come to nothing. But if you lay me upon the beach and step upon me, I will take you to your sister."

When they had traveled some distance, the spear dropped once more to the ground, and said to Kauilani, "See that great wiliwili tree standing near the sea, leaning out over the water? Climb to the top of it and look along the beach until you see a bright rainbow over the water. Under the arch of the rainbow is a beautiful girl catching fish and gathering seaweed for her grandparents. She is your sister Lepe."

Now, as I have said before, Lepe's beauty when she was in her girl's body was so radiant that the very colors of the rainbow rested in the air around her. Rainbows stayed over her little house when she was in it, arched over the pool when she bathed in it, and followed her everywhere.

Of course, Kauilani saw his sister when he had climbed to the top of the great wiliwili tree, and he was anxious to make himself known to her. He ran to the house of his grandparents and told them who he was. They were glad and happy to have him with them, but when he said that he had come to see his sister, they told him he must be patient awhile.

Palama, his grandmother, pointed out the little grass house where Lepe lived, but warned him, "You must not go into the house; that is forbidden to all except herself. When she is asleep, then you must catch her and hold her until she is willing to accept you as her brother. And while you hold her, I will chant for your good luck."

Poor Kauilani could not understand the strange procedure, but he dared not ask too many questions and he decided to do as he was told.

Lepe was changed into her bird body when first her brother saw her asleep. Quietly he tiptoed into the grass house and held her in his hands. But she struggled free and flew out of the house and high into the air. Swiftly she flew until the incantation that her grandmother was making came up through the air to her; then she began to fly more slowly.

Her grandmother's chant told of her brother's victories on Kauai—how he had killed the sea monster and restored his father's lands. Slowly she flew and finally circled around and around until she was near Kauilani. "Who are you?" she asked. "Where did you come from?"

Eagerly Kauilani answered, "I came from Kauai, the land of our father. I am Kauilani, your younger brother."

Love for the brother she had never known came to her then, and she changed from her bird form and stood before him, his beautiful sister. And so they lived with their grandparents on Oahu: Kauilani, with his feather cape, magic girdle, and magic spear; and Lepe, who remained a girl, never again becoming the beautiful bird she had been.

An Incident in the Niihau Channel

IT HAD been an unusually stormy winter. First came the kona storms with rain and wind and blinding lightning, blowing up from the equator and filling the mountains with fog and water. Then came the cold gales from the north (the kiu it was called by the Hawaiians) and it came with a roar and a rush, slamming doors, rattling windows, bending the tall palms almost double, and making us all shiver. The wide ocean channel between Niihau and Kauai had been slashed into a turmoil for months, and I sometimes wondered, when I gazed across the strip of angry water, if it would ever lie smooth and sparkling again.

But finally the summer months came on, the trade

winds began to blow steadily once more, and the channel quieted down. The water was a ribbon of blue and rippled lazily in the sun. Now the Niihau boat could cross again in safety. You can imagine our joy when one morning Kapahe, the big kanaka captain of the boat, walked in, and handed mother a letter from Grandma Sinclair, inviting us all over to Niihau to pay her a visit.

Of course we could go! There was great excitement among us children. What fun it would be! Mama and Papa had a hard time keeping us under control during the week of preparation for the journey. We began getting ready, sorting and packing and working like beavers.

At the end of the week, back came the big whaleboat, and word was sent for us to meet it at Pupu Pakai, a tiny little landing place on the shore below Kekaha. The boat was to leave at three o'clock in the morning, so we were all put to bed and everything made ready to leave. It was dark as pitch when Makae, our nurse, came along with a lantern and called to us children.

"Get up," she cried. "We're off for Niihau. Wiki-wiki! The carriage is ready and loaded."

We tumbled out in a hurry and hustled into our clothes. Not much sleep that night; we were too excited. We were off to Niihau to visit our jolly Scotch grandmother, and it had been a long time since we had last seen her.

It was very dark when we started out. There were no street lights in those days but, thank goodness, it was only a short way, and the kanaka boys with their sharp eyes had no difficulty in finding the landing. Sure enough, lying there with her bow just touching the sand, was the big boat.

As our carriage loomed up in the darkness, the crew ran up and unloaded our baggage and stowed it on board. Then they sat down and all began to smoke and talk.

We all sat on the sand and waited for the word to go, but no one made a move and finally mother said, "What's the pilikia? What are you waiting for? Let's be off!"

At that, old Makae came over to us. She had been sitting and gossiping with the boatmen. "If you give the order, we will go at once," she said. "But the sea has come up and a nasty surf is breaking on the reef. The channel is narrow, as you know, and hard to follow because it is so dark. The crew is afraid the boat might be swamped going out, and then it would be hard to find the little children, as we would have to feel about for them in the holes in the reef—so if you don't mind waiting, we will go out at dawn. Hoomanawa nui— have patience," she said. So hoomanawa nui we did.

The grownups gathered in little groups on the landing to await daybreak. Some of us children curled up nearby and went to sleep. I remember how the murmur of soft Hawaiian voices in the darkness and the creaking of the boat against the pier drifted in and out of my consciousness. I lay on my back with my arms under my head and tried to count the stars until my eyes blinked with sleepiness and they became only pinpoints of silver light that pricked my tired eyelids. Then I turned over and snuggled against Papa's warm thigh and soon was fast asleep.

Dawn came, and the sea quieted a bit. Kapahe, the captain, gave the word. "On board, everyone!" All of us children awoke with a start when the big Hawaiian boys picked us up and tossed us into the boat. In no time at all, we were on our way. The little night clouds were scurrying across the sky, trying in vain to escape the sunrise. Already the eastern sky was pink from the sun that was still hidden beyond the horizon. We slipped down the channel and through the outer breakers into the open sea.

It was getting light rapidly, and we could begin to see into the distance. Suddenly, to our surprise we saw the dark silhouette of another boat anchored outside. It was a big boat and belonged to some natives living in Waimea. As we came nearer, we could see that it was loaded to the gunwale with men, women, children, and household goods. They had come down from Waimea to join us, and called to us as we came alongside, asking permission to go with us as it was a long way over and the sea was liable to get rough again.

The captain turned to my mother, who gave her consent, and the two big boats then started off on the twenty-mile trip to Niihau—the little island that had been bought by my grandmother during the reign of Kamehameha V and that could now be seen in the early daylight, lying serene and peaceful across the channel.

The old whaleboat was heavy in the water, and we made slow progress. Soon the wind began to blow. It whipped our clothes and buffeted us. I watched the women's and girls' hair blow about their heads and in their eyes, and laughed to see them twist and turn this way and that to keep a clear vision. The men worked feverishly to make everything fast. Stronger and stronger came the wind. It whistled and moaned in its fury, and stirred the sea into mountainous waves that crashed against the boat's sides and pitched and tossed us about like a feather in the breeze. Only when we were lifted on the crest of a huge comber could we see the other boat that was traveling with us.

None of the Hawaiians seemed too concerned about the storm that raged about us. They still laughed and called to each other above the noise the wild winds made. But some of us began to feel a little upset and wished the sea would calm a bit. It wasn't nearly as much fun as we had thought it would be. Secretly, I longed to be safe and sound with my little Scotch grandmother, who was waiting for us on Niihau. As we looked across the tumbling sea, the island seemed unusually far away, and we seemed to be making no headway against the wind and sea.

"Will we ever get there?" I wondered. Just as I was questioning in my mind, along came an extra big comber. High—high—high into the air we were lifted, until it seemed we were suspended in space; and in that fraction of a moment we all saw with horror that the other boat had been swamped by the same huge wave. Our boat wallowed around in the sea—it seemed like hours—before another big comber caught us and carried us on its crest so that we could see the swamped boat once more. All the Hawaiians were in the sea, some holding the boat's bow against the wind, some bailing. Captain Kapahe and his men steered our boat as close as possible so that we might help, if it became necessary.

In the swamped boat, we could see a little girl two and a half or three years of age. She was wide-eyed and smiling, and not at all afraid. Suddenly, another great wave rolled over the boat, and we all gasped with fright. The little girl had been swept into the boiling sea.

My mother was frantic. What would become of that tiny child in such a sea? "Save your child!" she cried to the big kanaka woman who was swimming near the boat. "There! There she is! Save her!" my mother called.

"Oh, never mind her," the child's mother calmly replied. "She's all right. She won't sink, but this will!" With a laugh, she held up huge iron kettle for all of us to see. She was treading water and holding the kettle she had bought in Waimea and was taking home to Niihau. It was a great treasure. Most likely there was not one like it on all the island of Niihau.

We all kept our eyes on the big waves, trying to locate the little girl, but we couldn't see a thing of her. No one seemed unduly concerned, but I kept remembering her big eyes and her smile and didn't want anything to happen to her. My mother watched anxiously at my side, but we couldn't see her anywhere.

Finally the Hawaiians succeeded in bailing out the boat, and all climbed aboard. The precious iron pot was safely lifted up, and then the mother turned to look for her baby. Just then a huge wave curled over and there in the foam was the child, paddling around in her watery cradle. With one big brown arm, the mother reached for her and gathered her safely to her ample bosom. The little girl and her mother were then pulled into the boat. As the child was bundled into an old coat, she smiled and waved at us. Why had we worried? She hadn't been afraid. We continued on towards Niihau without further mishap.

Maui Fishes Up an Island

MAUI sat in front of his mother's house sulking. He wasn't at all happy. He had just come back from the beach, where he had watched his brothers go off in their canoe for a fishing trip. And they wouldn't take him with them.

"Lazy!" yelled one of them. "Shiftless!" jeered another. "Lazy and shiftless, lazy and shiftless!" they teased in singsong fashion until they were away out in the water and Maui couldn't hear them any more.

Maui sighed and poked viciously at the insects crawling around on the ground. Even his mother had no time for him, because she was busy making tapa cloth. It wasn't as if Maui cared that his brothers wouldn't play with him—at least that's what he said to himself—but he did wish somebody would pay just a little attention to him once in awhile. He liked to go fishing, but it really was true that he didn't catch very many fish—and that's why his brothers called him lazy and shiftless.

The fact of the matter was that the brothers were jealous of Maui. He could do such marvelous things. He lifted the sky one day, and another time he killed Puna, the great eel. And he could outrun his brothers and surpass everybody at any kind of sport. For Maui, the only one in the family to be so gifted, was born with supernatural powers.

Of course the family never complained about the good things that Maui did. No, that was a different story. He invented a barb to put on the end of a spear so that the fish wouldn't wriggle off. The barb worked with birds, too. But those things didn't help Maui now. As he sat there feeling sorry for himself, he heard a sudden commotion at the back of the house. He ran to see what it was, and found two of his mother's sacred alae birds fighting over a scrap of food. In fact, one of the birds was almost dead, and while Maui busied himself quieting things down a wonderful idea came to him.

"I'm going to do some fishing," he declared to himself. "Maybe I can't catch ulua and pimoe like my brothers can, but I'm going to fish for something at the bottom of the sea that they could never catch. I'll show them how to really fish."

Maui continued to mumble to himself while he decided what he needed for his wonderful catch. Everything had to be selected with great care. First came the fish-hook. That had to be very special indeed — like no other fish-hook in the whole world. In those days, all the hooks were made out of bone, and the kind that Maui wanted wasn't even on the earth. It was way down in the underworld. And it belonged to a strange creature. It not only belonged to her, it was part of her.

Maui set off to the underworld. It didn't take him long to find the old woman; she was so unusual that everyone knew her. Part of her was dead, and the other part alive. From the side of her that was dead, Maui took a bone — her jawbone — and out of this he made his fish-hook. Maui was very proud of his hook, but he wasn't ready yet to show it to anyone, or to tell anyone what he was doing.

Next came the bait. This had to be selected just as carefully as the hook. It had to be magic bait, and different from anything ever used in the world before. Maui thought and thought. As he neared his house, he heard the sacred alae birds quarreling again. "Just the thing," he murmured. "Besides, if I take one," he excused himself, "they might stop fighting."

Now he was practically ready. Just one more thing— a line, a good strong line. But that was easy to get. He took the strongest of the olona vines and wove them carefully and tightly into a line as strong as steel. And now for the great catch!

Shoving his hook and bait into his basket, Maui once more went down to the beach. His brothers were there getting ready to go fishing again. "Here is Maui," they laughed scornfully. "Here is Maui, come to go fishing. And what do you expect to catch?" they mocked.

"Let me go with you," begged Maui.

"No," cried the brothers, and pushed their canoe into the water and paddled away before Maui could jump in. This time, though, the brothers weren't so lucky with their fishing. After spending a long time out in the water, they were forced to come back, and they had not caught even one fish. To add to their discomfort, who should be patiently waiting for them on the beach but Maui.

Much to their surprise, though, Maui did not tease them. He just begged them to go out again and take him with them. Finally they consented, and Maui leaped into the canoe and away they all went.

They had paddled for about a half an hour, and the brothers thought they had gone far enough, but not Maui. "Further, my brothers, further out. That is where the ulua and the pimoe are." So they paddled a little longer.

The brothers let down their lines and waited and waited, but no fish came. They were beginning to get fretful. They turned to Maui and started to scold him again. "Where are the ulua and pimoe that you were talking about?" they demanded.

"Not yet," answered Maui. "We must go still further." So the brothers paddled out into the sea until they were almost exhausted. "Let's go back," they wailed. "We still haven't caught anything."

The only answer Maui gave to that was to hoist a sail on the canoe. With the wind behind them, they sailed far, far out into the ocean. One of the brothers let down a line. In a few moments he felt a heavy tug on it. It was only a shark. They had to cut their line to let it go free. Bitterly disappointed, they turned on Maui. "You are just as lazy and shiftless as you ever were," they grumbled. "What are we going to do now? You've brought us way out in the ocean and you haven't helped us a bit."

Maui listened for a minute. "Wait," he said. "I will show you something." He reached into his pocket and brought out the magic hook—the hook that was baited with the struggling alae bird. The brothers were fascinated. They watched the line sink into the water. Down it went—deeper and deeper until they could no longer see the bait. But still it sank until it reached the bottom of the sea.

Here lived Kaunihokahi, Old One Tooth, whose duty it was to hold the land securely to the bottom of the sea. When the sacred bird came near him he took it in his mouth. And the magic hook that Maui had made was held fast in his jaws.

Maui quickly fastened the line to the canoe. Soon he felt a pull on his line. "Now!" he cried excitedly to his brothers. "Paddle as hard as you can! Hurry!" The pull on the line was so heavy that Maui had to help paddle too. They all felt a great weight on the canoe. It grew heavier and heavier until the brothers could hardly make the canoe move at all. "Help us, Maui," they begged. "We can't pull much longer."

Then Maui began to chant a magic verse. As he chanted, the brothers could feel the great weight move with them. It was a little easier now. And they struggled on, laboring against the terrific load behind the canoe. At last, one of the brothers, resting himself, turned and looked behind him. He screamed in terror. Frantically he clenched Maui's arm and pointed a shaking finger at what he saw.

Behind them, a huge land mass was rising out of the water. Land and mountains! It was wonderful! Unbelievable! But then something else happened. One of the brothers, weak from astonishment, dropped his paddle. It fell on the line that was fastened to the jaws of old Kaunihokahi and the line snapped. The land, that had not yet come to the top of the water, broke and fell back to the bottom of the sea. Thus it was that Maui pulled up only an island. If the line hadn't broken, he would have brought up a whole continent, and all the eight islands that we now today would have been joined in one. At any rate, this great deed of Maui's was a wonderful bit of fishing, you must agree!

A Kauai Kahuna in Yellowstone Park

THE summer of 1927 found me wandering over the northwest on a sightseeing tour, accompanied by my son Val and my two little girls, Anne and Betsy.

Starting out from Hawaii on a great white ocean

liner, we thought we were going to visit only a few states. But upon our arrival in San Francisco, the children decided we were going to see a great deal more of our beloved land than I had first planned. And so we kept on and on, until finally one day we found ourselves in the famous Yellowstone National Park. This weird place with its spouting geysers, springs, and oddities of nature fascinated my family, and we decided to stay a while, taking up our abode in the beautiful Old Faithful Inn.

I had been there before, and took great pleasure in showing the places of interest to the youngsters. Some geysers were the same; some, like the Giant, that had played for me twenty-three years before, were dormant. A new one, known as the Grand, was then the largest and most active.

While staying at the Inn, we met many interesting people. A young doctor and his bride from Maryland became our companions, and together we explored the wonders of the Park.

Everyone we talked to agreed that the Grand was the finest geyser and the most spectacular, but no one knew when it played. When I asked the hotel clerk, he referred me to the head wrangler. Out we went to the yard where the riding horses were kept. Of course, the man agreed that the Grand was grand, indeed, but he couldn't say when it would shoot again, for it was as unpredictable as the most temperamental glamor girl.

"It played about four days ago, and it might go off today, anytime between two o'clock and midnight," he said, but that was the best he could do for us.

Lunchtime came, and I noticed that the dining room was all too small to accommodate the crowd of diners.

They were standing in line. I asked the head waiter if he could save me a table for dinner. At first he gave me an emphatic "No!" But when I slipped him a nice crisp bill he agreed to hold a table until six-thirty, but not a minute later.

We motored over to the Grand and took a look. It was two o'clock, and the big pool lay simmering in its heat, but with no sign of active life. We waited an hour. At three o'clock, a big ranger and several hundred tourists came along.

"Say, ranger," we called to him, "when is it going to play?"

He stood over it and listened. Then he shook his head and said, "Not a chance. Not a murmur in the pool. She won't play today." And with his party of disappointed tourists, he turned away.

"What's the use of staying?" my son Val inquired. "There's no use waiting around any longer. Let's go!"

We had just about decided to leave the Grand when Betsy noticed that our friends, the doctor and his bride, had taken out their books and were sitting down to read and wait a while longer.

"We will look at some of the smaller geysers," I told them. "But we'll be back around six o'clock."

When we returned, the doctor and his wife were still there. It was nearly six o'clock and still the Grand showed no signs of activity. I looked over at the hotel and thought of the table reserved for us. I knew the youngsters were hungry, too. Something had to be done!

Then I remembered the old Hawaiian kahuna of Polihale who taught me years ago how to make an altar and how to pray to the ancient gods of Kauai. The old kanakas, or Hawaiians, once called me a kahuna. Aha! I

81

had an inspiration. I would be one again!

So I said to the doctor, "Have you ever heard of Pele, the great goddess of the volcanoes who lives in Halemaumau? She is very powerful, and her jurisdiction extends all the way from Hawaii to the faraway island of New Zealand. We, in Hawaii, believe in her, and I haven't the slightest doubt that her power extends to the volcanic lands of the Yellowstone."

Then I walked over to the simmering pool of the Grand and began building a small pyramid of rocks, even as I had seen the old kanaka priest build his, and on top I placed a coin and sealed it with a pebble. As I built, Anne and Betsy also built two small ones. Being little girls, and not liable to arrest, they broke off flowers and capped their altars, as we do in Hawaii.

Standing by my altar, I called out in my best Hawaiian, "O Kane! O Lono! O Pele! Wahine Hookanu, kokua mai nei keia keiki o Kauai, etc., etc.," asking her to make the geyser spout and to let me get to the dining room in time for dinner.

I finished, and taking off my cap I bowed over the altar. At that very moment, I heard my son, Val, yell, "Look out, Pa!"

Boom! went the Grand. Up flew the boiling water in one great torrent of steam, high over our heads!

A source of emotion swept through me like a wave. "Pele, I thank you," I said. Though I stood close by the edge of the geyser, not a drop of water fell on me. My prayer was answered. I stepped back a bit and viewed the glorious sight.

We entered the dining room as the clock struck six-thirty.

The next morning I was met by a delegation of tourists, headed by my son and the doctor. "We want to shake your hand," they said. "You are the first real medicine man we have ever met. Now do us a favor. Come along with us and get the long dormant Giant to show for us."

Some contract! The Giant hadn't played for over eight months, and was considered dead. I felt flattered, but the teachings of my old kanaka kahuna came to me. "Don't crowd the gods. If they do you a favor, wait a bit. You may need help later."

Thanking them, I excused myself and promised that the next time I came to Yellowstone I would do my best to persuade Madame Pele to exhibit to us the glories of the Giant.

Kawelu, the Shark God

LONG before the arrival of Captain Cook, and most likely long before the Hawaiians ever landed on Kauai, the cruel shark god Kawelu took up his abode in the Wailua River. He had an eye for beauty, for of all the three big streams that are found on Kauai — the Waimea, the Hanalei, and the Wailua — the last is perhaps the most beautiful.

The first Hawaiians to reach Kauai landed on the sandy beach at its mouth, and, being enchanted with the big river and the smaller one near it, settled there and made it the center of royalty. There, they built *heiaus*, or temples.

Kawelu must have eyed the newcomers with suspicion, but as they multiplied and spread up the valley, building grass houses and planting taro, he found they were a blessing in disguise.

He lived a dual life. He had the power to change himself from a shark into a man as it suited his purpose. Kawelu lived far up the river near where the gorge begins. He had two houses, one on land, and the other in the sea.

Even today, you can see where the one on land stood, for a huge rock shaped like a tent marks the place. Down in the river beneath the surface lies another immense rock, and there he lived when he was a shark. On the edge of the river can still be seen a great flat rock shaped like a poi-pounding board, where he was supposed to have pounded his poi.

Across the river from his house, he had a taro patch, and when he took the shape of a man, he would work in his taro patch and toil away as any other Hawaiian would. For a long, long time no one suspected he was not a human being. When the natives passed his house on the way to the sea to fish, he would call out, "Aloha, where are you going?"

If they answered, "We are going fishing," he would answer back, "Good luck!" But if they were only going visiting, he made no reply.

For many years life went on in this friendly way, but in time the families who lived up the river began to be suspicious. They noticed that on the days this strange man wished them luck, they always had bad luck, and always one of the party was lost at sea. Sometimes a swimmer would just disappear, leaving no trace. Sometimes a man would cry, "Look out for sharks!" and then vanish.

One day they hid a boy in a place where he could watch. After the fishermen had passed on toward the shore, the boy was surprised to see the man quit his taro patch, cross over the river to his house, and then

84

plunge into the river.

The boy ran to the river bank and gazed into the clear water, expecting to see the man, but to his horror he saw instead a huge shark dart away from under his water house and go swimming out to sea.

At first the boy was so excited he didn't know what to do. But he soon got his wits, raced down to the path, and dashed across the sandy beach to the water's edge. There he stood and called and called to the men swimming far out, but the trade winds were blowing and his little voice could not be heard. He waved and shouted, but the men did not see him and kept on fishing.

Of course the shark god claimed his victim as he had done before. When the rest of the men reached the shore, the boy told his story. From that time on, no Hawaiian fisherman ever told where he was going.

Many a time as I have ridden along the shore, out toward the Barking Sands, I have met men loaded down with nets and rods on their way to fish. When I have asked them where they were going, they invariably answered, "Awana."

I asked one of my paniolos, or cowboys, who spoke good English, what they meant by "Awana."

"Oh," he answered, "that word means they are just wandering, not having any special place in mind. Of course they know where they are going, but it is bad luck to tell anyone where you are going to fish."

The Fish-Hook of Pearl

AIAI'S descendant and I met once on a trip I made up into the mountains. We all sat talking around the camp fire one evening, and when I expressed an interest in Kuula and Aiai, he asked if I would like to hear the story of the fish-hook. Of course I said that I would, and as the embers glowed and the woods took on the mystic shadows of night the old man began to speak.

Kuula, the father of Aiai, lived many, many years before the first white man set foot upon our Hawaiian shores. In those days life was very simple and our ancestors enjoyed their days here among all the beauty you, too, have grown to know and love so well. Their labors were for the most part only those which were necessary to sustain this carefree life. Fishing was the most important work the early Hawaiians did. Not only were they proud of their skill in the art but also a man's position in the community was often reckoned by the size and quality of his catches. Fish was the main food for the family, and if he was clever enough to catch more than he needed, he might become very wealthy.

Kuula was such a marvelous fisherman that each time he went out his canoe was filled to overflowing with the very finest fish. He had a canoe not five nor eight fathoms long but ten fathoms in length, so that you can imagine how many fish it took to fill it.

He was skilled at handling the lines, but there was also another reason for his success. He owned the most wonderful fish-hook that anyone had ever seen or heard about. This fish-hook was so unusual that it even had a name. It was called "Kahuoi."

One day Kuula was fishing, and not catching much, when a bird came out of the sky and flew low over the spot where he sat holding his line. In his beak the bird carried something that glinted and shone in the sunlight. As it flew over him, the bird opened his beak and the shiny object fell to the bottom of the canoe. When Kuula picked it up, he found that it was a most beautiful fish-hook, delicately fashioned of the smoothest pearl shell.

He immediately placed it on his line and after that, whenever he went out in the canoe, the bird—which was named Kamanuwai—came and sat on the edge of his canoe. Kuula would take the fish-hook, Kahuoi, and gently let it down into the water. At once the aku would begin throwing themselves into the canoe. Kamanuwai would continue to perch on the canoe, eating fish to his heart's content and looking so pleased with himself that it made Kuuala smile. Sometimes, indeed, Kamanuwai grew so heavy from eating so much fish that he had trouble taking off from the edge of the canoe.

Kuula grew rich from his large catches. Now it happened that one day he was fishing outside Mamala, and the king of Mamala was fishing there, too. The king caught few fish and none of them fine ones. Just as he was becoming tired of his poor luck, he noticed Kuula and his canoe, and saw hundreds of aku jumping around the hook that the fisherman had let down.

"How is it that fellow can catch hundreds of aku while I can catch no fish at all?" he asked his attendants.

The attendants told the king the story of Kuula and the famous hook, Kahuoi. When they had finished their tale, the king commanded them, saying, "Go and bring this wretch, Kuula, to me. I wish to behold him, and I must have for my own this magic hook." So poor Kuula lost the precious fish-hook and after Kahuoi was gone he caught no more aku.

He felt sorry for the bird who had given him the hook and said sadly, "Kamanuwai, I can no longer catch aku fish—and of other fish I can not catch enough for my wife and me to keep our poor stomachs from lying upon our backs. My friend, there is no way now that I can replay you for what you have done for me, but perhaps some day I will be able to."

Kamanuwai listened, and though he returned for several days he finally grew so weak without food that he flew away to his home, and there he roosted with his eyes half closed from hunger. To this very day the place where the bird roosted is called Kaumakapili, which means "roosting with closed eyes."

Kuula and his wife became poorer and hungrier each day. It was at this time that a son was born to them whom they named Aiai.

Tears filled Kuula's eyes as he looked upon him, and he said to his wife, "Auwe! So long I have wished for a son, and now he is here. He is a beautiful child and would grow to be a fine man and a comfort to us in our old age, but we must send him away. We cannot care for him properly, and without food he would surely die. Auwe! Auwe! Strange is the way of the gods."

On the following day they took the child, Aiai, and put him in a lauhala basket which they had lined and padded. They placed the basket in the stream and went back to their grass hut with heavy hearts.

The basket floated down the stream, and when it was just above the place where Kamanuwai roosted with closed eyes, it was caught and held fast by branches which overhung the water. On the same day the king's small daughter came to bathe there and found the basket. She was charmed with the baby and bade her attendants take him back to the king's house.

There he was cared for, and as he grew older he and the king's daughter became so fond of one another that when he was at last grown to manhood, they were married.

But one day Aiai's wife became ill, and calling him to her she said, "If only you coud bring me some fish, I think I would be well again."

Aiai took his rod and went fishing. He caught a few fish and brought them to her, but after awhile she again became ill and again longed for fish—this time aku fish.

Now in the meantime it happened that Aiai had come to know his father and had heard the story of the fish-hook and how the king had taken it. He said to his wife, "I cannot bring you aku fish unless I have a canoe and a fish-hook of pearl."

Suddenly she remembered the wonderful fish-hook her father had once used, and went at once to see him.

"What do you want, my daughter?" the king asked.

"A canoe and a pearl fish-hook for my husband," she replied.

The king gave his daughter a pearl fish-hook and sent a servant to her house with a canoe.

When Aiai saw the fish-hook he was overjoyed, and taking the canoe he went down to the sea.

A bird flew low and watched the shining fish-hook. It rested on the edge of the canoe as Aiai paddled out into the ocean. The bird's eyes were half-closed, but suddenly it opened them wide and watched intently as the fisherman lowered the shining hook. Aiai and the bird Kamanuwai recognized each other and knew that at last there would be plenty of aku for them both.

But no aku came. The bird closed its eyes again, and emitting a harsh croak it flew away.

Aiai returned to his wife with a troubled heart and told her of the day's events. Again she sent him to bring her aku fish, and he said to her, "It may be that the king has another pearl hook. Go to him once more and ask for one. Tell him that in the calabash where he keeps the fishing nets and hooks he used long ago, there may be another pearl fish-hook."

So the king's daughter went again to her father and told him, "I have come for a pearl fish-hook so that my husband may go out and catch me the aku fish that I long for."

"Have I not given you the pearl fish-hook?" the king asked.

But his daughter persisted, saying, "In the calabash that you used long ago there may be another pearl fish-hook."

The king ordered this calabash brought to him and after searching amongst all that was in it he at last found the pearl fish-hook that he had taken from Kuula. He gave the hook, Kahuoi, to his daughter and she hurried home to place it in the hands of her husband.

Aiai immediately took his father's canoe and the hook and went fishing in the place where his father used to go. As he started seaward the bird Kamanuwai flew down and lighted on the canoe. It opened wide its eyes to watch him let down the shining hook.

When they came to Mamala the aku began to jump. They threw themselves into the canoe by the hundreds, until even that ten-fathom canoe was deep with them. It became so heavy that Aiai needed all his

90

strength to paddle it back to shore.

Kamanuwai ate of the fish until the sheen came back to its plumage, and it was once more a wide-eyed, strong-winged bird.

It was also a very wise bird, for it took the wonderful pearl fish-hook and flew away with it. But whenever Aiai set out in his canoe, the bird brought the hook to him. The hook, Kahuoi, was never again allowed to fall into a stranger's hand.

The Village Belle of Pokii

OVER in the village of Pokii, near a big taro patch, dwelt an old Hawaiian and his wife and daughter. He was a crusty old man, and none of us liked him in spite of the fact that he was one of the most industrious of all the villagers.

He lived in a large grass house; his taro patches were always clean and full of taro; his calabashes were always full of food; and twice a week he pounded his poi.

His wife, too, was hard working and kept his house in splendid order. They were a thrifty couple who minded their own business.

When people living in the district had to turn out to do their number of days' work for the overlord, or konohiki, as the Hawaiians called him, the old Hawaiian was always ready and did his work well.

Everyone liked his daughter. But who would not admire her? She was the prettiest girl in the whole village, and her name was Hilo. As she grew up, all the young men for miles around came courting her, but to all she only smiled and seemed to turn a deaf ear.

One morning, quite early, I ran through our house and out onto the lanai. I stopped short in my tracks when I heard someone sobbing. I looked around and saw Hilo sitting on the grass near the front entrance. I went up to her and saw the tears streaming from her beautiful brown eyes.

"Why are you weeping? Is there anything I can do to help?"

Quickly she grasped my hand, and looking at me with pleading eyes, said, "Oh, Elika, find your papa and bring him out here. I am in a frightful pilikia. Please bring him right away!"

I patted her bowed head and said, "Don't cry any more. I'll find him for you." Then I ran down the long road in search of father.

I soon found him. "Come with me, Papa!" I urged excitedly, grabbing his hand and pulling him along.

"What's happened? What's happened?" he kept asking me as we hurried back toward the house. But as always, he came willingly enough with me.

When we came up to Hilo, she had stopped crying, but her eyes were troubled and my father held out his hand to help her to her feet. She stood up and looked into my father's kind face. Her lips trembled as she spoke.

"Kanuka," she said, "my heart is breaking, and I am ready to die. You must help me." Her eyes filled with tears and father patted her hand tenderly.

"Tell me about it," he said in a low, understanding voice.

Hilo dried her tears with the back of her hand and continued. "Last night, my father told me I was to marry a man named Pua. He lives in Hanalei Valley and is very rich, with large taro lands and many horses. He has bribed my father to let me be his wife, but I hate him. He is so old, Kanuka—older than my father, and has had two wives already who have both died. Now he wants me for number three."

My father listened to Hilo's story, and I could tell he felt very sorry for her. "Did you tell your father you didn't want to marry the man?" he asked.

"Yes, of course," Hilo answered. "I cried No! No! No! but he only laughed at me and said I was to be married next Sunday and then go home with him to Hanalei." Then shyly turning her head away, she spoke softly. "Besides, I am in love with young Paleaiki, the son of Palea. He and I have been sweethearts for a year, and were to have been married when I reached nineteen years. Save me, Kanuka! You are konohiki and have so much power."

True enough, father was konohiki, but he doubted his authority went as far as meddling in the matrimonial affairs of the people living on the land. Still, he told the poor girl that he would see what he could do.

My father was a man of his word. He went for his horse and rode down to the village to see Hilo's determined parent. For a long time he talked and argued with the old Hawaiian, who only laughed and sneered at the very thought of having his plans for his daughter's marriage go awry. He insisted that she should marry the man he had chosen for her the following Sunday.

"I have no use for the young men of this village," he said angrily. "They are lazy and shiftless. They have no money and no ambition. I have picked out a man of wealth. My daughter will marry him. She will do as I say." So that was that!

93

Sunday morning broke clear and bright, and everyone turned out to attend the wedding, for great preparations had been made. People awaited the arrival of the bridegroom with bated breath. How would the old fellow look? What would he be wearing? Was he really as old as rumor said? How could Hilo's father give his beautiful daughter to such a man? Such were the questions the men and women and young people whispered among themselves.

Finally he was spotted far down the road astride his big black stallion. He had ridden over from the nearby town of Waimea, and was all decked out in brand-new top boots and blue denim pants and shirt. In the excitement of seeing the old bridegroom, the young bride was completely forgotten for the moment.

When he had been greeted by Hilo's parents and introduced to the crowd that had gathered, he asked to see his future bride. But where was she? No one knew. The bride had disappeared. Word flashed over the village that Hilo had vanished and must be found at once.

A great search began. Men rode up to our house to say the girl was gone and to ask Papa if he knew where she was. Of course none of us knew. Papa laughed, saying that she had run away, no doubt.

One whole month went by, and then the second and third, and still no trace of Hilo.

While waiting in Waimea, the old gentleman made friends. When the third month had passed and no trace of his bride-to-be had been found, he quietly married a big and buxom lady of Waimea, much nearer his own age. Together they returned to his taro patches in Hanalei.

The day after he left with his bride, a light knock

sounded on the door of our house. When Papa went to see who was there, he stepped back in great surprise. There stood the runaway Hilo.

"Come in! Come in!" he invited. Then he called Mother and all of us to see her, and soon news of the arrival of Hilo had spread to the village and everyone came to welcome her home again.

"Where have you been?" was the question on everyone's tongue. And this is the story she told us:

"It was Saturday evening, and the sun was just about to sink into the ocean. I was so sad, thinking about my wedding to the old man the next day, that I wandered to the beach and sat on a big rock on the reef. I was weeping and moaning at my fate when a big shark came swimming right up to me.

"To my great surprise, he began talking to me. He asked me why I wept, so I poured out my tale of woe. He took pity on me and said he would save me from such a fate. Then a strange thing happened. He told me to jump on his great back, and I didn't hesitate to do as he said. Away we went through the surf at lightning speed!

"After a while, I found myself in a big cave with ocean and cliffs all around. He told me to get off, and to wait there, so I did. Each day he brought me food and I lived in the great cave for a long time.

"Yesterday, after he had brought me my food, he told me all was well and I was to return to Pokii. I jumped on his back again, and he brought me back to the same rock where I had been sitting when he found me. I climbed from his back and up onto the rock, but when I turned to thank him for all he had done, he was gone."

No one said a word for a long minute, but we knew

the shark god had taken good care of Hilo, for she was more beautiful than ever and looked well kept.

The whole village, as well as the children, believed the story implicitly. Her father knew that if the shark god had interfered with his plans, he could do nothing about it. He consented to the marriage of Hilo and Paleaiki, who had waited patiently for her return and had never once despaired.

The wedding was a great success. And now I must tell you a funny thing that happened. Hilo was lovely in a white holoku, and when Paleaiki rode up on his best horse, he looked grand in his big coconut hat, new denim pants and shirt, carrying in his hands a pair of big, blacktop boots with a red seal stamped on the front. He had slaved and saved for a month, and with ten big trade dollars he had bought these wonderful boots—the pride and joy of every kanaka boy.

He tied up his horse and walked barefoot to the church. There he pulled on his boots and strode manfully up the aisle to meet his bride. But as he walked the length of the church, it was apparent that something was wrong. Paleaiki was plainly disgusted and upset about something. It took all his courage to go through the wedding ceremony.

No sooner was the knot tied and the minister had pronounced Hilo and Paleaiki man and wife, and he had come out of the church with his beaming bride on his arm, than he jumped on his horse and galloped madly over to the nearby store where he had bought his boots. His face red with anger, he almost tore them off his feet and hurled them at the astonished clerk's head.

"Take your boots," he yelled at the cringing little man. "They're no good! They don't squeak."

Alas, the shiny boots had not advertised to all present at his wedding that they were brand-new!

The Ditch the Menehunes Built

SEVERAL of us were sitting around the campfire one night many years ago. We had been telling stories all evening long, stories of our adventures and stories of old Hawaii. The ones I liked best were those curious ancient tales that had been told by father to son, generation after generation.

Beside me on the ground sat an old Hawaiian. He was smoking his pipe and gazing thoughtfully into the fire. He had been silent throughout the evening, just listening to the stories. Now he spoke in a soft quiet voice. "Have any of you ever been to Waimea Valley on Kauai and seen the Menehune Ditch?"

"Yes," said one. "I have. I remember it because of the rocks. They're differnt from any I've ever seen before. They look as if they had been cut by hand, yet there isn't a man living today who can chisel stone like those. I'm a stonecutter myself, so I know. I've tried."

The old Hawaiian replied:

No wonder! The menehune built that waterway, and it is true, not a person has found the secret of cutting rocks as those folks did. They lived so long ago that today we know hardly anything of their traits and habits. My grandfather said they were dwarflike people, gifted with supernatural powers. And strangest of all, the menehune worked only at night. Every job they started, no matter how big, they finished in one night. And so it was with this ditch.

97

It is supposed that it was built during the reign of King Umi. Part of his lands were dry, flat plains. But the soil was rich and fertile, and when the scant rains did fall the land produced fine crops. King Umi was an ambitious man and dearly loved by his people. He did everything he could to make them more prosperous. One day as he was visiting the dry country, a thought occurred to him. Why not bring water down from the mountain springs? Then the farmers could irrigate the fields and there would be good crops all year round. But how to get the water down? That was the problem, indeed! King Umi pondered for days, but couldn't find any answer. Finally he called in his engineers. They, too, went out and looked over the lands. They suggested one thing or another, but all their efforts resulted in failure.

The king was bitterly disappointed. He sat in his garden one day thinking of his problem, when suddenly there appeared before him an ugly little dwarf. The king looked up startled. "What is this?" he thought to himself. He had never seen such a creature before. It was dressed from top to toe in brilliant green, and wore on its head a tiny crown of emeralds.

As if reading the question in King Umi's mind, the little dwarf spoke first. "I am the king of the menehune. For a long time now, I have been watching you and your men struggle to bring water to the valley. But I can do it. My men and I can do it!"

King Umi's eyes fairly sparkled with joy. He leaned forward and held out his hand.

"If only you could! I will pay you anything you ask."

The dwarf replied, "I will. Tomorrow you shall have your ditch, but on one condition." There was a pause before he announced the strange condition. "Six months from tomorrow you must give one fish to each and every one of my men, including myself. If you can do that your problem is solved."

"What an unusual request," thought the king. Nevertheless, he was beside himself with joy.

"It shall be done," he exclaimed, jumping to his feet. "Six months from tomorrow I will have a fish for you and a fish for every one of your workers." With that, the little dwarf vanished.

The king could hardly wait until dawn to see if his wish had come true. The day dragged out and the night seemed endless. At daybreak, he arose and hurried out to the lands. Lo and behold! There was a long, long ditch stretching as far as the eye could see up into the mountains. And running through the ditch was the clear, cold water from the springs. It was not long before the water covered the fields. The people were excited over their new gift, and the king was happy and satisfied.

But now to collect the fish. King Umi called all his men together and told them to catch moi, as many as they could. And so, day after day, week after week, the men caught and dried moi. For six months the men fished and finally they had enough. At least, they thought they did. King Umi sent a messenger to the king of the menehune that he was ready now to pay. The appointed place was a small hill near the Waimea Canyon. Puu Moi it is still called, and here the dried fish were brought.

All day and all night the men of Waimea toiled up the long slopes of the mountain carrying bales and bales of dried fish. It seemed they would never get done. But by sunrise of the appointed day the fish were all collected in one spot. And then the two kings set to work.

One fish to each menehune workman. They worked all day and by sunset the last of the fish had been given away. But when the last fish was gone there were still menehune left, long, long lines of them, lines extending to the west, over hill and valley, as far as the eye could see.

King Umi sank in his chair dismayed. He turned to the king of the menehune. "Give me a little more time," he pleaded. "Another six months. I know I'll have enough then to pay you."

"All right," replied the king of the menehune. "I do not mind giving you more time, bt this you must do. Give all my men a fish at the same time on the same day. And furthermore, since you failed today, all the fish you have just given away must be forfeited." So saying, the dwarf vanished again. And, with him, the long line of menehune.

Poor King Umi was discouraged. He thought he would be bound forever to fish for the menehune. He didn't see how he could ever get enough fish to pay his debt. With bowed head and bent shoulders, he journeyed sadly back to his palace. He had no more than arrived when he received a visit from Kapuai. Kapuai was a wise man and knew well all the fish laws of Hawaii.

"Why don't you catch shrimp?" he suggested to the king. "Shrimp are fish, and they're easy to catch. One shrimp to each menehune would pay the bill."

"Kapuai," cried the king excitedly, "you are a great man! We will be saved after all."

Again the king sent a call for all his men. This time they must not fail. If they did, the menehune would take away their ditch as quickly as they had built it. The men set to work at once. They fished from dawn until dusk. They even fished by night with torches. Even the boys fished—and some of the women. The people grew tired, but still they kept on, for weeks and months.

They covered every bit of swamp and marsh where there could possibly be a shrimp. Basket after basket was heaped to the brim and hauled away to the trysting place. Every cart and every container that could be found were filled with shrimp. There were millions of them caught and millions more. It didn't seem possible that so many shrimp existed. The men fished until the very last possible moment.

All too soon the time came for the appointment, and the two kings met again. They started in at sunrise. And all day long as the menehune filed by, each received one shrimp. King Umi thought the line would never end. But it did. Just as the sun began to sink into the ocean west of Niihau, the last one of the menehune received his pay.

King Umi was exhausted. He looked down into the basket and found just two shrimp. Those were all that were left of the thousands and thousands of baskets carried up. He picked up the two of them. Handing one to the king of the menehune, he said:

"Oh, king of the menehune, just these two shrimp are left. Take this one and I will keep the other. Now our work is done."

And that is why there is a mountain on Kauai called Puuopai—the Mountain of the Shrimp.

Hawaiian Navigators

THE schooner lay at anchor in the bay of Waimea, Kauai, rocking gently on the rollers as they passed her on the way to the beach. The captain was busy taking in supplies of poi and fried fish, for besides the cargo of raw sugar, he had just been notified that Governor Kanoa and his retinue wished to take passage on his vessel to Honolulu.

In the little sleepy village of Waimea, all was hustle and bustle and excitement as the faithful servants packed up the clothing and baggage necessary for such a visit of state, not to mention suitable presents for his royal master, the king.

Boatload after boatload of food and baggage were taken on board and finally the crew were ready for the passengers. One by one the retainers were picked up by the stalwart boatmen, dressed in malos, or loincloths, carried through the surf, and put into the waiting rowboats. Finally the old governor himself was picked up and carried out to the waiting rowboat. Soon he was safely stowed on board the schooner. Away they gaily sailed for Honolulu.

Now, the distance from Kauai to Oahu is only a hundred miles or so, and the schooner should have arrived in port within a couple of days.

All was merry on the ship. They sang and ate and slept in a happy frame of mind. They were all off on a grand holiday spree and would soon see the glories of Honolulu, the capital city, not to mention all the wonders of the royal court.

Thus, they sailed on and on. Days went by. Finally

the food supply was exhausted, and still the port of Honolulu was not in sight. Having nothing else to eat, they began to eat raw sugar. The gay, carefree atmosphere changed to one of tension and worry. What was wrong? Why were they not in sight of land? The Hawaiians could tell the haole (which means white person or foreigner) captain was worried, but the captain would speak to no one.

Finally the situation began to look desperate, and he decided to tell his troubles to his illustrious passenger, Governor Kanoa.

"Governor," he said, "we have sailed and sailed these many days, but so far have not been able to find Oahu. We are lost completely. What shall we do?"

The governor looked quietly at the captain. "Don't you know," he said, "that all these days you have been sailing directly away from Oahu? Turn your ship around and sail straight back, and you will find land."

The captain groaned. "That is impossible, your excellency," he replied. "I do not know which way to steer for land."

Fortunately for the lost schooner, a whaler appeared on the horizon shortly thereafter. Sighting their signals of distress, the whaler came up to the schooner and sent a boat alongside to find out the trouble.

The captain replied that he was not only out of food, but he was trying to find Honolulu; that he was lost. The whaler sent over a boatload of provisions and told the captain to turn his ship about and sail straight back the way he had come.

The food was accepted with great thankgsiving, and the captain, in a crestfallen manner, ordered his ship to turn back. The next day, to their surprise and joy, the mountains of Oahu loomed in sight. The old governor was much elated and laughed heartily at the haole captain.

"I knew you were wrong," he said. "I could tell by the look of the ocean which way you should steer. In the future, do as I tell you and you will have no difficulty in finding land."

The schooner soon arrived safely in port. The governor had the pleasure of meeting his king, who entertained him royally. From that day to his death, old Governor Kanoa was famed as a navigator, and again proved how much at home the Hawaiians are when sailing the seas.

A Night on Molokai

THIS happened long, long ago, when I was a very little boy, or most likely before that—sometime in the 1860's.

Away back in those early days of Kauai, one of the chief sources of income came from the sale of hides and tallow. There were thousands of fat cattle on my father's big ranch at old Waiawa, but not enough cooking pots to make tallow. The pots used were the big iron ones like the whalers used to extract the oil from the blubber of the sperm whales.

Hearing that a man on Molokai had some of these iron pots for sale, father sailed for Molokai and finally landed at Kaunakakai. There he met a man whom we will call Mr. X, who owned the pots.

They rode up to his home in the hills to look them over, and finding them satisfactory, father agreed to buy them.

It being late, Mr. X invited father to dinner and to spend the night, and showed him a small room at the head of a flight of stairs.

After dinner they sat on the lanai with Mrs. X, a Hawaiian woman, until bedtime. Then they gave my father a small kerosene lamp, and he climbed up to his room. It was hot and close, so he opened the upper sash of the only window in the room and was soon in bed.

Somehow, and for some strange reason, he felt uneasy. There was something queer and uncanny about the place. He simply couldn't go to sleep. He lay on the bed and looked out the window. The room was pitch black, but the night was clear. Suddenly, he saw something moving at the window! He thought it was a monkey for a moment as it was dimly in view against the faint light of the sky. Then it vanished! Suddenly there it was again! It seemed to swing in through the window, though he could hear nothing drop to the floor.

Positive that something had dropped into the room, he sat up in bed and kept his eyes on the faint light coming in at the window. And as he looked, and to his horror, two hands appeared from nowhere and stretched out right over him. He grasped the two wrists and sprang out of bed, dragging his prisoner over to the door.

Now, his prisoner was a small man who danced about, trying his best to free himself; but father held him in a viselike grip. Fearing the intruder carried a knife, he was afraid to let one hand go. He held both wrists in one hand and holding him tightly, unlocked and opened his door. My father dragged him down the stairs and called loudly to his host.

When Mr. X appeared, father told him what happened and demanded an explanation. All he did was

105

gaze at the intruder, who turned out to be a very small Chinese. But before he could say anything, his wife came bustling into the room.

"Hello, Ah Sing!" she cried out. "You big lapuwale (rascal)!"

She turned to father. "Let him go," she demanded. "I'll take care of him." She grabbed him by the shoulder, dragged him to the door, opened it, and threw him out.

"Get out of here wikiwiki (quick), you big lolo (crazy)," she cried, and slammed the door. Whereupon she turned on her heels and left the two men.

Father returned at once to his room. He didn't sleep much after that, though it was past midnight. At dawn, he was glad to get an oxcart and haul his pots to the schooner. Soon he was sailing back to Kauai. He never returned to Molokai.

We children loved this story, and when father took us by the hand and gripped us tight, we could easily understand how he held the little Chinese; but what the Chinese was doing in the room always remained a mystery to me.

Many years passed, and one day I found time to visit the famous Molokai Ranch. Riding up in the hills I came upon two men out hunting, and to my surprise and joy I discovered they were the sons of the man my father had visited so long ago, and that they remembered him well and recalled his visit.

The little Chinese man came to my mind at once. Now I might find the answer to the riddle of the strange night my father spent on Molokai so many years before. I asked them about him.

Yes, they remembered him well. He had lived in a little tenant house for many years and did odd jobs around the place. He was very fond of opium, and when he had enjoyed a good long smoke, he would tell of the wonders of China and of his beloved Canton. His dream was to get enough money to return to his homeland, but he never worked hard enough to earn the home passage. He was dead and buried when I visited the friendly island, but the men told me how, just before he died, he awoke from a deep sleep and as though in a trance clasped his two hands together and cried out, "The haole (white man)! His hands! He held me like a vise. I only wanted a little silver to go home, but he was too quick."

And that, my friends, cleared up the old mystery for me.

Halemano and the Princess Kama

HALEMANO stirred restlessly in his sleep. "Kama," he whispered. The dream girl turned and smiled at him.

"Come," she beckoned. "Come with me . . ."

Halemano awoke and found himself sitting at the edge of the couch, his hand touching the table beside him. "Gone!" he whispered. "And her name!" He caught his breath. "Oh, why can't I remember her name?"

Halemano rose and walked out into the cool garden. Here the early morning sun was just touching the tips of the flowers. He was disturbed. He couldn't shake himself from his dream.

Every night for a long, long while he had seen in his dreams the vision of a beautiful girl. He called her by name and even talked with her. He could remember how she looked — the long dark hair, sometimes braided around her lovely head, sometimes falling loosely around her shoulders. He could remember the clothes she wore, and the wreaths, and the flowers, even the scent of her dress. But her name and what they said to each other — these slipped away from his memory the moment he awoke. Abruptly he was shaken out of his thoughts.

"Halemano! Halemano! Where are you?" It was his sister Laenihi calling. "I've been looking all over for you!" she cried, catching sight of him at the far end of the garden. Halemano could hardly answer her. As she came closer, she could see the anguish on his face.

"Why, Halemano, what is the trouble? Are you ill? Please tell me." She took his arm and led him down the path to the beach. "Tell me, Halemano. Perhaps I can help you."

Halemano unburdened his trouble to Laenihi. She nodded her head wisely. "It is in Puna," she explained, "where the women wear the lehua lei, and have scented tapa for their dresses. It is there, too, that they wear the hala wreaths around their heads. Do not worry. I think I can help you."

That night, after Halemano went to bed, Laenihi crept into his room and sat quietly beside him while he slept.

When he awoke the next morning, she said gently, "Kama is her name. The Princess Kama of Puna."

"The Princess Kama of Puna?" echoed Halemano. "She is beautiful, Laenihi." He paused. "Tell me how I can meet her."

"That is very difficult," his sister replied. "You see, the princess is the loveliest maiden in all the land. There are two kings who want her for their bride. They have been sending wonderful gifts to her, and not only to her but to her parents, too. However, the princess has never seen either of the two kings. Nor has she seen anyone for a long, long time except her little brother. The two live together on an island far away from everyone else."

"But, Laenihi," interrupted Halemano, "why is it that way, and how do you know these things?"

"Oh, my brother," chided Laenihi. "Have you forgotten my magic powers? The reason Princess Kama is kept alone is that her parents know that it will not be very long before she will reach the very height of her beauty. When she does, they will give her in marriage to one of the two kings. Until that time, no one must speak to her, or even see her.

"But do not be discouraged, Halemano. I think I know a way for you to see her."

Laenihi chuckled silently to herself. She had not told her brother all she knew. It was three days before Halemano saw his sister again. He spied her running along the beach. It was but a moment until she was in the garden. She carried in her hands a hala wreath, a lehua flower lei, and a scented tapa dress!

"Laenihi!" cried Halemano excitedly, when he saw what his sister had. "You have seen her! You have seen her!" Halemano fairly danced with joy.

"Sit down, my brother," laughed Laenihi, "and I will tell you all about it. When I got near the island, I saw the Princess Kama and her little brother swimming in the water. I changed myself into a brightly colored fish so that they would be sure to see me. And they did. The little boy put me into a calabash and took me into the house. That night after they had gone to bed, I changed back to myself. I stood beside the Princess Kama as she slept. She was restless too, just like you. And then a very strange thing happened. I heard her say one word —Halemano. And then she awoke. She was frightened when she saw me, but when I told her I was the sister of the one whose name she had just uttered . . ." Laenihi paused.

"Yes, yes, go on," cried Halemano, impatiently.

"She was very happy," replied Laenihi simply. "And she gave me these things of hers to give you."

"We'll go at once," declared Halemano. "You must show me the way."

"No, not just yet. There are certain things we must do before we go. First we must make some toys. They will be for Princess Kama's brother."

They set to work. There were little wooden birds that floated on the water; a toy canoe which they colored red; and little toy men to paddle the canoe. There was a kite, brilliantly colored, one that would fly high into the sky. And lastly, some little figures about a foot high, which looked just like people. Halemano and Laenihi put the toys in a canoe and started off for Puna. As they neared the shore, Halemano let the kite rise into the sky.

Sure enough, Kama's little brother, playing on the beach, saw it. He called out, "Oh, let me have that!"

Halemano paddled the canoe closer and gave him the kite. Then the boy caught sight of the rest of the colored toys. He touched one and then another. Laenihi laughed to see the youngster so delighted. They gave him all the toys except the standing figures. These the boy wanted most of all. But Halemano held them firmly.

"You may have these, too," he said, "if you will bring your sister to us." Off the boy ran. He was back in just a few moments, and with him was the Princess Kama!

110

There are no words to express the joy of Halemano and Kama when they met.

It seemed but a moment till Laenihi cried out, "Look on the beach!" People were running excitedly into the water and swimming towards them. Some were launching canoes.

Kama burst into tears. "They know I shouldn't be here. They know you are not the king of Puna or the king of Hilo."

Halemano did not answer her. Nor did Laenihi. They were busy with their own paddles, and in a flash the canoe darted out into the sea. Again Laenihi called upon her magic powers, and soon the canoe was far beyond the reach of the angry people.

When they reached home, Halemano and the princess were married. The two loved each other dearly, but their happiness was doomed to last only a short time. They had forgotten the two kings.

When it was discovered that the princess had been carried off, the two kings grumbled to each other. "We have given her and her parents much of what we owned, knowing that one of us was to have her. And now a mere common lad has taken her away. We'll make war upon these people and punish them."

The two kings called their armies together and descended upon Halemano's people.

Halemano and Kama fled for their lives. They hid by day in caves, or whatever shelter they could find. And by night they traveled across the mountains and lowlands. Finally they came to the island of Maui. They were poor now, and instead of living in state and having plenty, they had to dig the ground, and live as a farmer and farmer's wife. Poor Princess Kama was entirely unused to this sort of living. And she was not to be blamed for wishing desperately to be back amid the luxuries she had always had.

It seemed fated that one day, as she walked along the beach, she saw a large number of bright red canoes. They were the canoes of a king. In a moment, a tall figure left one of the canoes and came towards her. It was Huaa, the king of Puna. Yes, Kama was soon persuaded to go with him.

Halemano, when he discovered what had happened, was heartbroken. There was nothing for him to do now but return to his own home. As before, he turned to Laenihi for comfort and help.

"I think," said Laenihi, "if you will learn how to sing and chant verses, you may win the princess back again." Halemano couldn't see how that would help, but Laenihi was firm.

So, for a long time, Halemano studied and trained himself to sing and to chant verses. As time went on, people invited him to come into their homes and entertain them. Halemano's fame grew. And as his fame grew, so did his fortune. He visited the wealthy and lived among kings. But always in his heart he loved Kama. And all the songs he sang he sang for her, even though she wasn't there.

One day Halemano was invited to a great festival. It was a very important occasion. And Halemano decided to chant his favorite story for the guests. As he was finishing his song, he saw someone coming towards him, in all her grace and beauty.

Halemano told in his song that he had forgiven her. As she came nearer, Halemano saw tears in her eyes. But they were tears of happiness. Both knew now that their troubles were over. Yes, they did live happily ever after.

112

Hina, the Woman in the Moon

WOMAN'S work is never done from early morn to setting sun. That's an old familiar saying. Sometimes we men have not believed it, but always the women-folk do. And just for the sake of — shall we say, gall-antry? — I'm going to tell the story of Hina, who was constantly burdened with her many household tasks.

Many women just grow so weary performing end-less tasks that it seems they no longer have time to enjoy the world in which they live. Life itself becomes a burden to them.

Hina, the lady of our story, was such a woman.

As the years went by, Hina grew more and more weary. All day long she sat outside her house, beating out tapas for clothes for her family, making cloth from the bark of a tree by beating it into shape. When dark-ness fell and she could no longer see to work, she would have to take down a heavy calabash and carry it filled with water to the house. Often she stumbled in the dark, and sometimes she would trip and fall, spilling so much of the water that she had to go back for more. Then there was the cooking, poi to make, fish to catch, and even the repairing of the grass hut.

There was no one to help her. One of her sons sailed from island to island robbing people. Her favorite daugh-ter had left her home and gone to live with the wild people in the forest. Hina's husband had become very bad tempered, and no matter how hard she worked he always thought that she should work harder and ac-complish more. Hina felt that she was an unloved, neglected, and unappreciated wife and mother.

The poor woman became more and more weary, until she feared she could go on no longer. She would think to herself as she worked, "Auwe! If only I could go far, far away from this house and find a place where I could rest myself! A place where there was much less work to do; where I could take a pleasant walk in the cool woods or bathe in a little mountain stream; where I might just sit quietly in the shade and do nothing for a whole day."

One day her grumbling husband said to her, "You miserable, lazy wretch! All day long you do not do as much work as one boy could do in an hour. What a sorry thing you are to call yourself wahine (woman). Go, then! Take a net and fish up some shrimps from between the rocks so that I may have them for my dinner!"

Another job to do! Alas! Hina felt she could bear no more. As she fished amongst the rocks, rebellious thoughts plagued her mind.

"Perhaps the tide will grow strong here," she mused. "Then it may pick me up and carry me out into the sea. I should have no strength to withstand it. It might be a pleasant thing to float in the soft blue water. Or a heavy wind may blow up and carry me far up into the sky. As a kite I would be born up, and where I would come to rest no one knows. Surely the place I came to, wherever it might be, would be better than this poor life I lead here. What does it matter? Auwe!"

The rainbow that spanned the blue sky above her head heard Hina and felt great pity for her. From its home high above the clouds it began to let down a part of itself. It was as though someone were unrolling a lovely, multicolored ribbon. It fell slowly and gracefully, closer and closer to the earth, until finally the very end of it touched the rocks and blended into the blue-

114

green waters right at Hina's feet!

The light dazzled her eyes and for a moment she gazed with awed amazement at the spot where the rainbow touched the water. Then slowly her bent form straightened. With her eyes she followed the rainbow's beam, searching the skies for the place from which it had come.

Then from somewhere in the azure spaces a clear and gentle voice spoke to her. "Daughter of the earth, I have seen your great struggle and heard your wish to leave this place. I have sent you a road by which you may leave the world. What you will find above it, I cannot say."

Hina hesitated a moment and then with the net still in her hands she began to climb the arching pathway from the rocks up into the heavens. She thought to herself, "I will go up the rainbow and then over to the sun. There I will rest myself."

She climbed higher and higher along the rainbow's arch. As she ascended, the rays of the sun beat down upon her. Still, holding the net over her head, she went on.

After a while she had climbed above the clouds. There was nothing to shelter her from the sun's fierce rays. They burnt her terribly. Her throat was parched and the skin of her body felt drained of all moisture, dry and drawn and wrinkled like old parchment. Her lips were cracked and her head spun, while objects floated and danced crazily before her eyes. Still she would not stop, so great was her desire to escape the earth. Though she could no longer walk, but only crawled along on her hands and knees, she continued upward. Finally the fire of the sun's rays tortured and shriveled her so that she could go no further. She lost her unsure foothold entirely and, slipping back along the rainbow arch, she fell down, down, down to earth again.

It was night. Yet in the darkness she could dimly see her husband on his way back from the pool with a calabash of water. He was stumbling along and saying ill-tempered things about her. When he saw her he had no words of welcome, but only of abuse. "Hina!" he cried. "You no-good wahine! Where have you been? Why were you not here to bring the water? Auwe! To be such a luckless fellow to have you for a wife!"

Now that the sun had sunk beyond the horizon and its rays were no longer upon her, strength gradually returned to Hina.

"I will go to the moon," she decided. "It must be very quiet and peaceful there."

Hina went into the house and hurriedly filled her calabash with all the earthly things that were precious to her. As she was leaving with the calabash in her hand, her husband looked up. "Hina!" he shouted angrily. "Get me some supper. I am hungry and have waited too long for my food. Come away from the doorway. Stop your dreaming. Go, and be quick about it!"

Hina neither hastened to obey his commands nor did she seem to fear him any longer. He had been so intent upon his grumbling that he had not realized that his wife had been acting strangely. When he saw her carrying the calabash, then he sensed that she was planning on a long journey.

"Where are you going, my wife?" he inquired wonderingly. "And when will you return? You have not asked my permission to go visiting," he added more sternly.

"I am going to the moon," Hina said quietly. As she

spoke a beautiful lunar, or moon, rainbow appeared in the evening sky. While she watched, the rainbow's curved pathway moved until it touched Hina's tired feet.

When she saw the path, Hina gave a little cry. "The gods and nature have been good to me. I am coming!"

Without a moment's hesitation she began to climb the rainbow arch and was almost out of her husband's reach when suddenly he leaped up in one final effort to catch and bring her back. But he could not stop her, although he managed to catch one foot in his last frantic grasp. He held on with brutal strength and though he was at last forced to release it, Hina's poor foot was twisted and broken as her husband fell backward on the ground.

With her crushed foot Hina still climbed heavenward. Though she limped and was in great pain, she was happy as she struggled along. When she came to where the stars were, Hina paused, chanting to them and asking them to show her how to get to the moon. The stars showered their silvery light upon her and the way to the moon sparkled before her from their radiance.

The moon welcomed Hina. She entered its strange lands and was given a home of her own where she might stay for the rest of her life. Grateful tears welled in Hina's eyes and her heart was filled with peace at last.

Look up at the moon on any lovely Hawaiian night and you will see her. There she sits, her foot still lamed, and with her calabash by her side. The Hawaiians do not call her "Hina" any more. She is known as "Lono Moku," or "Lame Lono."

Some say that instead of the calabash, she took with

her a tapa board and mallet and that she still beats out tapa cloths. Some old Hawaiians say that the soft fleecy clouds seen around the moon are really fine tapa cloths that have been beaten out by Hina, or "Lono Moku," the Woman in the Moon.

The Hermit of Kaunakakai

NOT TOO many years ago, near Kaunakakai on the island of Molokai, there stood an old, weatherbeaten frame house in a coconut grove by the sea. It was a shadowy, desolate spot and lonely, too. An angry surf thundered ceaselessly on the barren shore and restless winds moved uneasily through the palms, making grotesque dancing patterns on the empty sand.

In the house lived an old man, a hermit, whose queer habits had earned him a fearsome reputation. In time, it was whispered among the good people who worked on the nearby plantations that the man was a kahuna. The story spread that he had been heard muttering strange chants in the night to Uli, the goddess of the dreaded anaana. The townsfolk who knew of the place regarded it with awesome fear and passersby were careful to give the old man a wide berth. Those who did meet the old hermit spoke to him only briefly and with the greatest politeness.

The first to break the kapu was a young man who worked on a nearby plantation. For the purpose of our story, we shall call him David.

One day David and a companion, having a holiday, took their jug of okolehao down on the beach for a celebration. The old hermit was quietly sitting in front of his house mending his net. The two young men paid no attention to the old man and lightheartedly frolicked on the beach, between sips from their jug.

After a while they tired of their sport. David by this time was quite drunk. He began to tease the old man and, finding himself quietly ignored, he grew louder and bolder.

His friend begged him to curb his tongue and respect the kapu, but David felt daring, headstrong, and mean. His voice became louder, his tone and bearing more insulting.

The old hermit stood it for a while. Finally he got up and brought, from within his house, six pieces of hau wood. Carefully selecting a spot in the sand, he took each stick of the hau wood and stuck it erect in the sand. Then, when the sticks were in place, the old man beckoned to David and explained.

"Each stick," he said, "is a day. Today I put them here. Tomorrow I take one out. The next day another. The next day another. The next another." He halted his chant of doom and looked at David with dark, terrible eyes. Then he muttered slowly, "With the last stick, you die!"

As soon as the last fatal words were spoken, David's friend fled as fast as his legs would carry him. But David remained brazen and unmoved. He sneered and his face was dark with anger. "You cannot frighten me, kupuna kane," he shouted. "I am young and strong and I have many years to live. I do not believe in any old kahuna anaana." With that, he kicked over the sticks the old man had set before him and walked away after his friend. But, as he looked back, he could see the old hermit patiently lining up the sticks again. It gave

119

him an uneasy feeling, but he shook it off and continued on his way home.

Word of David's encounter with the dreaded old man had spread fast through the plantation village. Before he reached home, David noticed that his neighbors were staring at him in morbid fascination. His mother greeted him with tears in her eyes. The story went by word of mouth from house to house in Kaunakakai—out to the plantations; up through the hills among the paniolos riding herd on their cattle; with fishermen out to sea—until not only all of Molokai, but Lanai and Maui, too, knew that within six days the young man would die.

That night, David tried desperately to sleep. He lay in his bed and listened to the sobbing of his mother in the next room. He tossed and turned, until his bedclothes were rumpled and knotted. As the night progressed, each normal sound took on a new and fearful meaning. Was that shrill sound in the night an akua, an evil spirit lurking in the darkness? When finally he did doze, he awoke screaming from a nightmare, in which shadows leaped from the face of the moon and threatened to engulf him.

When dawn came, David's mother found him sitting on the lanai, moodily watching the sun rise above the morning mist.

On the plantation that day, his friends were kind, but he could see that they tried to avoid him when they could, and chose to work at a distance from him. David brooded throughout the day. He was hurt, resentful, and more than a little frightened.

The next day, as he was returning from the fields, he heard the women in his mother's house wailing, "Auwe-e." The mournful lament curdled his very soul.

On the third day he found his family making leis. When he asked why, they said, "Because you are dead!" Dead? To his own family he was dead! He tore himself frantically from his mother's sorrowful embrace and ran, stumbling blindly, through the canefield, not caring where he went.

Finally, he went to the old kahuna and apologized for his rudeness. The old man, sitting beside the three upright sticks, did not answer. He looked at David again out of those dull, terrible eyes and took out one more stick. "Only two sticks remain," he said, and turned his eyes out to where the sea was lashing furiously at the coral.

That night, the frightened villagers could hear David wandering blindly through the canefields, crying out in the darkness like a lost, wounded animal. When he came home at last it was morning. He was covered with mud where he had fallen. His clothes were torn. His eyes were red-rimmed and bright with fever that none of civilization's drugs could cure.

His sister met him at the doorway to their home. Failing in her other sweet, youthful attempts to console him, she plucked the orchid from her hair and offered it to him. He took the delicate bloom in his trembling hand and sadly smiled his gratitude at her. Then, when he looked again at the flower, he saw that it was slowly wilting, dying from the touch of his hand. He fainted from the impact of the horror on his tired brain.

On the fifth day, David desperately went to see the old man again. Kneeling in the sand, he begged the hermit to spare his life, but the old man just turned his eyes out to the rolling waves in answer to all the despairing young man's pleas. David's friends had come with him to visit the old man, but they kept

121

themselves at a respectful distance while he was talking with the hermit. As David arose to leave, he could hear their mournful "A-u-w-ee" like a death knell in the distance.

That afternoon, the head luna and several of David's haole friends went to the old man and pleaded with him to put a stop to the tragic affair. But the old man would not enter into talk. Silently he sat, looking out to sea. They came next to David and argued with him to resist. But it was too late. That night one stick remained.

The next day, they found David. He, who had been a laughing, healthy man only a week before, lay dead in the sand. The old man was gone; he has never been heard of since that day. And David held the last stick, clutched in his dead hand.

The Phantom Goat of Honopu

WE HAD left Haena before daybreak in a big, flat-bottomed boat. It is always best to start early to avoid the wind that generally rises with the sun. As we traveled south, we soon were able to see the Napali coastline. What an inspiring view it was! One by one, the valleys opened up and then closed like a book. Hanakapiai, Hanakoa, then the large valley of Kalalau, famous for its taro. And there were the great caves and the sparkling waterfall called Kolea, gushing out of the cliffs near the caves. How beautiful they all were in the early morning light!

Then we saw the famous arch of Honopu. The little spring Waialoha, in the center of the arch, tossed down its shower of drops that looked like quicksilver in the sunlight.

Honopu is not so large as Kalalau or Nualolo, but it is one of the most picturesque of all the Napali valleys and the most difficult one to enter. On the ocean front of the Honopu arch are two small beaches. High sand dunes lie behind them, with the cliffs rising straight up some eight hundred feet.

The two beaches are separated by a narrow arch like a hog's back, and somehow or other the waves pounding against the base managed through the centuries to cut the arch through the hogback. It is large — some three hundred feet long and about one hundred feet high at its center.

The river that comes down the valley dashes over a perpendicular cliff for some two hundred feet and lands on one of the beaches, but prefers to turn to the right, run through the arch, and enter the sea on the other beach. All these cliffs are cut as smooth as though by a power shovel. The only way out of the arch is along the reef at the end of the hogback, but if the surf is running high, this reef is impassible.

At the center of the hogback, the cliff has been worn away a bit, and you can climb up. It is not exactly an easy trail, but if you hold on and keep your head, you can make it all right. And once through the small cliffs, you climb up and go over the top of the arch and enter the valley that lies above.

Since few people care to risk going to it, it makes a very private and ideal place for those who know the sea and cliffs. It is safe enough in summer but not recommended as a winter resort, for if the large typhoon swells should come up, you would have to stay in the arch until they subsided.

Since the beach on the south side is the better place to land, we passed the first one and then headed in for shore. It was still early in the morning when our boat rounded the cliff that guarded the entrance to the cove. Our boat captain was an expert. He swung the cumbersome flat-bottomed boat toward the shore. As we raced in on the swells, he kept one eye on the shore and one on the sea. He slowed down the outboard motor for a second, caught the onrushing swell, and as the stern of the boat rose he gave her the gun, and the boat riding the huge wave shot up onto the beach and lay almost high and dry.

We passengers and crew jumped out and unloaded the boat and then slid it up on the dry beach above high water. We were quite a party—my son, Val; his friend George Hogan; five members of the crew; and myself. Four were Hawaiian boys and there was one Japanese, who, fortunately, turned out to be an excellent cook. We soon had packed our supplies over the trail and sand dunes into the grand Honopu arch. It is a delightful place in which to camp, and so far as I a concerned there is no place like it in the whole world.

We had left Haena so early that we had had no breakfast and took time out for ham and eggs. After finishing a hearty meal, we picked up our rifles and started off to try to get fresh meat for camp.

The trail led down to the beach and along a ledge of rock only a little above the sea. The trail was a tricky one. We passed the guns from one to another around one particularly tight spot, and finally rounded the top of the hogback. Looking down, we could see our boat and the landing on one side and, on the other, a beach almost identical in contour. And while walking over the top of the arch, we had a marvelous view of the whole valley.

We were looking for goats. After a while, we spied some, high on the slopes on the south side of the valley. Val and George decided they would climb up and stalk them. It was quite a large herd, some twenty goats perched on a small ridge. As the boys went up a little valley, the goats did not suspect danger until Val and George opened fire at them.

The surprised animals fled in panic and headed straight for me. As there was a lot of lantana where I was, I climbed upon a big rock and waited.

On and on they came, nearer and nearer. Sometimes I could catch a clear glimpse of them, and then they would be hidden again in the lantana. Finally I caught sight of a big brown billy and fired. As he dropped, a shining black billy came into view. He had three white spots on his right side all in a row. One was as big as a small saucer; one was as big as a silver dollar; and one was the size of a dime.

I swung on him and fired and down he fell and lay as dead. Two large kids, just right for camp meat, now came out of the lantana. I fired again and luckily got them both.

Some of the boys ran up to get them, and as they ran ahead I heard something rushing in the lantana. Suddenly out came the black billy with the three white spots, the one I had just shot. As I swung to fire at him again, he ran in line with the boys. I held my fire, and the goat vanished around a rock. I ran to the rock and around the cliff for some distance, but the black goat was gone. I searched the cliff and the valley at my feet, but he simply was not there.

We went on hunting, and when we had as many

goats as we could carry we started back to camp. We had passed over the arch and were heading down the steep cliff toward the ocean when two old nanny goats appeared right in front of me, and trotted slowly away toward the stream.

George borrowed Val's rifle and began shooting at them, but his bullets did no harm, and they soon disappeared from view.

I was in the lead, so we started on our way again. Just at that moment, a big black billy goat ran past me. I ran forward a few steps to get a better look at him, when all of a sudden something hit me with great force. I was stunned. I felt as a halfback does in a football game when a powerful guard throws him back for a loss. I just crashed to the ground and a sharp pain shot through me.

I sat up and found I could hardly breathe. I thought my back had been stove in. When I was finally able to take a long breath, I felt something pop back into place. Then I realized I had broken a rib.

Val rushed up to me to inquire if I were hurt, but I said, "Oh, no, just a bit shaken." I managed to pick up my gun and my goat, and we climbed on down to the ocean. I was mighty glad to be back in camp.

The next day, all the boys climbed the cliffs to look for wild kids. I remained in camp with one of the boys who was a better fisherman than cliff climber. His name, oddly enough, was Spring Water. He had an excellent voice and entertained me by singing and playing his ukulele all the morning.

At about eleven o'clock, a great crashing sound broke the quiet of our camp. Something had fallen from the high cliff, making a great noise and sending up a huge cloud of dust. What was it? It must have been a large boulder.

Spring Water was sitting near the entrance of the arch and I called out, "A big stone fell just now; did you hear it?"

A few moments later I managed to get to my feet and walked over to the nearby stream to get a drink. Before returning to my bunk in the sand dune, I decided to go and look at the big stone.

Imagine my surprise, when I got there, to find instead of a rock a big black goat lying dead on the ground!

I called Spring Water, and he came running to me. He stared in amazement at the goat, and then stooped down and turned it over. Will you believe it? There on the dead goat's side were three white spots all in a row. One was as big as a small saucer; one was as big as a silver dollar; and one the size of a dime!

Spring Water stood and gazed at it for a while. Then, turning to me, he inquired, "You know that is the same goat you killed yesterday, don't you?"

I nodded. "Yes, it is the same goat all right. See! His whole right shoulder was shattered by the bullet. But though I thought I had killed him and I saw him fall, still he ran past me and completely vanished from sight when we were returning to camp."

Spring Water studied the goat for some time before he spoke, and then he said, "Do you know what happened? I will tell you. Those two old nannies were only spirits to lead you into trouble, and when you did not follow them but instead went forward, all you saw was the spirit of the dead billy. He hit you with all his force and knocked you down, while all the time the real billy was lying dead on the cliff. And now he falls down on the beach just to shame you."

127

We let him lie where he had fallen, and when the rest of the party returned to camp they could hardly believe their eyes when they saw the big, black billy goat with the three white spots lying there so near our camp. Of course, they all agreed that it was his ghost that had laid me low in revenge.

Later they dragged him away and tossed him into the ocean. I planned to return the next year; but the blitz came and the Napali Coast was closed to all hunters. I will have to wait. But to all of you who go hunting some day in Honopu Valley, if you see a big black billy with three white spots, leave him alone or you may get into a worse jam than I did!

The Arrow and the Swing

HIGH on a mountain peak, in the days of long ago, there lived a boy with a wonderful arrow. His name was Hiku and he was as strong as he was handsome. He hunted and roamed over the mountainside all through the year.

One day Hiku decided that he wished to see other parts of the island and learn how the people there lived. He took his arrow and went down into the lowlands. Soon he saw several boys casting arrows into the air, and he asked if he might cast against them. The first arrow he shot went straight over the heads of the other boys, across the planted fields, and fell to the ground before the door of a grass house.

Now this was the house of a beautiful young girl, Kawelu, the Princess of Kona. However, even though she was a princess, Kawelu did not live in royal state but preferred to live in much the same manner as her neighbors.

Hiku followed the arrow to the spot where he knew it had fallen and, seeing one of the princess's attendants, he asked politely, "Did you see an arrow fall nearby?"

However, the woman at once replied, "No, I have seen no arrow fall."

But Hiku persisted. "I know that the arrow fell here. Are you sure you have not seen it?"

Then the princess, hearing voices outside, called to Hiku, "Would you know your arrow from any other arrow?"

"Know it?" Hiku replied. "Why, my arrow would even answer me if I called to it."

"Call it, then," said the princess. "And we shall see if it is such a wonderful arrow."

So Hiku called, "Puane! Puane!" And what do you think happened? A clear little voice was heard answering him, "Here I am!"

"I knew it!" cried Hiku. "You have hidden my arrow!"

Hiku entered the house of the princess and there, sure enough, he found his arrow. But Hiku became so fascinated by all the beautiful and precious possessions he saw in the princess's house that, instead of leaving immediately, he wandered from one to the other, thinking that each one was more exquisite than the last. But more beautiful than anything his eyes beheld was the Princess Kawelu herself.

Hiku forget his home upon the mountain and his wonderful arrow. He looked upon Kawelu and loved her. At the same moment, Kawelu realized that she liked Hiku more than any young man she had ever known.

Hiku stayed on the lands of the princess for five days. Kawelu would talk with him during the day, but she always ate her meals with her lady attendants, and she neither offered him food nor told him where he might find some. Soon he was hungry and a little angry. And as the hours passed he became angrier and hungrier.

"Why does she not give me food?" he asked himself. "Is it because I am of lower rank? But that is no excuse for allowing me to starve to death!"

On the fifth day he was so angry and so very hungry that he took his arrow and, leaving the house of Kawelu, he strode straight up the mountainside toward his home.

When Kawelu saw him going, she ran after him calling out to him, for she knew now that she truly loved him and wished to have him for her husband. But Hiku did not look back even when he heard her quick steps behind him. In fact, he was so angry that he made an incantation to hold her back, calling upon the maile vines and the ie vines, the ohia trees, and all the other trees to close up the path so that she could not follow. Still she came on, struggling against the tangled vines in her path. Though her clothes were ripped to shreds and her body scratched and bruised, still Kawelu climbed on.

She cried out to him, "Oh, Hiku! Wait for me! Tell me that you hear me. I beg you to stay but a moment. Save me from these thorns and vines that cut into my flesh and twine themselves about me. They are choking me and I shall surely die!"

Hiku heard her plea but he was still so annoyed with her that he would not listen, nor would he turn back. As he climbed the mountain with long, sure strides he gave no sign that he heard her. Soon Kawelu was left behind him, hopelessly tangled in the underbrush. He could no longer see her nor hear her pleading voice.

When at last Hiku reached his parents' house, he was still full of anger. But as he arose the next morning he found that his anger had left him. To his surprise he realized he was still thinking of the beautiful young Princess Kawelu. His mind and heart were full of memories of her lovely brown eyes and her great beauty. As time went on he found himself thinking of her almost constantly.

One day as he was going up the side of the mountain he found himself singing a song for Lolupe, the god who brings together friends who have been lost to each other. When he reached home that afternoon, there were strangers in the house.

"Who are these people?" Hiku asked his parents. "And why have they come?"

"Kawelu, the young Princess of Kona, is dead," they answered him. "And these people have come for timbers to build a house around her dead body."

Hearing this, Hiku wept with remorse and anguish for his great loss. Immediately he left his family and went to pray to the god Lolupe, for whom he had been singing that very day.

Lolupe had taken the form of a kite, because as a kite he could fly high into the air and travel faster in search of what people had lost and prayed to him to find.

That night Lolupe heard Hiku's prayer and, coming to him in a dream, he told him where to find Kawelu and how he might go there and bring back her spirit to the land of the living.

"This will not be easy, Hiku," said Lolupe in the dream. "But if you love this girl enough to try, I will help you all I can. Go to the wood and gather thousands of morning-glory vines. Fashion from them the two longest ropes anyone has ever seen, and to each one fasten the seat of a swing. Take the ropes out over the ocean and, when you are just above the spot where the spirits descend into the land of the dead, let down the two swings to the ocean's depths. Be sure that you are seated on one of them." Then Lolupe also told him what to do when he at last found himself in the kingdom of King Milu.

Now Hiku could not have done these things alone, but he was very lucky and had friends who wished to help him in any way that they could. Hiku and his friends gathered vines and plaited them into ropes so long that they were scarcely able to carry them to the largest canoes. They started out upon their journey, and when they reached the spot designated by the god Lolupe the men lowered the great rope swings. Down, down, down they went, with Hiku astride them. The gods had given him the power to breathe under water and had caused him to have the appearance of those who had gone into the land of the dead.

Hiku came at last to the place at the bottom of the sea where dwelt the spirits of all those who had left the earth.

He began at once to swing himself back and forth. All the spirits in this lower world were without cares and played all day long like children. When they saw him, they also wished to swing. But Hiku would not let them, for he had a plan. Presently he saw the spirit of Kawelu standing beside Milu, the king of the dead.

Soon King Milu came to Hiku and signified his desire to try the new plaything. Hiku gave him one of the swings. Some of Milu's spirit subjects came and began to swing him, and Hiku saw that Milu was delighted with this pastime.

Going over to where Kawelu stood, Hiku said to her, "Come, here is our swing." He brought her to where the second swing hung, placed her on the seat, and began to swing her. As he did so, he sang songs to her of the world of the living, but she did not remember them and seemed to have forgotten him and everything that had happened before she came to this world below.

After a while Hiku got on the swing himself, holding Kawelu on his lap, and they continued to swing backward and forward on one swing while King Milu was swinging on the other. When he was sure that Milu was completely absorbed by this new diversion, Hiku pulled on the morning-glory rope.

This was a signal to his friends above, and they began to pull on the swing. Up, up, up they came! Suddenly a weird thing happened. As they neared the sunlight, Kawelu began to grow smaller. She shrank and shrank. First she was smaller than a child, then smaller than a doll. This horrified Hiku, but he remembered the god Lolupe's instructions and knew that, if he wished to save the one he loved so dearly, he must not fail to do as he had been told. He continued to hold her more firmly. Soon she was the size of a little bird, and by the time he had reached the top of the ocean she was so tiny that he held her clasped in the palm of his hand.

When they were once more upon the land, Hiku went directly to the place where the body of Kawelu lay. It was protected by the little timber shelter the people had built and surrounded by beautiful flowers. Then, still holding the spirit firmly in his hand, Hiku knelt down by Kawelu's body and placed his hand tightly against the sole of her foot. Thus the spirit entered Kawelu's dead body and finally reached her throat. There the spirit remained.

Gathering the precious body up in his arms, Hiku carried it to the home of Kawelu's parents, where the women gave Kawelu the famed lomi-lomi massage (an art in which the Hawaiian people are especially skilled). The lomi-lomi warmed the still body and, as Hiku watched anxiously, life returned again to his beautiful Kawelu.

These two, Kawelu and Hiku, lived long years together in a place halfway between the mountains and the lowlands. They wove many wreaths for each other and sang many songs. But no matter how happy or how busy they were, they never forgot to leave offerings for the god Lolupe.

The Legend of the Rolling Head

MANY, many days have passed and many hula moons have come and gone since those primeval days on the island of Maui when Pilikana and his sister, Keikiwaiuli, lived in a crude hut on the northern outskirts of Lahaina. Pilikana was very fond of his sister, and when she married Mahikoa, he was filled with happiness and rejoiced that love had come in to Keikiwaiuli's life.

Those were happy days for the families of Pilikana and Mahikoa. Pilikana was fond of gathering his nieces and nephews about him in the evening and, by the light of the burning koa log, he sang them many meles of Maui and his carefree pranks, and told many stories of the kind that children love to hear. Mahikoa sang meles too, but they were chants of evil kahunas and of dark and frightful happenings. His listeners always experienced a cold sense of fear, for reasons they were unable to explain, whenever Mahikoa chanted his weird and fearful tales.

Keikiwaiuli often spoke to her brother about Mahikoa's strange habits. "I love him and respect him as my husband," she once said, "but I find him strange, and there are times when I am overcome with fear of him. He speaks of death in such a way that it seems something he has known more intimately than we mortals should."

Pilikana chided her for daring to speak of her husband thus, and Keikiwaiuli never spoke of the dark misgivings in her heart again.

One evening, Mahikoa said to Pilikana, "Our quarters are becoming cramped. Tomorrow, let us go up into the mountains for a supply of ahos for a new house." Pilikana quickly agreed, for he knew that near Wahikuli, right above Kaanapali, grew the kalia, which furnished the choicest ahos. Ahos were thatching sticks, you see, that furnished the finest battens for even chiefs' dwellings.

The next morning, after making preparations for their journey, the men set forth, and all day they cut and trimmed ahos.

As the day waned and twilight deepened, it began to rain and there was an uncomfortable chill in the air. The men spoke of returning to the village for the night, but Mahikoa insisted that they remain in the mountains in order to get an early start on their labors in the morning. Pilikana finally agreed and they decided to remain in the shelter of a nearby cave overnight. Before lying down to sleep, however, they gathered a great quantity of wood, which they placed around the

135

cave for a fire to keep them warm during the night. Then, after lighting the fire, Pilikana and his brother-in-law lay down and went to sleep.

Around midnight, Pilikana was startled into wakefulness by the great heat of the fire, which had painfully blistered his feet. He noticed then that the fire was consuming his brother-in-law's feet, but Mahikoa slept on.

Pilikana tried to awaken him, but there was no response from Mahikoa. The fire burned on, and Pilikana's efforts became increasingly more frantic as the flames devoured Mahikoa's legs. The flames crept along the body and, although sickened by the black smoke and the stench of burning human flesh, and nearly overcome by the smoke, Pilikana tried in vain to quench them. The flames continued their creeping journey and soon Mahikoa's stomach, then his chest was gone. Pilikana could hear the sputtering sounds of the fat in Mahikoa's body being consumed, and the sharp cracking of the bones in the intense heat. Finally, when the fire had reached the neck, Pilikana gave up in despair and ran down the mountain toward his home.

During the course of his journey homeward, Pilikana was climbing a hill and preparing himself for the hard task of facing Keikiwaiuli with the sad tale of the tragedy. Suddenly, he heard a voice call his name. It sounded like Mahikoa! A feeling of dread crept over him, that changed to crazed fear as he looked behind him and saw Mahikoa's head rolling up the hill behind him.

"Wait," Mahikoa's voice cried out to him. "Let us return home together. Wait until I catch up with you."

Pilikana, now completely terror-stricken, ran madly

to escape. The head continued rolling after him and calling to him.

Pilikana, with the head behind him, raced up one hill and then over another. While descending the second hill, Pilikana looked behind him again. The head was gaining on him. He could see Mahikoa's distorted features and tongues of flame shooting out from the rolling head. He could hear Mahikoa's voice calling out, "Oh, head! Oh, head! Restrain Pilikana so that I may catch him."

On and on they raced toward the wild tangle of the valleys. As they reached the plains above Puulaina, Pilikana realized that he was weakening and the head was gaining on him. His breath was becoming short, and he could feel the muscles in his legs tightening and becoming knotted from the strain of the chase. Avoiding the road homeward, he swung into a shortcut to the seashore by the trail heading for Keonopoko, on the western side of Mala.

At this point, an old kuala, or prophet, saw Pilikana stumbling toward him in the distance, and in close pursuit the rolling head of Mahikoa. The prophet turned to his companions and said, "If this person running toward us is not overtaken by that head before he reaches us, he shall live. If he is caught before he reaches here, he shall die." His friends were filled with fear, and urged the old kuala to continue on their journey to Kaanapali.

"No," he replied. "We must wait, or this man shall be overtaken by that head and die."

He told his companions to take a bamboo and split it into small strips, which they did at once.

Pilikana could hear the head rolling right at his heels as he neared the group. When he came up to them, his strength failed and he collapsed in a heap in front of the old prophet. The others, meanwhile, lashed at the head with their strips of split bamboo until they thought it was dead.

Pilikana came out of his faint after a while and told them of his journey and his experiences with his brother-in-law. After that, the prophet and his companions continued on their journey and Pilikana returned home.

When he had arrived home, his sister asked, "Where is Mahikoa?"

Pilikana looked at her quietly a moment before he replied. "Keikiwaiuli," he said, "I thought your husband a man, but I know now he is an akua. You have married into evil and we can only hope the pilikia (trouble) is now at an end. Your husband tried to kill me this very day."

"Kill you!" she said. "How?" And when Pilikana told her of what had happened, she wept silently. "I see now what my heart has always known. It is well that he is dead," she said.

As they were talking, the prophet appeared outside the house. While he had gone on his way, he had received an intuition that the spirit-head would reappear. The head had been merely stunned by the thrashing, and the wise old kuala realized that Mahikoa's family, and Pilikana too, would be killed by the akua unless he could destroy the evil spirit.

When he came up to where Pilikana and his sister were conversing, the prophet said to Keikiwaiuli, "Wahine, I have not come to console you in your grief. Your husband is dead, but his spirit still lingers and will return to visit grievous pilikia upon your household. Tonight, your husband will return to you in the bodily form you knew. He will appear before you and ask you to return and live with him, but if you agree you are accepting an invitation to death! Take your children and we will all wait within your brother's hut for his return tonight."

That night, as the prophet had predicted, Mahikoa appeared and called out to his wife to return and live together with him. Keikiwaiuli remained hidden in the shadows of her brother's hut and trembled with fear. She was mute with fright. Then the old kuala sprang from his hiding place and chased Mahikoa, but the akua escaped into the darkness of the forest.

Late the next afternoon, the prophet told Keikwaiuli to take her children and return to her own house. "Your husband will return again tonight, this time as the head that pursued your brother. You will hear three whistles. The first will mean he is at a distance. With the second, he will come closer. The third whistle will mean he is close at hand. When you hear this, hide yourself in the furthest corner of your house, lie down, and remain still. You will know he is outside, for the light will show his presence. Hide yourself well so that his search may be delayed. He will ask that you give him his son, but if you comply it will mean death."

Keikiwaiuli followed the old kuala's instructions, and at midnight, while dark clouds swept across the face of the moon, she heard the first whistle, then another. With the third whistle, she hid herself and waited, trembling with fearful expectancy.

Soon she heard Mahikoa's voice calling her. "Oh, Keikiwaiuli," it said, "please come outside."

"I will not," she replied. "It is raining, for the mountaintop is shiny."

"Then," said Mahikoa, "let me have my son, for I

have a ripe banana to give him."

As she refused, she could hear the head rush in and search around in the dark for her. Keikiwaiuli dashed out the door, and as she did, the prophet and her brother blocked the doorway. The door was closed and the house set afire. Through the crackle of the flames they could hear the head pleading to be set free. Finally, as the flames consumed the house, there were twelve reports when the head burst. The head was no more. The prophet departed and peace came again to Pilikana and his sister.

Kalakoa or the Five Little Pigs

LONG ago, before the day of the automobile and the paved road, the west side of Kauai was a fairyland. The Hawaiians called it the Kuahivi.

It was a long day's ride up into this land, but one felt well repaid for the tiresome journey. Upon entering this section the traveler found forests of koa and lehua trees and tall kauilas, the hardest wood known. It was from kauila wood that the Hawaiian warriors of long ago fashioned their famous spears and war clubs. In the valleys were open glades and cool, sweet water running over the rocks, making many beautiful little waterfalls between masses of tall ferns and vines. Many of these little streams had such romantic names as Nowaimaku, meaning the tear drop. Kokee, Noe, Elekene nui, Elekeneiki, and Waineke, the stream full of bulrushes. Wild cattle roamed the woods and came to the little streams to drink. Wild pigs were plentiful and, in the cliffs of the Waimea Canyon and along the Na Pali

Coast, wild goats offered hunters endless thrills. Cattle were hunted with rifles alone, but pigs were hunted with the aid of dogs, and many a good dog lost his life cut to pieces by the sharp tusks of a huge boar.

Over forty years ago, I made a camping trip into this wilderness. The legislative session of 1903 was just pau, or finished. I had had 120 hectic days there, and now that I was home at last I wanted a real rest. To make the vacation plans nearly perfect, James Judd, an old and dear friend, had agreed to come along and enjoy his well-earned rest with me. We had been friends since childhood and it was somewhat startling to realize that James was now Dr. James R. Judd, only recently returned from the famous Medical School of Vienna, Austria.

Arriving at our destination, we pitched camp on the edge of a small grove of lehua trees near the bank of Kokee stream. It was the most luxurious camp I have ever had and consisted of three large tents: one for James and myself; one for the two cowboys; and the other for my cook, Willie, and his wife, Okio. There was a big fly which served as dining room and kitchen and a small tent for supplies. No coming back to camp tired and hungry to start dinner by candle light! No, indeed, I was going to camp de luxe for once in my life!

Every day we rode and explored the woods, hunting some days, loafing others. One day Mose Kua, one of our cowboys, came riding into camp in great glee and handed over a small black pig. "There were several others," he said, "but I could only catch this one. They are in the meadow called Kanaloa Huluhulu."

We took the pig from Mose, promptly built a pen, and put the little fellow into it. The next day James and I were passing through the meadow on our way back from a goat hunt when James shouted, "Look! There are four little pigs. They're about the size of the one we got yesterday."

I followed his gaze and there, indeed, were four small pigs wandering about.

"They have evidently lost their mother and don't know where to go," I said. "It's our chance!"

Jumping off our horses, we ran to catch them. Three were black, but the other one was black and white and much huskier than the others. We chased them into some long grass and one by one we grabbed them. The three blacks were now in our bag, squealing their little heads off, but the black and white one was still going strong.

"James," I cried, "let me hold the three while you catch the fourth!"

Off he ran. It was a great chase, but finally he caught the pig and came puffing back, his face dripping with perspiration. "You are a nice one," he muttered. "You used to be light on your feet. Why don't you go after this pig instead of calling me to do it? I am half dead!"

"You are wrong," I replied. "I did it out of kindness to you. The last time I was in New Haven, you were a football hero and I figured you would be expert at chasing the pigskin."

When we returned to camp that afternoon all four pigs were put in the pen and the little family was again united. We gave them a pail of water and a trough for food. They drank the water but consistantly refused to eat. The food was strange. Haole food was no good; they wanted fern roots dug out of the ground by mama pig.

Several days went by and they grew thinner and thinner. We discussed the situation, which by now had become a real problem. What were we to do? Surely something had to be done. It wasn't right to turn them loose as they were too young to forage for themselves; but it was a tragedy to see them die of starvation. There seemed to be no satisfactory solution.

A day or so later, James and I were looking for wild cattle and in a loney valley we came upon a patch of poha bushes full of ripe fruit. We picked them all, brought them back to camp, and poured them into a pan. I picked up one and idly tossed it into the pig pen. Like a flash, one of the pigs struck quickly with his front foot and, as the fruit popped out of its paper shell, he grabbed it and swallowed it. I had found something they understood at last.

We tossed the pohas in one by one until they were all gone. But the pigs wanted more. We spent nearly all of the next day gathering pohas, which the pigs continued to devour greedily, and soon they began to eat the white man's food as well. Our troubles were over and all five of the little fellows were soon thriving. Within two weeks they were a goodlooking family. The black and white one was their leader and we had christened him Kalakoa.

One day all of us men were out of camp, each on his own pursuit. Willie had taken a shotgun and gone after wild chicken. James and I, and the two cowboys, were off to explore the Nualolo cliffs for goats. Little Okio was all alone in camp.

Enjoying a day off, she was lying down on her bed with a novel when she heard a strange noise. It sounded something like this: "Oink, oink, oink!" The sound came nearer and nearer. She looked toward the door of her tent and, to her surprise, there came Kalakoa leading his gang. He stood and looked at her for a moment and then walked off with all the other pigs following in line.

I'll wager you wonder how they had managed to get out of their pen. Okio did too, and when the rest of us heard about it we were just as puzzled. However, we later found the answer. Kalakoa had dug a hole under the bottom rail of the pen and all five pigs had squeezed their way to freedom.

Okio sat watching the little procession. There was only one thing to do—drive them back into the pen. She picked up a stick and began trying to herd them back, but to no avail. They ran faster and faster away from camp. Finally, they crossed the open meadow where we kept our horses, and the last she saw of them they were running up the hill and into the lehua forest.

Okio was exhausted and, returning to camp, she threw herself on her bed weeping bitterly. What would the men say when they learned of their loss? The thought was too terrible to bear, and she sobbed again.

As Okio lay feeling unhappy, she thought she heard the strange "Oink, oink, oink" far in the distance. She sat up and gazed out of her tent. True enough! To her amazement, along came Kalakoa, followed by his gang, marching back to camp. Straight up to her tent door they came and looked in, then hurried on, "oink, oink, oink," back to their pen, where they all crawled under the rail again.

Once inside, they hurried over to their trough looking for food. Finding it empty, they set up the loudest squealing you ever heard, just as though they were telling Okio, "We are hungry! Come and feed us! Why all this delay?"

Okio rubbed her eyes and looked again. Sure enough, they were all there, all five of them. She hurried to the kitchen and snatching up all the food she could find, she filled their trough to the brim.

Once again peace and happiness reigned over the camp, and Okio went back to her novel with a big sigh of relief.

Soon our vacation was over. Camp was struck and our packhorses loaded. Of course the pigs must go along. We arranged it so they could travel comfortably. Each little fellow had his own bag, with a hole cut in it for his head to stick out.

As our cavalcade filed off, I glanced about to see that everything rode well, and there was Kalakoa! There he hung on a packsaddle in his little bag, looking as proud as punch. His head was held high and his shiny little eyes missed nothing. He was off for new places on a big strong horse, in company with some of the best cowboys that ever threw a loop over the head of a wild bull. Adventure lay ahead and he was ready for it!

The Wahine of Lalohana

LONG long ago, in Hawaii Nei, there lived a king whose name was Konikonia. He was a good and kindly ruler.

One day, the young king directed his fishermen to set forth in their canoes and catch some fresh deep-sea fish for the community. As was the custom of the village, the king and his people gathered on the beach to bid aloha to the fishermen.

Soon the outriggers were far from land and the exciting hunt for the fishing grounds began. After a time,

145

the fishermen came to a spot that appeared suitable, and they let down their lines. Soon after they hauled them in, and from each canoe came an outraged cry, for all the hooks had been cut from their lines as if some strange undersea creature had removed them with a knife.

The paddles flashed in a hurried rhythm as the fishermen sped back to tell their king what had happened. They explained to Konikonia that the affair was even more puzzling and strange because none of them had felt their lines quiver as they would have if a fish had nibbled at the baits.

When they described the place where this strange event had occurred, the king recalled other puzzling happenings of which he had heard about that particular fishing grounds. Konikonia sent a messenger to the hills for a wizard, or kahuna, in order that he might consult with him on the matter.

When the kahuna had appeared before the king, he smiled and plucked a tiny bit of seaweed from one of the lines. "I see," he said, "that your fishermen let down their lines over Lalohana."

"Lalohana, a country under the sea?" Konikonia asked, frowning. "Strange that I have not been told of this place before."

"Few men know of it," the kahuna remarked. "It is located just below the surface where your fishermen rested their canoes. The lines were cut, no doubt, by the wahine of Lalohana. Hina is her name, this beautiful woman of the sea. All alone, she lives in a house of coral beneath the waves. Her brothers, who were given charge of her, have gone to a place far off."

Konikonia pressed the old kahuna to tell him more about Hina. As the kahuna went on to describe her beauty, her gentle, timid nature, and the lilting music of her voice, the young king felt his heart leap up. Somehow, he knew this was the wahine he had so often met in his dreams, and he longed to see her and have her for his wife.

After first warning Konikonia that, if he was not the man whom Hina would wed she would disappear from his sight, leaving him unhappy and forever haunted by her beauty, the kahuna told the king how she might be brought out of the sea to him. The king eagerly agreed to follow the kahuna's instructions. He called his craftsmen before him, and soon the entire village was happily engaged in carving a large number of images. Large as a man, each had dark hair, eyes made of pearl shells, and malos of brightly colored cloth.

At last the great task was completed, and the men of the village, led by the kahuna, set forth with their canoes laden with the images for the spot where the hooks had been cut from their lines. When they came to that part of the sea, over the country of Lalohana, the kahuna instructed the men to lower one of the images to the bottom of the sea. Then, another image was lowered and then another and another, all securely held by ropes, one above the other. The line continued to the top of the sea, where other images were left standing in caves that went in a line to the beach. Others were left in a line that led a direct path to the king's house. The last image was left standing just outside the king's house.

When all the images were in place, the kahuna blew a loud blast on his pu ohe, which is a trumpet made from a shell.

Hina, the wahine of Lalohana, heard the pu ohe and came out of her lonely coral house. There she saw the image of a man standing near her door. She was fascinated by the dark color, the wavy black hair, and the shining pearl-shell eyes. Her brothers had been gone a long time, and she had not seen even the image of a man since they had left her.

She came closer to the image and touched it. As she did, she saw there was another image just above her, and she swam up and touched that one too. All the way up to the top of the sea she went, following and touching each of the images.

Hina was delighted when she came to the surface of the sea and found that there were canoes, each with an image standing in it. As she approached the beach, she was thrilled to find that each succeeding image seemed to be more beautiful and colorful than the one before. Finally, she came to the last one in front of the king's house. It was taller than the others, beautifully proportioned, with black hair shining in the sun and a brilliant red malo around its form. But now Hina was tired; she had come a long way from her home beneath the sea. She lay down beside the image and soon was sound asleep.

Hina awakened to find the image gone and the king standing quietly beside her. She saw this big, bronzed man beside her, the hair in dark ringlets, the kind, soft wisdom in his eyes. She knew then that she would never return to Lalohana. Konikonia saw Hina's sweet, serene face, her smiling lips, the bright innocence of her eyes, and he, too, knew that he loved this beautiful wahine and must make her his queen. In that moment, a love was born that has lived through the ages in the legends of Hawaii Nei.

Legend of the Flood

IT WAS not long after Hina had come from Lalohana that she learned to speak the language of Konikonia and his people. Often while talking with the king she would speak of the precious belongings she had left in her house of red and white coral in the faraway land beneath the sea. Her most valued possessions, she said, were hidden in a large calabash, and how she longed to sea them again!

So often did she speak of it that Konikonia decided to send one of his best divers down to the white and red coral house under the sea to bring the calabash with its priceless treasures to the anxious Hina.

With her careful instructions to guide him, the diver had no difficulty in finding the calabash and he soon returned with it in his arms.

Now Hina, as we have said before, was the moon goddess. Ever since she had come to live with Konikonia, the moon had been missing from the sky, and the people were saddened and puzzled by the phenomenon.

No longer could the fishermen plot the tides. No longer could happy lovers gaze enraptured at the heavens while the queen of night bathed the earth in enchanting silver. No longer could the brown-skinned children play games by Hawaiian moonlight.

That night, after the diver had returned, Hina retired quietly to her chambers and opened the calabash. Out floated the round, full moon and quickly rose into the heavens. When the moon shone brightly in the sky, it was called kena by the natives. When it cast a luminous path upon the sea, it was known as ana.

Hina knew that when it pointed a luminous path to the island where she now lived, her brothers would see it when they returned to the land of Lalohana. Hina was distressed.

One night as she looked out to where ana was shining upon the sea, she saw signs in the water that told her that her brothers had returned and were searching the ocean for her.

She ran to Konikonia and said, "My brothers will be here shortly. Soon they will come upon this land in the form of pao'o fishes. There shall be a great tide that shall reach the tops of the mountains."

Konikonia listened calmly to what his beloved Hina told him; and when she had finished he called his people and told them: "Gather your belongings and prepare for a journey away from the sea, for soon there shall be a great flood of waters upon the land. We shall seek refuge," he continued, "on the tops of the highest mountains in our land."

Soon the caravan was moving upward into the green hills beyond the village, led by Konikonia and Hina. As the people looked behind them, they could see what Hina had said was coming to pass. The ocean had risen above the beaches, and the homes they loved so dearly had already been smashed by the great rolling surf and carried away in the violent swirl of the onrushing torrent. And the pao'o fishes were there, too, searching everywhere for Hina.

On and on the water swept inland, and while the royal couple with their people climbed higher into the mountains the flood crept through the green valleys and rose higher and higher, until it brimmed over the hills. Still the pao'o fishes continued to search for Hina, probing every cave, every volcanic fissure, every shadow and depression in the earth.

Then, with the water almost at their feet, Konikonia and Hina told their people to climb the tallest trees on the tops of the mountains. They, too, sought refuge in a great treetop.

When the water had risen to cover the highest peaks, the pao'o fishes found no more land over which to search for Hina, and soon the waters began to recede. When the mountains reappeared above the flood, the people clambered down from their points of safety and watched the water gradually go down, down, down until it reached sea level once more. An overwhelming joy filled the grateful hearts of Hina, Konikonia, and all their people.

Soon the hot sun dried the earth, and the people were able to return to their land and rebuild their houses and cultivate the fields again.

Hina lived on in happiness with Konikonia, and together they ruled a contented people in the rich land beside the ocean.

The Love of a Chief

LONG, long ago on the island of Kauai lived a young chief whose name was Lohiau. He was greatly beloved by his people and always took an active part in their affairs.

Lohiau liked to plan new games and amusements in which they might all participate. And he entered into the sports with all the zest of any young athlete.

Upon one of these gay occasions, large crowds were gathered on the beach of Haena. Someone suggested they all join in the hula dance, and soon Chief Lohiau was leading the dancers to the accompaniment of gourd drums and chanting voices from the admiring crowd.

Now, Lohiau was an excellent dancer and all eyes were upon him. The goddess of hula dancers was present, although invisible to the merrymakers. She watched the young chief's graceful movements with appreciation. Suddenly the spirit of wanton mischief overcame her and she decided to let the beat of the drums—the steady tum, tum, tum—carry far over the sea until it should reach the ears of Pele, the dread volcano goddess who lived in her fiery cavern on the island of Hawaii. What would Pele think when she heard the drum beat? What would she do? Would she be angered, or would she come and join in the merriment? Who could tell? The volcano goddess was always unpredictable.

Pele's fires were burning brightly when the sounds of revelry finally reached her ear. Her restless spirit was in a mood for action. She decided to leave the care of her fires to her brothers and sisters and go to Kauai immediately to see what was going on.

As an invisible spirit she wafted on and on and over the sea in the direction from which the sound came, until she reached her old mountain retreat on the garden isle. From there she could see Lohiau dancing on the beach. His grace and charm captivated the goddess, and she decided to assume mortal form and join the merrymakers so that she might know him better.

To attract such a handsome person as Lohiau, Pele knew she must take her most attractive human form.

She became a beautiful young woman—more beautiful than any woman on Kauai.

Slowly she walked down the side of the mountain until she was near enough to see the young chief's rhythmic movements and to hear the crowd chanting. Catching the refrain, she joined in the dance and soon was in the midst of the dancing group. Everyone gazed at her wide-eyed. Who was this beautiful stranger? Where had she come from?

At first Lohiau was annoyed at this sudden intrusion, but at the sight of her graceful figure, her charm and beauty, he became captivated by the unknown dancer, and soon was doing everything within his power to entertain her.

Not many days after their meeting, the young chief and Pele were married. Lohiau loved his bride dearly and remained always in her presence. If Pele had been a mortal, she never would have been able to withstand his charms, but, because she was a goddess, she remembered her fires that must be tended on the Big Island, and she knew she must soon return to them.

"I must leave you, my husband," she said. "I shall not be gone long. Please do not try to stop me." Lohiau would not hear of a separation, but one morning Pele had disappeared as mysteriously as she had come.

Lohiau was heartbroken and could not understand what had become of his beautiful bride. He had his men search the length and breadth of the island, but when a month had passed and she had not been found, Lohiau believed the cruel shark god must have devoured her.

Now, when Pele reached her home on the big island of Hawaii she was angered to find that her family had neglected the great fires of the volcano. It took all her time and constant watching to put them into flaming order again. While she worked, she had little time to think of Lohiau, but when the fires once more were burning brightly, her thoughts turned to her mortal husband, and she realized that she loved him more than she had believed possible.

Since she must watch over the fires, she was unable to go back to him. She decided to bring Lohiau to her home. But how to get him there? He would not know the way. Whom could she send on such a dangerous journey? She knew her brothers and sisters would refuse to go, because the way was beset with cruel akuas.

Now Pele's youngest sister had superhuman powers, and if she would consent to go, then Lohiau might safely come to her. But Hiiaka, the sister, was away in Puna living as a mortal.

However, she finally consented to go when Pele had called her home, and soon she was on her way, with two paddlers handling the big double canoe in which she traveled. At last they reached the beautiful shores of Kauai and, as they beached the canoe, Hiiaka glimpsed the escaped soul of Lohiau, who had died from grief. It beckoned to her from behind the rocks a moment and then vanished into a large cave in the distance.

Hiiaka hurried ashore. She knew she must capture it if her journey were to be successful. She ran up the beach and into the cave, where she finally found Lohiau's soul hidden in a niche in the rocks.

Keeping it well out of sight, she carried it from the cave to the Tower of Silence, where Lohiau's body was still lying in state, constantly guarded by his faithful attendants.

Hiiaka, seeing the attendants pacing back and forth

before the bier, knew she must become invisible if she were to reach the body and restore the soul to it. Using her magic powers, she was able to reach Lohiau's side without being seen by the guards. Quickly she pushed the soul back into the body and then lomi-lomied, or massaged, the stiff limbs until they became warm, and life returned to Lohiau's body.

Then Hiiaka again took the shape of a beautiful woman. When she suddenly appeared before the attendants and told them to carry the weak body to a grass hut near the sea they could scarcely believe their eyes. But they obeyed her, for they had seen the return of life to Lohiau, their beloved chief.

Hiiaka had the men make their chief comfortable in this restful place, and there she nursed him tenderly until he had become strong once more. It was not long before Lohiau was once more mixing with his people. They marveled at first, but not for long. In these days the affairs of men and gods were mingled together, and nothing seemed too strange or impossible to these open-minded, happy Hawaiian people.

Hiiaka waited until Lohiau was strong enough for the long journey before she told him why she had come to Kauai. How anxious he was to be on his way! And soon they departed together.

Lohiau traveled as a prince of high estate, and upon all the islands they were royally entertained. Lohiau consented to these delays in his journey because he believed such homage would please Pele and make her realize his power. But how little he knew of his god-dess-wife's disposition! Hiiaka grew weary of the delay and worried silently because she had seen her sister's wrath before and knew Pele would be angry because they had not hurried to her.

155

Finally they came to Hawaii and Lohiau was in high spirits, for he believed that he soon would see his beloved. But Hiiaka felt troubled, and it was not long before she knew there had been reason for her fears.

Pele had become angry and jealous. She had brooded over the delayed expedition and, remembering the beauty of her youngest sister, she had come to believe that Lohiau had been unfaithful to her. Poor, innocent Lohiau was unprepared for the goddess' vengeance. But Hiiaka knew the great power of her sister and knew that Pele would do some evil thing if she had become truly jealous. Tearfully, Hiiaka tried to tell the eager Lohiau of her fears, but dared not. Finally she bade him a sisterly farewell and turned to leave him.

Now, Pele, watching unseen by Hiiaka and Lohiau, saw her sister kiss the one she loved. Believing the worst, she rushed from her cavern home and tore the ground apart between them and ordered her sisters to kill Lohiau at once.

Even when Lohiau understood his great danger, he did not waver. The brave chief chanted an appeal to his jealous wife, asking forgiveness and telling of his mighty love for her. Everyone who heard believed him innocent—everyone but Pele. She refused to listen and insisted that her sisters destroy him immediately.

One sister defied the goddess and reached out to touch his hands, but when she took them in her own, his turned to stone, and she fled in fright. Pele's other sisters wept as they were forced to obey her angry demands. Each one touched poor Lohiau and soon he had been turned into a big, cold stone.

When Pele saw what had been done, she went back into her cavern home. After a time her anger died and she began to feel sorry for what had happened to brave Lohiau.

Her sister, Hiiaka, wept bitterly and would have nothing to do with Pele. At last Pele's heart was touched, and one day, when she found Hiiaka alone, she admitted that it had been wrong to put Lohiau to death, and even confessed that when she took human form she was subject to the frailties of human beings.

Hiiaka finally forgave Pele. The sisters promised each other that they would never again take human form and bring unhappiness upon people with whom they might associate. They had learned that it was not wise to mix their affairs with those of mortals; and when they did, only pilikia, or trouble, followed.

The Wreck of the Thunderer

THE valiant little schooner *Thunderer*, her sails proudly expanded in the wind, was slowly beating up the channel between Niihau and Kauai, loaded down with a full cargo of wool bound for Honolulu from the lonely isle. Loading the ship had been strenuous work, and everyone on board was tired when the heavy-laden vessel dropped anchor for the night in Waimea Bay. The crew was eager for a respite from the sea and begged permission to spend the night ashore, before proceeding to Honolulu the following day. The captain agreed, and the crew sallied forth with the characteristic enthusiasm that a night's liberty ashore brings to a sailor.

The delights of Waimea completely enthralled

the crew. So much so, in fact, that when the next morning was more than half spent, not one of the crew had reported back to the *Thunderer*. There is no available record of the opinions expressed by the old haole captain, but he swept into Waimea like a kona gale in search of his truant crew.

It took him several days to round them up; but at last everyone was on board and the *Thunderer* was ready to continue her voyage.

However, by that time things had changed. A strong head wind was blowing from the south and the schooner could not get away. Dark, glowering clouds scudded across the sky, swept along by violent kona winds. And as the tempo of the wind increased, big southerly swells began to roll into the open roadstead of Waimea.

The little schooner tugged grimly at her anchor as the wind increased in strength and the surf grew larger and larger. Heavily burdened by her cargo though she was, she wrestled gamely with the angry surf. But gallant as her efforts were, she was being steadily overcome by heavy seas and the savage intensity of the gale. Finally her anchor began to drag. Back she went, back, back, back—stern forward, on toward the cruel-edged reef, against which mountain-high waves were smashing with thunderous fists! The *Thunderer* was doomed!

Then, as the uneven battle progressed and the *Thunderer* was forced to the line of surf, the crew of Hawaiians all jumped overboard and swam ashore. But the poor old captain, who could not swim, was left on his ill-fated ship to trust to luck, which at the moment appeared uncertain and gloomy.

Finally the little schooner struck the reef. She groaned and wallowed like a stricken animal as the waves poured over her and pounded her against the reef with huge sledgehammer blows. Crowds gathered on the beach to watch the fearful surf dash the little vessel to bits against the jagged coral. They could see the old captain doggedly hanging to the mainmast. With each lurch of the ship and engulfing wave, he had all he could do to keep from being swept overboard.

The waves mounted in a thunderous crescendo and had already snapped the first mast like a toothpick when the captain lashed himself to the mainmast. All hope gone, he was prepared to go down with his ship, in the tradition of the sea. The mainmast began to wobble and, through a gaping wound in her side just above the waterline, the sea poured into the *Thunderer*, giving her a heavy list to starboard.

"Poor old fellow," the people on the shore said, "he's a goner." But nobody in the crowd made a move to help the doomed captain, even when it was apparent that the ship was going to pieces fast.

At this moment a young Hawaiian girl (I think her name was Mele) was attracted by the crowd and came down on the beach to see the excitement. She was only eighteen years old, but large, beautifully proportioned, and strongly built. Her dark, eloquent eyes glowed with the lively vigor of youth, but they were serious as she pointed out to where the *Thunderer* was floundering in the surf. "Look!" she cried out. "There's a man on board that ship. Why doesn't he come ashore before the ship goes down?"

"He can't swim." The reply came from one of the crew members, who was resting on the beach near Mele. His clothing was still wet and he was trembling from the exertion of his swim and the tension of the experience. Mele stood there looking at him for a moment and then she asked in a puzzled voice, "Has no one gone out to try and save the man who cannot swim?"

The sailor's voice had a scoffing note. "Who can save a man in such a sea?" he said. "We had trouble enough saving ourselves."

Mele bit her lip and looked hard at the surf for a moment. A conviction came into her eyes and her lips set in a firm determined line. Without further hesitation, she threw off her holoku, calmly ran into the boiling surf, and swam out.

The people on the beach couldn't believe their eyes. "Kahuhu!" they shouted in amazement.

Graceful as a dolphin, Mele swam on, ducking under the tremendous waves, moving steadily and smoothly out toward the reef. Not once did she look back or show any sign of fear. She was still swimming strongly and wasn't even out of breath when she reached the ship.

"Haole!" she called to the old captain, who had disengaged himself from the mainmast and was sitting on the after hatch with a look of total hopelessness in his eyes. He looked in the direction from which he thought he heard a voice. The old man blinked. Was he going mad from the ordeal? There was a girl swimming toward him! He closed his eyes, shook his head and looked again—she was still there. Perhaps it was a mermaid!

Mele was growing impatient with the delay.

"Come, haole, jump in and come ashore."

"But I can't swim," the captain replied in a nervous, uncertain voice.

Mele laughed. "That's all right, jump!" There was something in the note of her voice that gave him confidence. He jumped, clothes and all. Just as he cleared the ship the mainmast fell, hitting the deck and splintering the after hatch where the old captain had been sitting only a few moments before.

Spluttering and gasping for air, the old man came to the surface and began to struggle to remain afloat with weak, panicky efforts. But when Mele took him in hand, he stopped struggling and placed his faith in her skill in the water.

With the captain in tow, Mele set out for the beach, ducking him under the fierce combers and stroking firmly and surely in the rush of the waves. As they neared land, the men on the beach joined hands in a human chain to help them ashore.

Someone handed Mele her holoku and, when the hubbub died down, she walked over to where the captain was resting after being treated for shock and exhaustion. The old captain wasn't able to say all he felt, but gazed up at Mele with a look of inexpressible gratitude. Tears brimmed in his eyes. His lips moved speechlessly in a vain attempt to convey the emotion in his heart—an emotion too big for words.

Finally he searched through his pockets for some token of appreciation to give the girl. He found only a coin, the last one he had left, and offered it to her wordlessly. A kindly expression moved across Mele's face.

"Keep it;" she said softly, "you need it more than

I do. Besides, what I did was only fun." With that she walked quietly away.

Red Horizon

YOUNG Doctor Jamison, new county physician in Kona on the Big Island of Hawaii, sat beside an old-fashioned oil lamp. It was past two o'clock in the morning.

"I have tried everything I can for that young man," he was thinking. "All the medicine in the world won't help a person who firmly believes he is doomed to die. If I could only replace his pagan beliefs! But I've tried that: the books I've read, the stories I've told him. None of them took his mind off the spell that cursed kahuna has cast upon him."

The doctor lifed his eyes to the ceiling. "God, help me," he prayed. He stood up, reached for the lantern, and started toward his bedroom. Just as he reached the door of his study, he heard a knock on the outer door.

"Doctor-san! Doctor-san!" came an excited voice. "Doctor-san! This man too much sick," Jamison heard someone say to him.

He opened the door wide and looked into the face of Yamguchi, the old Japanese coffee grower.

"What's the matter?" he asked.

"Me look, me find old Hawaiian man. I think so he fall down. Him leg too much sore."

"Where is he?"

"Me too much tired," the Japanese continued.

"This man all way carry."

"Where is he?" Jamison repeated impatiently.

A groan came from the darkness at the foot of the steps. In the shadows, Jamison saw the form of a person doubled over.

He carried the groaning man to the lamp and looked at his face. It was that of a gray-headed native, wrinkled in pain and agony.

Dr. Jamison reached into his medicine bag for a pair of scissors with which to remove the blood-soaked trouser leg.

The knee was covered with a mass of coagulating blood. Jamison examined it carefully and, with some cotton gauze and hot water, he proceeded to clean the wound.

"What time did you find him?" Jamison asked.

"I think so maybe twelve o'clock me find this man," Yamaguchi replied.

Jamison felt the man's pulse. "I must work fast. He may have bled too much to pull through this, but there is still some hope of saving him."

As Jamison bent forward again, he looked up at Yamaguchi and asked, "Who is this man? Do you know him?"

The Japanese looked down at the haggard face, thought for a moment, then said, "This man, Hawaiian call kahuna. Him sometime good, sometime too much bad. This man . . ."

Jamison's hands paused in their work. He turned his head slowly and looked at the Japanese. "Who did you say he was?"

"This man Hawaiian call kahuna," Yamaguchi repeated.

Jamison straightened up suddenly. "The kahuna,

you say? Is he the only kahuna in this part of Kona?"

"Yes, Doctor-san."

Jamison's eyelids narrowed. "So this is the kahuna," he said half to himself. He looked at the kahuna again and spoke to the unconscious form before him. "Which one shall live?" he asked. "If I stay here with you all this coming day, it may be you who will live. If I leave you now, you are sure to die by the next sundown. You are old. If you die, Kamuela lives. If you live, he dies. He saved my life once; now I'll save his."

"Where you go now?" Yamaguchi asked, as Jamison started toward the door.

"Never mind. Go home."

Jamison saddled the white horse the people of the county had given him, and started down the narrow trail which led off through the shadows.

"Starting this early should get me to Kealiakai sometime before sundown," the young doctor said to himself.

Toward the latter part of the afternoon, Jamison reached the ridge overlooking the little valley of Kealiakai. Below him was a little wooden hut surrounded by graceful coconut palms. It stood near the edge of a curving stretch of jet-black volcanic sand. Back of the hut the leaves of the banana grove waved lightly in the faint breezes from the sea. Jamison leaned forward and patted the horse affectionately. "We are here early, Keoni."

The doctor guided the horse down the hillside through the dense growth of lantana bushes and kukui trees. Jamison then urged the horse into a gallop, and in a moment reached the hitching post beside the hut. He jumped off and ran up to the partly open door.

The rays of the sun behind him cast the outline of his shadow upon the smooth lauhala mat on the floor. On several layers of soft mats, beneath an open window, was the prostrate figure of a young native. He seemed to be fast asleep. At the head of the youth was a native girl. She kept her gaze on the face of the one she loved, and occasionally wiped tears from her long lashes with the back of her hand as she dipped long ti leaves into a calabash of clear water and placed the wet leaf on his forehead.

"Aloha," Jamison whispered softly.

She looked up at him sadly. Her eyes lit up momentarily because she was glad to see him, but she was too sad to smile.

Jamison stepped in, tiptoed across the room, and knelt beside her.

"How is he today?" he asked softly.

"I don't know," the girl answered. "He has been asleep since last night. I am afraid he will not wake up again."

"I've got good news for him today. We must wake him up and tell him about it," Jamison whispered in a confidential manner.

The girl looked up at him with a puzzled expression on her face. "What news have you? Tell me."

"The kahuna is at my house now. By the time the sun sets today, he will be dead. He was badly hurt last night. I know he will die. We must tell Kamuela. We must wake him up."

The girl looked back at the drawn face of Kamuela and said, "But I have tried to wake him up all day and he still sleeps."

Jamison put his hand on Kamuela's naked chest, leaned forward, and whispered, "Kamuela, wake up! Wake up, I want to tell you something that will make you very happy."

Kamuela did not stir. His eyelids did not flutter. No part of his body moved. Except for his very faint breathing, he showed no signs of life.

Jamison felt the native's pulse. It was very weak. Gently he leaned forward and with his fingers opened the closed eyelids of Kamuela.

"There's no question about it! The fellow is in a coma," he said to himself. "I hadn't expected this so soon. Now, how am I going to tell him about the death of the kahuna?" he pondered.

Jamison leaned back and sat on the floor. He stared at the tops of the coconut palms through the window above him. He noted by the deepened hues that it was not long before sunset. "I think I'll walk down to the beach and watch the sunset. Lehua, poor girl, musn't think I've given up hope," he said to himself. He stood up to leave.

"Are you going now?" the girl whispered anxiously.

"No, I'll be back soon," he answered.

When Jamison stepped outside the hut, the sun was setting in a colored sea beneath the lower edges of huge clouds gilded with gold and topaz. Farther along the horizon, other clouds had piled one upon the other and were massed there in purple and black confusion. From the western horizon to the sands of the beach, the ocean heaved and lifted slowly like a multicolored rug from some Arabian tale. The surface of the sea had assumed all the colors in the sun-tinted heavens above it and had mixed them with somber blues and lighter shades of green. The leaves of the coconut palms, too, had caught a tint of gold.

"It does not seem that such a glorious sight as this could be accompanied by death," he muttered half aloud, running some sand through his fingers. "Such a

166

sight as this quickens the heart of the living. It should arouse the dead."

The sun was not far from the horizon now. Jamison was thinking aloud. "If Kamuela has watched the sun dip into the ocean every day and has thrilled to this glorious picture, I wonder if it would reach some responding process in his subconcious mind now?"

The lower edge of the sun was almost touching the water. Suddenly Jamison straightened up. "I've got it! I've got it!" he said excitedly. "I'll bring him out here now."

When Jamison reached the hut, the shadows were much deeper than they had been before, but Kamuela was lying just as he had been, and Lehua was still by his side, tearfully gazing into his face.

Jamison leaned over, gently picked up the prostrate form in his powerful arms. "Come with me," he said aloud to the girl.

One-third of the sun had disappeared below the horizon when Jamison reached the sandy slopes again. He laid Kamuela down gently with his feet toward the sunset. "Lift his head up so that he may look at the sun," he told the girl.

"He cannot see," she answered a little amazed.

"Never mind. Do as I say," he insisted.

She knelt beside the unconscious native, placed one arm under the back of his head, and lifted it until his face was bathed with the red and gold rays of the setting sun. Jamison then lightly parted Kamuela's eyelids. Half of the sun had now set, but the colors had become more deep, and crimson predominated.

"Look, Kamuela! Look at the sun set today," he whispered softly. "You have seen it set many times before; see it set now. For the kahuna, this is the last sunset.

See the sunset, Kamuela — the kahuna is dead, he will see no more. The sun you see setting now, Kamuela, is setting for the last time for the kahuna. He is dead," Jamison repeated.

"Live! Live to see the sun rise tomorrow."

Only a small part of the sun remained above the horizon, but the colors were still vivid. Kamuela's heartbeat was still faint.

"Live! Live to see the sun rise tomorrow. The kahuna is dead. The sun sets for him."

The pulse which Jamison could scarcely feel began to increase in rate, became stronger and more steady.

Jamison took a deep breath, sighed, and looked into the sad eyes of Lehua, and smiled. Kamuela had heard — he would live to enjoy many more Hawaiian sunsets.

How Maui Snared the Sun

MAUI was hanging up the last of his fishnets to dry when he heard it! He stopped abruptly, his arm suspended in mid-air. There it was again, a sigh. Curious, he bent his ear to the wind to catch the sound once more. Quite plainly now he heard it, a long, deep sigh, and then a sob.

Maui threw down his net and strode up the short path to his house. There in the lengthening shadows of twilight he saw his mother. She was on her knees beating out tapa. With almost every stroke she sobbed — deep sobs that shook her poor, tired body.

Maui hurried to her and lifted her from the ground. "No more today, my mother," he said gently. "You are

168

tired, and besides the sun is gone."

"That's just it," she sobbed, laying her head on his shoulder. "There's never enough light in the day. I no more than get started with my work and the light is gone. It takes me weeks to make enough tapa for our clothes." Hina cried now without restraint, the tears streaming down her face. "And the garden, look at the garden." She pointed a trembling finger at the plants and the fruits. "Years, Maui, it takes them to grow, years. All because they can't get enough sunlight." Maui listened to her and consoled her as best as he could; listened until she had cried out all her troubles. They disturbed him, the tears and the troubles. He felt sorry for his mother.

That night, after everyone had gone to bed, Maui crept out of the house and walked slowly to the beach. Along the shore, in the undisturbed quiet of the night, he paced up and down, up and down, thinking of his mother and turning her problem over in his mind, over and over again. As he thought of her tears, his face darkened, and he shook his fist at the sky. "You won't go fast when I'm through with you," he vowed silently, thinking of the sun that sped so fast across the heavens.

The next morning when the sun rose, Maui was still on the shore. He watched it as it came over the great mountain Haleakala. And he watched it all day—watched until it fell into the sea, splashing color all over the sky.

"But the sun will never go slower," said Hina sorrowfully when Maui told her what he intended to do. "He has always gone fast and he always will."

"No," declared Maui emphatically. "No, he will not. I will find a way."

"Well," advised Hina, "if you are going to force the

sun to go more slowly, you must prepare yourself for a great battle. The sun is powerful. Stronger than you, Maui. But go now. Go to your grandmother on the other side of Haleakala. She can help you. When you get there, wait until you hear the rooster crow three times. Your grandmother will come out then with some bananas. These are for the sun. He always comes through the great chasm of the mountain and stops a moment before starting the long climb into the sky. Now, when your grandmother lays the bananas down, you pick them up. When she finds they are gone, she will get another bunch. You must take those too. And any more she may bring out. Take them all. When she starts looking for the one who took them, then, and not until then, you may speak to her. Tell her you are Maui, the son of Hina-of-the-Fire."

That very night, Maui set out. He arrived at his grandmother's before the sun was up. Hiding in the bushes near the great wiliwili tree where he couldn't be seen, he waited. Suddenly, the stillness was shattered. It surprised Maui so much that he almost tumbled out of the bushes.

It was the rooster, who, with three long shrill crows, was announcing the day. The startled Maui looked around him. Everything was coming to life. He glanced toward his grandmother's hut, wondering when she was going to appear. Just then the door opened and the old, old woman hobbled out. She carried a staff to guide her about, for she was nearly blind. And under her arm was a bunch of bananas.

As she laid them down near the oven and turned to get some water, Maui reached out and grabbed the fruit. "I'll eat the old sun's breakfast myself," he muttered under his breath.

He was eating the last of the bananas when the old woman came back. Maui grinned as he watched her puzzled expression. "I suppose she thinks she put them somewhere else." He watched her hobble back into the hut and bring out some more of the fruit. And as she laid the bananas down and turned her back, Maui snatched these too.

The old woman was considerably bewildered when she went for bananas a third time. And when for a third time she found the bananas gone, she flew into a rage. "Who is here? Who are you — you who are taking the bananas for my lord, the Sun?" she called angrily.

Then Maui came out from the bushes. "I am your grandson Maui, son of Hina-of-the-Fire. Don't be angry. I have come here to ask your help."

"Well, what is it?" queried the old woman impatiently. She was still a little angry.

"I want to make the sun go slower," Maui replied.

The old woman listened to his story. Finally she nodded her head.

"All right," she said. "I will help you. First, you must get sixteen of the strongest ropes ever made. You must knit them yourself. Then, each of these ropes must have a noose. These you must make out of the hair of your sister, Hina-of-the-Sea. When you have done this, come back to me."

Off he went, scouring the hillsides for fiber strong enough to bind the legs of the sun. Then down to the bottom of the sea he went. There he found his sister and got from her the hair he needed to make the nooses. When he had finished weaving his rope and nooses, he proudly showed them to his grandmother.

"He can't get away now, can he?" cried Maui happily.

"That is good, Maui," replied his grandmother.

"Now, here is a stone ax, a magic ax. It has a great power and you will need it."

Maui set his nooses for the sun as you would set traps for an animal. Then he dug a hole beside the roots of the wiliwili tree, and there he hid himself. All was ready. He waited. In the deep, dark quiet around him, Maui felt rather than heard the forest waiting with him. Waiting and watching, nothing moved. The silence was heavy, hushed with the expectancy of coming disaster.

Suddenly, without warning, the tension snapped. The world seemed to tremble. It was the rooster ripping the silence with three long bugle calls! It wouldn't be long now. Soon the first ray of light, the first leg of the sun, groped its way over the mountain wall. The whole forest held its breath as it watched that leg catch in one of the nooses.

Maui himself watched anxiously as each leg appeared and caught itself. Finally all the legs had been snared except one. The sun was having a little difficulty hoisting this one over the mountain. But at last it, too, was caught and held tightly in the trap.

Maui sprang from his hiding place with a triumphant yell. He ran and gathered up all the ropes and tied them securely to the deeply rooted wiliwili tree.

"Now, what are you going to do?" yelled Maui to the sun. "I've got you tied so you can't get away."

The sun didn't have time to answer Maui just then. He was busy glaring at what had just happened to him. When he saw that his sixteen legs were held fast by the nooses, he tried to back down the mountainside and into the sea again. But he couldn't move at all, neither up or down. The ropes held fast, and the great wiliwili tree held fast too.

The sun could not get away. He roared at his captor, turning all his burning strength upon Maui. The two fought bitterly in a hand-to-hand struggle. Maui fought at first without the use of his magic ax, but the sun's intense heat was fierce. He waited for a chance and then whipped out the weapon. With this, he beat the sun; he struck again and again until he could feel the sun's power and strength lessening. Finally, with a last hot gasp, the sun collapsed. Never had he received such a beating!

"Give me my life, Maui! I will do whatever you want. But give me my life."

Maui was stern. "You may have your life, but on one condition. You must go slowly across the heavens. You can't race across any more. You are causing much misery on this earth by going so fast. The trees don't grow and the vegetables and fruits take too long to get ripe. You must promise me that you will always go slowly across the sky."

The sun didn't want to go as slowly as Maui wanted him to. They argued back and forth. Finally they reached an agreement. Yes, there would be longer days. For six months the sun would go as slowly as Maui wanted him to go. But in the winter, he could go as fast as he had been in the habit of traveling.

"Now," begged the sun, "will you please let me out of these traps?"

"Yes," laughed Maui. And he proceeded to let the rays, or legs, free. The sun was very tired, and even if he wanted to, he couldn't go very fast.

The next morning the sun, coming up through the break in the mountain, was badly frightened. There on the hillsides lay the ropes and nooses that had been his undoing the day before.

"Maui!" he called. "Why are you leaving these here?"

"Only so you will be reminded that you have made an agreement with me. If you ever forget, I will tie you up again."

But the sun has never forgotten the whipping Maui gave him. And if you climb the mountain Haleakala (The House of the Sun) you will probably see the great wiliwili tree and the ropes that Maui used to snare the sun.

The Sleeping Boy

THERE were certain events in my childhood days that stand out in my memory as sharply as a photograph, almost as though they had occurred only yesterday. For instance, that day almost seventy years ago. I think it was in the year 1876. I was a small boy playing in my father's office. He was looking over some papers when a knock came at the door. We both looked up and saw that it was an old Hawaiian woman from the village.

"Aloha, Kanuka," she said. Her voice trembled, and from her swollen eyes and sad expression it was plain to see that she was overcome by a deep sorrow.

My father looked at her quietly for a moment, and when he spoke his voice was kindly and reassuring. "Come in," he said. "What's the pilikia?"

The old woman bit her lip and large tears began to roll down her cheeks. "Auwe!" she said. "My troubles are great. My fine boy, Ku, died last night and I want a burial permit so that I can take him to his grave." With that she began to wail and rock back and forth, with her hands knotted in fists pressing tightly against her temples.

My father consoled her until she regained control of herself. Then he walked back to his desk, opened a drawer, and took out an official-looking paper. As part of his authority as agent, he had been authorized under the Kingdom of Hawaii to issue death certificates and other documents of a legal character.

He sat there solemnly reading the death certificate for a few moments. Then he picked up his pen. He seemed wrapped in deep thought. Finally I heard him say, "That's funny! I saw that boy only yesterday and he seemed to be hale and hearty enough." The old woman just stood there mute with grief.

My father's mind was made up. He laid the paper aside, picked up his hat, and told the woman he would go with her and look at the boy. And together they walked to the native settlement a mile or so away.

When he returned home a short time afterward, we asked if the boy were really dead. He had a look of deep concern on his face and there was a puzzled expression in his eyes. "I don't know," he said gravely. "He doesn't breathe and his heart is still, yet he doesn't seem dead. I told the woman to wait until tomorrow." He gave us no other reason for his decision.

The next day Father let me go with him to the home of the old woman. When I looked in the doorway, I saw the boy, Ku, lying on a mat. A cold shudder ran along my spine and I felt a little frightened. I was afraid to go into the hut, but my father entered and walked over to examine the boy.

After he had completed his examination, Father came out shaking his head. "This is very strange," he said; "he is dead and yet he is not."

This was on a Tuesday. Father returned again on Wednesday and called again late Thursday. There were, by that time, quite a number of natives gathered around the hut, some attracted by morbid curiosity and others to mourn for the departed Ku. Father spoke to several of them before entering the hut. Then he went inside and, after a few soft, consoling words to the mother, he went over and examined the boy once again.

Father was sitting there talking quietly to Ku's mother when suddenly, the sleeper gave a tremendous sigh. There was a gripping, awed silence in the room as everyone turned and looked at the boy. He sighed again. There were a few startled gasps in the room and some uneasiness, but the silence remained unbroken. The boy moaned slightly, sighed again and stirred on the mat. Then, as everyone stood amazed, he sat up, blinked his eyes, and looked around.

Finally, the boy's mother, clearing the excited natives out of her way, came close to her son. Pressing her tear-stained face against his, she kissed him and said, "My poor Ku, where have you been?"

The boy smiled. "Where have I been? I have had the most wonderful time. Three days ago I died and my soul went to Polihale. I was just going to jump into Po, but an akua there told me that I wasn't ready for Po yet. He sent me to wander on the rim of the Waimea Canyon. When I reached the place called Kaana, I met a lot of other spirits, who, like myself, were not yet ready for Po. They greeted me in the friendliest manner, treated me kindly, and we lived very happily together."

At this point in the boy's story, one of the fascinated listeners asked, "Who did you meet?" Ku at once mentioned a name. "He told me he was a great warrior," the boy added. Suddenly an old man in the crowd shouted, "It's true! What the boy says is true! When I was a small boy, that man he speaks of was a great fighter in the king's army. He was killed long ago. I have not heard of him since and no one else knows about him." Ku mentioned names of other people, some of whom had died recently and others who had died many years before the boy was born.

Ku paused in his story and told his mother he was very hungry; and while she bustled about the little hut preparing some food for him, the boy turned back to the crowd with a serious look in his eyes. Finally, a little wahine sitting at the boy's elbow piped up in a timid, half-frightened voice,

"This land of Kaana you speak of, was it more beautiful than Hawaii?"

Ku looked at her a moment before answering and smiled.

"Yes, Leilani," he said, "it was the most beautiful place I have ever seen." He sighed and looked dreamily into space. Then, he continued his story.

"When I first arrived at Kaana the other spirits wove a lei from a rainbow and bade me aloha. There were strange, delicious fruits and beautiful flowers. Bright-colored birds sang all through the day and there was sweet music in the air all the time. We sang meles all day and in the evening we had hulas in the moonlight. When we decided to go to sleep at night, the mene-hunes brought a soft cloud and laid it on the rim of the canyon like a punee in the sky. In the morning the mountain mist would wake us. It was such a beautiful life and I was so happy," Ku said, "but it's all over now."

"This morning," he continued, "an akua came to me

177

and told me I must return to my body. I said, 'No! No!' and ran down the canyon away from him, but he chased after me and soon caught me. He had a big sharp spear which he poked me with and ordered me to go. Sadly I went, and each time I turned to escape, there stood that mean old akua with the spear in my back.

"Finally we came to the lowlands. I walked up to the house, and as I came near I saw Kanuka. He was talking to people at the door." Ku mentioned the names of several of the people that my father had spoken to before entering the house. Then he added, with a grin, "When Kanuka stooped down to examine my body, I was just behind him, looking over his shoulder. And when he went over to sit down I turned to flee, but the akua blocked my path.

"'Go in,' the akua said to me, and prodded me again with his spear. I was afraid. I looked again at my body. It looked like a cold, black, empty cave. I tried once more to escape, but the akua held me with his spear. I crawled back into my body, and here I am."

Ku indicated that his story was ended; and while he embraced his mother the crowd slowly filtered away.

My father, meantime, waited until the crowd had left and walked over to shake hands with Ku. Not a word was spoken. When my father left the boy's home, he took the burial permit he had prepared and slowly tore it into small pieces and scattered them to the winds. And Ku, the boy who had lingered on the threshold of the tombs, lived on for many, many years.

Pele's Revenge

ONE balmy spring morning, many years ago, Pele, the fire goddess, awoke with a bored and restless feeling. She was weary of the sports she had enjoyed with her sisters in the fuming crater of Kilauea. Riding to the blistered lip of the crater on a wave of lava, she plumped herself down and sat overlooking the neat green fields of taro in the quiet valley below.

It was a brilliant morning. Laughing sunbeams skipped gaily over the plains of Puna and rippled on the swells of the blue-green sea. Big white clouds hung like leis around the tops of the mountains. But Pele paid no heed to all the beauty around her. She was restless and fuming with discontent.

Suddenly her roving eye caught a glimpse of color on the green slopes of Mauna Loa. She could see that a number of holua players had gathered on the neighboring hillside to hold a holua meet. There among the contestants were Kahawali and Ahua, the two hand-somest chiefs of Kauai.

Pele's eyes flashed with delight. Holua racing was one of her favorite sports and one in which she could display her supernatural daring and skill. Immediately she decided to enter the tournament. How amazed the holua racers would be when she entered the contest! She hurried to the fiery chambers, deep in the heart of boiling Kilauea. In a few moments she came forth, not as the wrinkled old hag who occasionally toured the countryside, but as a beautiful, tall, and slender maiden.

Pele planned her arrival at the course just as the two handsome chiefs were about to take their turn in the tournament. She carried her sled in her arm and ran her fingers slightly over the smooth bamboo runners. As she approached, Pele observed that the other sleds in the race were the typical papa holua, with bamboo runners fastened together by sturdy crosspieces and with stout poles, running the eighteen-foot length of the sleds, acting as handles. A steep hill, carpeted with pili grass and ferns, provided the course.

Down its sloping sides raced the contestants, head-first on their sleds. The object of the race was to see who could slide the longest distance down the sides of the hill. As Pele came near, she could see the holua players run out, throw themselves forward on their sleds, and shoot down the slippery course with lightning speed, laughing and calling out to each other. A crowd of spectators had gathered along the slope to watch the sport, and there was much cheering and laughter as they encouraged their favorites.

Kahawali and Ahua were at the starting line when Pele, in her disguise as the beautiful young maiden, took her place beside them. The two young chiefs noticed her beauty, but were more concerned with the contest, and after a glance returned their attention to the race.

The signal was given and the race was on! Pele flung herself upon her sled and flew like a bird down the grassy slope. The Kauai chieftains were amazed to see the young wahine flying by them!

When the race was over, Pele was far ahead of the two chiefs. Kahawali and Ahua ran over to where she was sitting, quietly fixing her long black hair. There was love and admiration for this daring wahine shining in their eyes. Pele greeted them with a friendly smile, and tucked the flowers they offered into her hair.

"You are, indeed, a beautiful creature," Kahawali sighed aloud.

"Yes, yes, indeed!" Ahua said.

"Will you do us the honor of joining in another race?" they eagerly asked her. Pele nodded her head in assent. The three young racers started back to the top of the slope. Pele smiled quietly to herself, for in those days it was a great honor for a woman to be invited to join men on equal terms in a game or contest of skill.

Side by side on their sleds, they again started down the green hill. When the race was over, Pele had again finished far ahead of the two young men. They raced again and again throughout the morning, and each time Pele won by a good margin. The two young men accepted each defeat good-naturedly, and their admiration for the beautiful and talented girl increased.

Finally, Kahawali, in a spirit of good fun, hid a rock beneath his kapa. With the added weight, he was able finally to outdistance his beautiful rival. Laughing among themselves, the two young men ran back to where Pele was sitting moodily and began to tease her about her defeat. Suddenly, they stopped! What was happening? What had they done? They were struck dumb by what they saw before them.

The beautiful young maiden who had so delighted them a few minutes before was being transformed by anger into a terrifying object that struck fear into their hearts. Her features took on sharp, vicious lines. An angry red fire kindled in her eyes and there was a bubbling froth on her lips. She was breathing heavily with wrath and black smoke curled from her nostrils. Alas, Kahawali and Ahua recognized Pele too late! A tongue of flame leaped between her lips and the two chiefs were panic-stricken by the scorching heat. They must escape! But how?

Madly they ran and flung themselves headlong upon their sleds. Flying wildly down the mountainsides between Mauna Loa and the sea, they could feel the hot, panting breath of Pele close behind them. As they ran frantically uphill, Ahua looked behind and saw Pele riding a flaming wave of white-hot lava, rushing closer to them every moment. "Hurry," he cried to his companion, "we must reach the sea!" That was it — the sea. If they could but reach its cool depths, Pele would be unable to harm them.

The entire island of Hawaii was trembling with the terrible force of Pele's anger. The fearful heat was opening huge cracks in the earth and the very rocks were being turned to cinders. Loud claps of thunder echoed through the valleys. Violent earthquakes shook the mountains. The sickening odor of sulphur was in the air.

On and on raced the frightened chiefs, with Pele so close behind them that she scorched the clothing off their backs. As they came closer to the sea their hope was renewed. They ran faster, and faster, and faster. Ahua, looking behind, could see the mountain streams disappearing in clouds of vapor from the boiling heat.

Then, just as Kahawali's foot touched the surf, he tripped on a reef. He struggled to his feet; alas, too late! Pele's flaming arms were about him and she drew him angrily to her bosom. He struggled for air as he was engulfed by the flames. Everything was a violent, ugly red. Finally, complete numbness swept over him. There was a rushing sound as he was crushed in a flood of molten lava. Kahawali struggled no more. Only a

182

ragged hill of lava now marked where he had stood.

Ahua, meantime, ran madly out toward the edge of the reef, where the sea was smashing itself into white foam on the sharp coral. Sobbing with relief, he threw himself into the surf—but not soon enough. Just as he disappeared beneath the water, Pele stretched forth, grasped his leg, and plucked her victim from the sea. Fighting with all his might, he struggled free at last. He lay weakly on the reef, too exhausted to rise. His leg had been withered by the fiery grasp of Pele's fingers, and he was unable to escape. He could do nothing now but await his fate. "Oh, no," he sobbed as he felt himself being drawn into Pele's arms. She held him close to her evil face and pressed burning kisses upon his protesting lips. He felt his life slipping away in her cruel embraces of fire and smoke.

A wave of repentance swept over Pele as she stood there looking sadly at what she had done to the young chiefs. Sorrowfully she recalled the handsome faces of Ahua and Kahawali. Beneath those two mounds of lava were two young mortals who had known health and laughter just a short while before. They had loved her and she had returned their affection with a crushing weight of terrible fire and painful death. Shame crept into her heart. Sadly she returned to her fiery chambers in the crater of Kilauea.

To this day, you may see, on the shores of Hawaii, two rugged hills. Despite centuries of violent winds and crashing seas, they have retained startling human outlines. "Puu o Pele" old Hawaiians call them, the two "Hills of Pele"—monuments to two men who dared to love a goddess.

Hunting Stories

FAR UP in the high mountains of Kauai on the western side of Waimea Canyon is a tiny stream called the Nawaimaka (the Teardrop).

In a little glade near the spring stood our camp. In ancient days bird catchers had lived there in a tiny grass hut and had named that spot Halemanu or the Bird House, but now a rambling wooden house stood there, with white moss growing on its ridge pole. It was a comfortable old camp, but the best part was the big fireplace at one end of the living room; and there every evening we gathered to enjoy the warmth of the crackling fire.

Every summer boys would come from Honolulu and as soon as we all were seated around the fire, some lying on the big skins of wild cattle, storytelling would begin. Hunting stories were the favorites and I will relate to you three of the many that have been favorites for years. In all three the number five figures.

In the first story, Charley Storeback is the hero. He was a part-Hawaiian carpenter by trade, but a hunter by preference. He had a fine .45 Winchester rifle and was an excellent shot. One day while leading a group of hunters through the woods, Charley came upon the tracks of a small herd. As he rode out of the woods into a small glade, he was surprised to see the band of cattle (there were five of them) sleeping on the ground right in front of him. Charley pumped up a shell and fired. When he had fired five shots, all the cattle lay dead.

Charley wouldn't tell about it but the next boy in

184

line described the hunt to me. "Suddenly," he said, "Charley stopped his horse and began firing. I looked ahead quick to see what he was shooting at. I saw nothing; but bang, bang, bang goes his gun! Then I see a big cow jumping up; but bang goes his gun and she fall flat on the ground. A big steer was on his feet and running like mad for the woods; bang again goes his gun and the big steer just pitch forward and fall dead upon the ground. We all begin to shout and yell with excitement; and then we see five cattle all lying stone dead! 'Charley,' we all exclaim, 'you're a wonderful shot! How can you shoot like that?' But Charley only smile and say, 'Well, boys, I guess we got enough beef for today.'"

And after all these years, Charley's record still stands unbeaten.

Now for the second story in which number five figures. This is also about wild cattle.

Four beautiful little rivers start at the Alakai Swamp and work their way down to the great gorge named Poomau, a side-arm to the Waimea Canyon. This large area is densely covered with lehua trees, ferns, and all sorts of other native brush, and is the watershed for that whole area — an immense natural reservoir. Into this wild country wild cattle found their way, and it was decided that they should be exterminated. A party of four of us, Charley, Brodie, Hines, and myself, made arrangements to visit that unexplored land and see what luck we would have.

The day before we left, a long, lanky youth of seventeen rode into camp. I knew him well. He was always called "B" and was a Honolulu lad on a two-week vacation. He arrived with a rifle and we invited him to join us.

At dawn the five of us rode away, headed for the hunting grounds. We crossed valley after valley. What pretty names they had, as beautiful as nature itself—the Kanaikinana, the Ka Wai Koi, the Waiakoali, and the Mohihi.

The cattle had been roaming those hills and valleys for some time. They had established very good trails, and we followed them until we reached the high ridge between the Mohihi and the impassable Koaia. Finally we picked up tracks and then entered such dense jungle that riding was impossible. We tied our horses and walked through the woods. We had three dogs with us, and as we came out on a small glade, they began to bark. We hurried forward and found a band of cattle. One glance took them in—a big bull, three or four cows, and two large yearling calves.

"Take the calves," I whispered. Bang! and down crashed the two calves.

We ran up to make sure they were dead. But I saw "B" race off through the woods and in a few moments I heard his gun roar. We were all turning to see what he was up to when a huge red cow came rushing towards us at full speed. Blood was streaming from her shoulder. "Better kill her!" cried Charley. We took a quick shot as she passed and the cow fell dead almost at our feet.

"B" came rushing out crying, "Did you see my cow? Did you see my cow? I shot her in the head."

"Was it a big red cow?" we asked him. "If it was, here she lies." He came up and gazed at his cow.

"You are a wonderful shot," we all told him. "Just see what you did. You are the first hunter who has been able to do that in all the years we have hunted; you made five holes in the cow's skin with one bullet."

"What do you mean?" he said. "She was running straight for me and I shot her in the face."

"Look," we said, "you hit her in the front shoulder and the bullet ran along the shoulder blade under the skin and then came out and entered her fat stomach and ran along under the skin and came out again and finally buried itself in her hind leg." And that is exactly what had happened. As far as I know, "B's" record has never been equalled.

And now for the tale of a goat hunt.

It was Christmas Eve and we were all gathered at the home of my cousin, Francis, and his charming wife, Lilly, to have fun and to light a Christmas tree. One of the party was a young Californian named Charley E., and when a shining new .30-.30 rifle that hung on the tree was presented to him, his happiness was complete. He immediately challenged me to a goat hunt which I accepted as a joke, but a month or so later he rang me up to say that he had four days' vacation and was coming to hunt.

He came, and off we went to the hills. On our right lay a deep gorge, the Hoea, lined for miles with high cliffs, a favorite hiding place for goats. We climbed out onto a ridge and spied a band of goats on the next ridge.

"Charley," I said, "if those goats get frightened they will run down the ridge they are on. They cannot get down into the Hoea Valley, the cliffs are too high. If one man sits there he will be right in the runway. Take your choice."

"I love to sit on the runway of deer," he said. "We hunt that way in California so I will take that station."

"Good," I said. "Hide yourself well," and we parted. I went up to scare the goats and he went down to the end of the gulch. After about half an hour, I came out above the goats and they immediately dashed off for the cliffs and safety. I trotted after them. When I reached the end of the grassland where the cliffs began, I saw the goats looking down into the valley.

I looked too, and there was Charley sitting on the top of the flat rock, his rifle in his lap and his white shirt shining in the sunlight. The goats didn't like this strange shining thing and were suspicious. As a big billy goat was the nearest to me, I fired a shot. Much to my surprise the bullet went through his neck and also through the neck of a nanny goat standing by his side. Both goats fell dead.

The shot startled the rest of them and they dashed madly down the end of the hogback right over to Charley, and in a few moments I heard his rifle begin to crack. One, two, three, I counted— sixteen shots in all.

I kept along the top and, looking down onto a ledge, I saw a big nanny goat with two kids and another young, fat nanny just right for mutton chops. I fired at the young nanny. At the shot, the mother nanny jumped to one side and, the ledge being only six feet below, I dropped onto it between her and her two kids. "He-he-he!" cried the kids. "Maa-maa," I replied in my best goat talk, and before they got their wits I lunged forward and grabbed the two kids and tied them. Then I dressed the young nanny. The mother goat had vanished.

I packed the three down into the valley to my left and found the two dead goats I had shot first. Then I laid them down and went to see what Charley had done. I heard him shouting. I hurried around the point of the ridge and saw him.

"I've got one," he shouted to me. "Look up there on the side hill!" And sure enough, there lay a big nanny! "This is a fine gun," he said.

"Yes," I replied, "you have done well. I heard you fire sixteen shots."

"By the way, how many goats did you get?" he asked me.

"Only five," I answered.

"You liar!" he replied. "You can't fool me. You only fired twice."

"That's all right," I said. "If I can show you five goats, will you take it all back?"

"Sure," he said, laughing at me. We walked around the point.

"Here is my gun and one goat. Come on. Here are two kids, and just a little over there you will see two more dead goats. Five goats is my bag."

He stared in amazement. "I give up, you win!" he said, grinning.

The Battle of the Giants

RIDING over the plains of Niihau once long ago, I saw a strange little hill standing all by itself in the midst of the flat land. It did not seem to belong there. It was a different soil and rock than the rest of the land, and I was curious as to how it got there; but no one seemed to know. Probably I never would have found out if I hadn't met by chance an old kanaka fisherman one day on the shores of Kauai.

We sat and chatted and I asked about the old inhabitants of the region and how they lived in the days before the white man came. As he talked, he began to boast about the men of Kauai—how big and strong they were. Suddenly pointing toward Niihau he said, "Do you see that small hill lying in the plain far from the main range of mountains?"

"Yes," I replied. "I have been there."

"Well," he said, "that was once a part of Kauai."

"Tell me about it," I begged. And this is the story he told:

"Hundreds of years ago a race of giants lived here in Hawaii. One great giant lived here in Mana and one lived on Niihau. One day they looked across the channel at one another and began to talk. First they bragged about their strength and size. Then they began to call each other names, and finally they got so enraged that they each grabbed a rock and hurled it at the other. The Kauai giant tore off a chunk of the pali back of Mana and it landed on Niihau, right on top of the other giant, and killed him instantly. His bones are lying underneath that hill, and if you dig in there you will find them. But the rock from Niihau fell short. It has a big white cross on it and lies just outside the breakers."

"I would like to see the rock from Niihau," I said.

The old fisherman took me in his canoe and we paddled out. Sure enough, there was the big rock with the white cross lying in the sea, easily seen in the clear water.

"You see," he continued, "the Niihau giant was fed on sweet potatoes and yams; he was not quite strong enough. But the Kauai giant ate poi; that is why he won the fight."

The Spear Bearer of King Kaumualii

THIS is a short story about the last king of Kauai. This great man's name was King Kaumualii. His bodyguard had been composed of splendid men; large, powerful, and afraid of nothing. In vain had Kamehameha tried to capture Kauai, but these fighting men had turned back every attempt. Finally, when King Kaumualii died in Honolulu, the guard disbanded and went back to their fields.

When I look at the long, black, kauila-wood spear handed on to me by my father, I think of the old spear bearer of King Kaumualii's guard and the story he told my father as he lay on his mat in his little grass hut in the village of Pokii.

Late in the afternoon on a hot summer day, a young Hawaiian boy appeared at our home in Waiawa. "My father is dying and wants to see you," he said.

Immediately my father joined him and away they went over the hot plain until they came to the hut. The old Hawaiian lying on a mat called to father to enter, and when he was seated he began to talk.

"Kanuka," he said, "I am an old man now and tonight I die and go to my people. But before I go I want to tell you this story. I was one of the king's guards. I was a big, strong young man working in the fields when the captain of the guards came and told me to come to the king's palace, as there was to be elected a successor to one guard who had been killed.

"I reported at once along with ten other young men. The judges looked us over and examined us, and finally five were chosen for the test: the poison test. They sat us in a row and gave to each man a seed of the koali, or morning-glory. We swallowed it and waited. After a few minutes they gave us another seed, and we swallowed it, and waited. 'You see,' he said, 'the seed of the koali is deadly poison, but you cannot detect it unless it is very strong, about the strength of six seeds. So if the guard cannot stand the poison of five seeds, he is not good as a guard; the enemy could kill him and he wouldn't even know there was poison in his food.'

"So the five young men sat and watched each other and took number three. No one seemed to feel the poison, but just as they began to hand out the next seed, one man fell back and died immediately. Number four was now given us. We sat watching each other, when two suddenly fell backwards and died. It was an uncanny feeling to see those two big men die so suddenly! But still we sat and swallowed number five. Only two of us remained and I looked at him; he was a good friend of mine. I did not want to die, and I didn't want him to die. I hoped we would both pass the test. We waited and waited! Suddenly my friend fell dead. I alone was left sitting there! I expected to die, but I didn't.

"'You are my man,' said the captain of the guard. 'The gods have chosen.'

"I was then taken before the priest and purified and annointed as a guard, and I was given this spear."

The old man drew out from under the mats a long black spear, made of kauila wood, and of most beautiful workmanship. "I carried this in front of the king, and any commoner who allowed his shadow to cross the path of the king, I jabbed with the hard, sharp point of this spear.

"I was a big man and a splendid fighter. No one could

poison me, but now I am old, and tonight I die. My king is dead. But you, Kanuka, are like a king on Kauai. Take my spear and keep it for me, and I will die in peace."

My father took the spear and shook the old warrior's hand. "Aloha," he said, simply.

"Aloha, Kanuka," came a faint reply.

Then turning his head away, the old Hawaiian quietly breathed his last.

The Three Old Ogres of Niihau

ONCE as Makaawaawa, my head cowboy, was racing over lava flows while vacationing on Hawaii, his horse broke through the crust and he fell headlong. The Big Island cowboys rushed up expecting to find him dead or crippled, but Makaawaawa sprang up, climbed on his horse again, and was away in the chase.

"Of course he is not hurt," said one of the cowboys. "Paakiki no kanaka o Kauai."

It sounded like an old Hawaiian saying, but no one knew its derivation until I met an old man from Niihau one day and asked him about it. He told me this story:

Once upon a time, long, long ago, three old ogres lived on Niihau near the landing called Kii. They were cannibals, and everyone who landed on Niihau was promptly killed and eaten.

One day a young chief named Ola decided he would rid the island of these ogres. He carved four little men out of lehua wood and put mother-of-pearl eyes in each one.

Loading them into his canoe, and taking some fish and poi and his magic war club, he paddled boldly across the stormy channel toward Kii. One of the old ogres was on the lookout, and when he spied something moving on the ocean, he called out, "I see a boat!"

"It's only a log!" came back the answer.

He watched for a long time, and again cried, "I see a boat and there are men paddling in it. They are headed straight for Kii."

When the ogres were certain it was really a canoe and was coming in to land, they hid behind the sand dunes and watched. Young Ola meantime drove his canoe safely through the breakers and ran it up on the sand.

On the beach was an old boathouse. He carried one of the passengers up and set him down against the wall facing the door. "Two go up, and one goes back," counted the old ogres. Then as Ola carried his three companions up beside the first one, the ogres could see there were five in the party. After Ola had set his four little men in a row, he hid behind the door and soon fell fast asleep.

The old ogres waited for some time and then one crawled up to the door and peeped in. When he returned to his companions he said, "They are still awake. I can see the whites of their eyes."

They waited a long time, then one crept up to the door again. There stood the four little men as before.

After Ola had slept for two or three hours, he awoke, ate some fish and poi, and soon felt his strength and vigor return. He then laid his four little men on their sides with their backs to the door, and again hid behind the door with his magic war club in his hand.

By and by one old ogre crept up and, seeing the men asleep, signaled the other two; whereupon all three crawled in.

The first ogre stooped over the nearest sleeper and bit him behind the ear to kill him; but instead he broke his long tooth!

"Auwe!" he cried. "Paakiki na kanaka o Kauai!" (The men of Kauai are tough)

"Paakiki we are, indeed!" cried the young chief, as he stepped out from behind the door. He swung his magic war club; and before the ogres knew what was happening, they had been killed!

Ola dragged their bodies to the beach and cast them into the ocean for the sharks and eels to devour. Then he loaded his canoe and paddled back to Kauai.

Great was the rejoicing among the people of Kauai. Niihau was free at last, and many families moved over and settled there.

The Modest Warrior

MANY, many wars have been fought and passed into history, and many Hawaiian heroes have nobly died in battle since those days long ago when warrior kings locked their armies in combat for the complete rulership of the island of Oahu.

Many centuries ago, that district which we now call Ewa was ruled by the iron hand of King Kahuhihewa. Not far away, in the beautiful area of Moanalua, lived his bitter rival, King Pueonui. For many years the green, rolling country between the two districts had been both the cause and location of fierce wars between the two kings; and their armies had fought unceasingly with neither side winning complete victory.

Among the warriors of King Kakuhihewa were two loyal friends. Kale and Keino were their names. All day long they fought side by side and when the shadows of evening fell they returned to their bivouac to share a hearty supper of poi and fish. Then, after they had eaten, they lighted their torches of kukui nuts and retired within their grass hut to rest upon mats of lauhala.

One night, after a hard day in the field, the two companions were resting on their mats and quietly watching the smoke drift lazily from the kukui nuts. They had been conversing in a sleepy fashion, but the conversation had struck a lull and neither one had spoken for some time. Finally, Kale propped himself up on one elbow and, turning to his friend Keino, he said, "What is it that you wish for more than anything else in the world?"

Keino stretched and yawned heartily before answering. He was a lazy fellow with a hearty appetite for the pleasant things of life and a deep interest in food, drink, and sleep. His face lit up with a smile.

"My wish is this," he said, "that we sleep late in the morning, until well past the crowing of the cock. And then I wish that we pull some ahuhu shrubs to intoxicate the fish and make them easy to catch. I wish that we have little work gathering the fish and that we catch a nice fat eel. Then that we return home, wrap the eel in banana leaves, and enjoy the smell as it cooks in the imu. Then I wish that we eat until our opus are full. And, after that, we can lie down upon our mats and watch the rats running among the lintels. That is my wish!"

Kale looked at his friend with amiable mockery in his eyes. "My friend," he said, "you talk like a man who has been starved for years." His hands tightened around his knees and a faraway look came into his eyes.

"Keino," he said, "my wish is one that I have thought about these many nights, when we have returned from our battles with the enemy to rest here in our hut. I wish that we may eat the sacred dogs of Kaku which bite the people. I wish also that we may bake the royal hog whose tusks are crossed, and that we may have the fattest amaama fish in the king's fishpond for our supper. And after we have dined in his royal fashion, I wish that the king himself shall bring to us the most delicate and intoxicating awa. And after we have drunk our fill of the awa that the king himself has prepared, I wish that he brings his most beautiful daughters to make them our wives. That is my wish!"

"Auwe, we shall both be killed for discussing things sacred to the king alone," Keino said. His voice was trembling with fright.

Kale laughed till tears filled his eyes. "My friend," he said, "you worry like an old woman."

Despite the fears of Keino, the two friends continued to repeat their dreams for ten nights. Meantime, the king had become curious about the lights burning in the hut of the two friends. In those days it was forbidden to burn the midnight oil without special permission from the king. Kakuhihewa became a little annoyed about the matter and decided to send a spy to learn the cause for such strange goings-on.

That night, the spy crept close to the grass hut and hid himself in the shadows of the eaves. He listened quietly while the two friends were talking and when he heard Kale's wish, he plunged a pahoa, or wooden dagger, into the red clay of the doorway. Then he sneaked away into the darkness to report his findings to the king.

When the king heard what the two warriors had been discussing, he was purple with rage. Calling his kahuna, or priest, before him, he ordered: "Have these scoundrels, who speak so lightly of the king, borne on the bony points of spears to the highest pali, to die for their treason!"

"Please, your majesty," interrupted the kahuna, "you should carry out the man's wishes, for it is decreed that it shall be he who will defeat Pueonui and gain for you the whole of Oahu!"

When Keino and Kale awakened the following morning, the first thing that greeted their eyes was the wooden pahoa that the spy had left sticking in the clay at their doorway. "Auwe," moaned Keino, "it is the sign of death. We have been discovered."

As he spoke, a band of warriors climbed the hill and approached the hut. They were armed with pololu, which were long spears, and newa, the typical war clubs of those days.

Keino turned to his friend. Cold sweat stood out on his brow and he was shaking with fright. "Our death is at hand!" he cried.

Kale did not answer his companion. He leaped to his feet and walked to the door with his newa in his hand and a determined set to his chin. "Keep your eye on them," he said.

When the band of the king's warriors came closer and surrounded the hut, Kale stepped outside. Raising his newa, he shattered the threshold with a single blow! One of the king's men stepped forward and said: "Calm yourself! We have not come here to harm you. We have been instructed to escort you in honor to the king."

So it came to pass that both Keino and Kale received

all the royal favors that Kale wished. Imagine their feelings when the king pressed shining calabashes of the awa he had prepared to their thirsty lips! Imagine their stunned amazement when he brought his handsome daughters and presented them in marriage to the young men! Not only did they receive charming wives, but each was provided with a separate hale in the royal village.

Shortly afterward, the war with King Pueonui was resumed. The warriors of King Kakuhihewa won several early victories, and Keino was soon strutting about the village like a mynah bird, robed in the brilliant red and yellow of a high-ranking officer. He had won great fame for having served in a battle in which Pueonui's army had been badly defeated.

Kale, meantime, was the subject of much whispering and ridicule in the village. All day long, it was said, he remained within the four walls of his hale and did nothing but sleep. It did not take long before word of the lazy habits of his son-in-law reached the ears of King Kakuhihewa. Proud as he was of the achievements of Keino, he was thoroughly disgusted with the antics of Kale.

But the king had been ill-advised. What really had been happening was something that only Kale knew. He had heard stories being circulated about him, and he was secretly amused. It was true that he slept soundly throughout the day, but what the villagers did not know was that, in the pitch-blackness of early morning, Kale would rise and slip quietly away. He wisely selected the hour when the enemy was soundest in sleep—as were the warriors of King Kakuhihewa.

Slipping past the enemy guards, he would race through the enemy's camp and kill their officers, and with their feather capes and helmets under his arm he would fight single-handed the enemy who blocked his escape. When he had completed his night raids, he would slip quietly back into his hut, and no one in the village ever saw him return. Kale's one-man raids on the enemy soon had the forces of King Pueonui badly shaken and disorganized. When Keino and the other warriors of King Kakuhihewa's army attacked later in the day, they won easy victories.

The actions of Kale would have passed unnoticed if it had not been for a farmer who decided, one night, to remain awake and guard his crops. He was hiding in the underbrush around his taro patch when he saw the huge figure of a warrior running at great speed. So unusual was the sight at that hour of the morning that he decided to keep a sharp watch the following night.

The next night, the old farmer waited as he had planned. Sure enough, at the same hour as the night before, the young warrior streaked past. The old farmer shouted and gave chase to the running young man. Kale did not stop. Finally, as a last resort, the old farmer hurled his spear at the fleeing young warrior. He had the satisfaction of seeing it strike Kale's wrist. The young man hesitated only long enough to break off the shaft and continued to run.

In due time Pueonui was defeated and Kakuhihewa took control of all Oahu. At a meeting of his local chiefs, he expressed his pride in Keino and made some bitter comments about his lazy son-in-law, Kale. But among the members of this council was the old farmer, who was a highly important chief. He told the king of the huge warrior who had really been responsible for the victory, and of the young man's strange actions when he had tried to halt him. "I wounded him in the arm and the point of hooked whale bone must, I think, still be imbedded in his flesh," the old farmer told the king.

Hearing this, the king ordered every man, woman, and child in his kingdom to appear before him, in order that a search might be made for the modest hero. No one had the wound the farmer had described. "Is there no one else?" the old farmer asked. "No one," answered the king, "except that worthless son-in-law of mine." The old farmer asked permission to examine Kale. And when he turned Kale's arm palm-upward, there was the telltale barb, buried in the flesh of his wrist.

At the farmer's suggestion, a servant was dispatched to the hale of the modest warrior, and when he returned he was loaded down beneath the weight of feathered capes and helmets that Kale had taken from his fallen enemies.

So delighted was the king with the modesty and courage of his misunderstood son-in-law that he decided to pay the young man the highest honor in the land.

Calling Kale before him, he placed upon the young man's shoulders the royal cape of yellow o'o feathers and upon his head the royal helmet. And so it was that Kale was proclaimed moi, or King of Oahu.

Hawaiian Superstitions

ONE of the earliest superstitions I learned was that, if you picked a lehua blossom, rain would come and spoil your day's outing. If you picked it on the way home, you had no rain. As a youngster this rule didn't mean anything to me, but in later years I could see the reason very clearly.

Every year in August, I led a party over the ancient trail running from Waimea on the west side up over high mountains and ending with an abrupt descent of four thousand feet into the Wainiha Valley on the north side. As soon as you left the airy glades of Kokee, the trail entered a dense forest and suddenly dipped down into a very deep gorge named Kauaikinana. When you climbed up to the top of the other side, the trail followed the ridge between that stream and the Kawaikoi. Here the weather began to change: you were on the fringe of the rain belt. Here grew tall ferns and strong vines, and without any warning you came out on a small meadow named Lehua Makanoi (The Lehua of the Dark Eyes); and in this meadow grew these short scrubby lehua bushes. Straggly and coarse, but they had the most beautiful flowers in the world—huge clusters of them on every bush.

The effect upon the first group with me was amazing. They shouted with joy and scattered over the ground plucking the beautiful clusters, forgetting all about the fact that we still had a two-hour tramp ahead of us to the end of the trail at the Kilohana of Hanalei, and on our return would have to pass again through this same meadow.

"Come on!" I called. "The trail soon becomes very hard to follow, and besides there is the old Hawaiian saying, 'If you pick lehua blossoms on your way out it will rain.'"

But they only laughed at me. The sun was shining brightly. Why worry about rain? They were a bunch of unbelieving malihinis. Finally I got the party under way, and we crossed the Kawaikoi river and climbed up into the dreaded Alakai Swamp. Alakai means to lead, and it lives up to its name. It is one of the most confusing trails you can find, and one can become lost very easily. Every little while someone would jokingly say, "Look out, it's going to rain!" Generally they made that remark as the sun came out from a cloud and it was hot. I just led along. At one particularly blind spot, I broke off some fern leaves and threw them in a line to mark the proper turn.

"What's that for?" they jibed.

"To find the trail on the way back when the fog is thick."

How they laughed! The guide was crazy. We left the swamp and entered the last short stretch of jungle, and just as we came out on the rim of the Wainiha the rain came. Black fog rolled in, and the whole north side of Kauai was lost to view. We could see nothing and the rain beat down on us. We stood eating our lunch with the water dripping off our hats, and then fled for home. Some of the younger boys took the lead and ran. When they came to the place of the fern leaves, they failed to see them in the fog, turned left, and were soon tangled up in an impenetrable jungle of scrub lehua.

Hurrying along after them, I came to the ferns and saw their tracks leading off the wrong way. I heard one fellow call, "Hi, Bill, have you found the trail?"

"No, it's lost," he answered.

I yelled, "Come back here!" and they came on the run. "Can't you follow the ferns?" I asked them.

"We didn't see them," they replied. "We didn't even look for them, it all seemed so foolish to us."

"Sometimes it pays to be foolish," I told them. And so a wet and disappointed party finally reached camp. The time wasted on the lehua blossoms would have been enough to get a good view. There really is some sound sense in the superstition of picking the lehua blossoms.

Clouds were used by the early Hawaiians to foretell weather conditions. They could tell by the clouds, the winds, and the rings around the moon pretty accurately what the weather was going to be.

However, I had a funny experience with cloud reading. It was during the First World War. I was riding home from Waimea towards Kekaha late in the afternoon. The sun was about ready to drop into the sea and the sky was flecked with white clouds. One of my cowboys was riding with me and, as we looked, suddenly all the little clouds turned into bears, thousands of them, and they were all heading west.

"Look, Mose," I said. "What do you see in the clouds?"

"Gee," he said, "bears."

"Russian bears," I said. "There has been a great Russian victory over the Germans." Sure enough, in a few days, when the steamer brought our mail and newspapers, they were full of the story of a great Russian advance through Poland.

A few months later, riding along the same road, about the same time of day, the same phenomenon happened. The sky filled with thousands of little white bears; they looked like teddy bears, and they were all racing full speed towards the east. "By George," I said, "the Russians have taken an awful beating!" Sure enough, when the papers came, there was the news of the terrible defeat of the Russians at Tannenburg and the slaughter of the Masurian Lakes.

No one in Koloa seemed to remember any ancient Hawaiian superstitions about clouds. I finally called on my old friend Louis Kilauano and his wife in Kekaha. Louis is now seventy years old. We used to hunt together up in the Kauai mountains. I asked them if they remembered their parents ever talking about clouds, but they shook their heads. Storm clouds, oh yes, and rings around the moon, but nothing more.

Louis and I got to talking of the countless times we had hunted wild cattle and pigs when suddenly the old lady said, "Pahu — pahu! Funny, just now I remember my mother sitting out in the grass late in the afternoon. She looked up at the heavens and got excited and began to point at the clouds floating past. 'Look!' she said. 'Pahus, pahus, several, they are coffins, coffins in the clouds.' And I looked and I saw them, and my mother said, 'When you see a pahu in the sky it means that someone of the royal family is going to die.'"

"Did anyone die?" I asked. "Do you remember? You must have been a very little girl at that time."

"Yes," she replied. "Soon afterwards we heard of the death of King Kamehameha V; and more, I now remember, my mother said, 'If you see many coffins or pahus in the sky, you are warned that there is going to be a war and many soldiers will be killed.' But," she added, "clouds don't tell much after all! A lady in Hawaii saw a zepplin in the sky on Saturday afternoon, December 6, 1941."

"Do you think that was sent as a warning?" I asked her.

"Pela paha, perhaps so, but what good did it do? The Japs came just the same and no one was expecting them."

"How about rainbows in the sky?" I asked her. "You have heard of the pot of gold that lies at the end."

"Yes," she replied. "Did you ever find one?"

"No," I admitted, "not yet, but I stood beside a pretty girl once in Kalaheo. A lunar rainbow was right in front of me and I felt it bewitching me; it faded out just in time."

"Oh, you men!" she exclaimed. "You are all the same; but I tell you, in the olden days when the queen or the young princesses travelled around the island, the valleys they entered would fill with rainbows to warn the common people that royalty was paying them a visit."

"I think you are right," I said. "I rode into a valley once and a gorgeous rainbow filled it from side to side. I felt like a prince."

"Oh, no!" she said. "Your father was called king, but you are just another commoner."

The north wind had been blowing steadily for two months and the sand dunes along the shore had been drifting. As I rode along with my big kanaka cowboy, Kanakaole, I spied a human skull lying at the foot of a drift. It had been exposed for quite a while and the sun had bleached it to a beautiful white.

"Kanakaole," I said, "you are pretty well versed in Hawaiian superstitions. Is it true that if you disturb a grave, bad luck comes to you?"

"Yes," he answered. "We Hawaiians believe that. It is a superstition as old as the hills."

"How about that skull lying on the sand? Would it be bad luck to pick that up?"

"No," he replied. "You can see that head is lost. Its grave has been destroyed by the gods of the wind."

I picked up the white skull and took it home with me. No bad results came to me, but years later my friend Honjiyo, a carpenter by trade, had a contract to put up a house on a nice flat piece of land near the shore. As his gang was digging in the ground to make a foundation, one of his boys came upon a grave two or three feet under the surface. It had evidently been there a long time, yet no fence or stone marked the resting place of this man.

The boy took out the bones, and Honjiyo told him to carry them away and dig a new grave. The boy did as he was told, but when he picked up the skull he quietly hid it in a bush nearby.

A passing Hawaiian fisherman happened to see what the boy did and said, "Eh, don't do that! Put the skull in the grave; by and by you will have bad luck."

The boy only laughed. "Don't be a fool," he said; "how can that skull hurt me? The man is dead and gone and I have wanted to own a skull for a year. Now I have got one."

"All right," warned the fisherman, "but look out!" and passed on.

The boy took the head home with him and was very proud of his new prize. A week went by. "Ha, ha!" he laughed. "That old fool can't scare me; nothing has happened to me."

Then things began to happen. One night he woke up with a start. Something stirred in his room and he smelled the faint odor of damp sand. He lay and trembled, but with daylight his courage came back and he went to work as usual. However, by the end of the week he was getting jumpy. He began to look daily at his skull. One night he had a terrible vision—a skeleton walked into his room and stood by his bedside. It had no head and yet he heard a voice saying, "Bring me back my head! I cannot rest," and he woke up screaming. "Get out of here! Get out of here!"

He became pale and ill. One night his mother heard him cry out, and when she went to him she found him gazing at the skull. "Don't make a noise," he said to her. "The skull is talking to me. I can see his white teeth moving, and he is telling me to take him back to his grave at Anahola and let him sleep with the rest of his bones."

They hurried with the skull to the new grave, where they reverently buried it beside his old bones; but the curse still worked. The boy just faded away, went completely crazy, and in a short time he too was laid in his grave. The terrible curse had killed him.

The Three Mo-os of Tahiti

ONCE upon a time, long years ago, there lived a family of huge lizards, or mo-os, on the island of Tahiti. Besides papa and mama Mo-o, there were a lot of young ones.

The young lizards played so many pranks on their older brother and two beautiful sisters that the latter decided to pack up and seek an island where there was more living space and peace. One bright day they said farewell to their weeping parents and swam away, out into the broad Pacific ocean.

Being used to an ocean full of islands, they had no idea how far they would have to swim, but they headed north. Day and night they swam along. For a while the water was warm, and then it began to get colder and colder. No rocks were to be seen, and they finally got so tired that they wished they had never left home.

Their strength was almost spent when one morning they saw land ahead. A long island lay sleeping in the ocean, and they could see a beach of white sand with the waves breaking on it. The two sisters wanted to go to this island, but their brother begged them not to.

"It looks bare and hot," he said. "I see another island lying only a few miles beyond, and it has tall mountains with clouds hanging on them. That means there are forests and rivers where we can rest and enjoy life."

But the two sisters would not listen to him. How human they were! They insisted on crawling up on the wide sandy beach to rest; and so they parted. The sisters landed on the island of Niihau, but the brother kept on toward Kauai.

When the hot sun beat down upon the two sleeping sisters they were too exhausted to crawl back to the ocean. They slept on and on, until they were finally turned to stone.

Many years later, when I was a small boy visiting my Uncle Frank on the island of Niihau, I rode with him along the shore and he pointed out the two sisters. They looked like two great coconut logs lying side by side and over one hundred feet long.

"They must be part of a lava flow," I said.

"No," he told me, "lava doesn't flow like that. The old Hawaiians say they are mo-os, and they swam here from Tahiti."

"Were there any more?" I asked Uncle Frank.

"I have heard that one went to Kauai," he said; "but where he ended up is a mystery to me."

The years rolled on and I grew up. Often I thought of the two black petrified sisters on Niihau, but I never got back to see them. The island of Kauai was a big one to get around on horseback. But when a Ford runabout fell into my hands, I began to explore my home island more thoroughly.

One day I drove down the old Koloa Landing road, and following a dirt road came upon the famed Spouting Horn. It was fascinating to watch this great geyser — to see an ocean swell come racing in from the open sea and splash up against the big lava at my feet, then a great column of white water roar up through an opening in the lava thirty, forty or fifty feet in the air. It had Old Faithful of the Yellowstone Park easily beaten. Old Faithful blew every fifty-eight minutes or so: but this one blew every minute!

As I watched the fountain play, I heard a queer sound coming from the ledge below me. It sounded like the hissing noise a snake makes when angry. I walked down onto the ledge and waited. A long swell came in and, as the column of water rose in a great fountain, the hissing noise sounded at my feet.

As I stood there an old Hawaiian fisherman came along, and when I spoke to him and asked him about the queer noise, he smiled and said, "Listen, and I will tell you all about it." We sat on the bank and he began to talk.

"Once upon a time a giant mo-o, or lizard, landed on Kauai. It had swum all the way from Tahiti. It was a huge monster but quite friendly, and the people called him Lehu. He landed at Lawai Beach and crawled up into the stream and lay exhausted for awhile. Then he

210

recovered his strength and wandered about the countryside. He went over to Koloa, and his favorite spot was the junction of the Poeleele and Omao rivers. He lived on Kauai for many years, and stories came from Niihau of the arrival there of two other mo-os who had become petrified as they lay sleeping on the sand.

"One day Lehu, feeling lonely, swam over to the island of Niihau to visit his two sisters. But when he found that they were dead, he swam back to his beloved Kauai.

"As he swam along the shore he was so fascinated by the fountains of the Spouting Horn that he came in close to land to get a better view. A long narrow lava tube lay under the lava where we now are, and the opening was under the water. He thought he would explore this strange tube. He crawled up into it. Unfortunately, some sharp rocks on the sides that let him slip in caught his legs as he tried to back out, and he was stuck fast in the lava tube.

"He wriggled and fought, but in vain. There he was doomed to lie, and now, every time a wave rushes in and wets him all over, he growls and hisses; and that is what you hear.

"The lava was too hard for Hawaiians of the long ago. They couldn't free him. And now, if we used dynamite to blow up the lava, we would only kill him. There poor Lehu is doomed to stay forever," concluded the Hawaiian.

I thanked the old fisherman. The mystery of the third and last of the three mo-os had finally been cleared up.

Her Name was Ilianu

THE strange thing about her name was that it was not Ilianu really. Her true name was Na Wai Maka. But how she came to be called Ilianu is our story.

She was the daughter of Makae, and her father was Makaawaawa. He was our cook and Makae was our nurse; and they were a handsome pair of Hawaiians! My mother had taught the man the art of haole cooking, and Makae had learned to sweep the house and make the beds. For many years they were a part of our family life at Waiawa.

The same day that I was born, Makae presented Makaawaawa with a son. They named him Makaawaawa-iki, and we grew up together. He was a fine-looking boy and as quick as lightning. He learned to speak English and I Hawaiian. We were inseparable throughout our childhood, whether at the beach or up at the camp at Halemanu.

When we were big, husky boys of four, we were much surprised when a new baby arrived. Makae was the proud mother of a little dark-skinned girl. The little girl was a beauty, with the clearest skin and wonderous dark eyes. She at once became the pet of the household.

A year passed and the baby began to toddle about. One day Makae came to my mother and said "Annie, I wish you would give my little girl a name."

Mother was very much flattered, for it was the first time she had been asked to name a native child. It showed great confidence in Makae to allow such a thing.

For several days mother thought about a name. It

must be a lovely name and an appropriate one for such a beautiful and dusky little maid. We were spending the summer at Halemanu at the time and, while still thinking about what to call the child, Mother's eye fell upon the little stream where we dipped our water, which was named Na Wai Maka, or The Teardrop. The little girl should be called after the brook!

"Makae," she called out, "I have a name."

Makae came running. "What is it?" she cried eagerly.

"Call her Na Wai Maka, The Teardrop. It is a beautiful name for your beautiful little girl."

Makae was delighted. "Oh, Annie," she said, "I knew you would find a suitable name. It fits her exactly."

All the other Hawaiians were pleased and the little girl was duly christened Na Wai Maka.

A year passed and we were all leaving camp. Makaawaawa-iki and I were big boys and rode proudly on our ponies, but the little girl had to be carried by her father.

As we rode along, a cold rain began to fall, and in a short time we were all soaked to the skin. The road became slippery and we made slow progress. Halting for a few minutes to adjust his pack, little Makaawaawa-iki rode alongside his father and looked at his sister. Then he began to laugh and laugh.

"Look at the baby," he cried; "she is shivering and her skin is all gooseflesh. She is a real ilianu!"

The rest of the Hawaiians in the party laughed heartily. Ilianu meant cold skin.

"Ilianu!" they exclaimed. "What a name!"

My Mother was shocked at the name and loudly protested, but in vain.

Gone was The Teardrop, and Ilianu she became.

Many years later, when I returned from college and was hunting for a maker of Hawaiian hats, the head man in the village said, "Go to Ilianu. She is the cleverest weaver of them all."

I went and found her sitting on the floor braiding coconut hats.

"Are you Ilianu?" I asked.

"Yes," she replied.

"Where is Na Wai Maka? What ever became of her?" I asked.

"Oh, she is gone," she answered, smiling up at me. "She was lost in the rain."

The Well of Last Resource

LONG, long ago, when the island of Oahu was still young, two children, a boy and a girl, were sitting wearily on a rock at the edge of a steep cliff near Waialua. They talked quietly between themselves as they looked out over the valley below, but their voices were tired and hoarse. Their lips were drawn down in sadness. Their eyes were dull and without the merry luster that lights the faces of happy children.

Mana, the young boy, knotted his fists with emotion as his sister, Noe, spoke to him. Big tears welled up in her dark eyes and flowed slowly down her cheeks.

"Mana," she said, "do you think our father will return from the wars soon?"

Mana made a manly effort to control himself, but he had a painful lump in his throat and had to wink his eyes to hold back tears.

"He is gone less than a moon, my little Noe," he answered her. "Sometimes," the young boy said quiet-

214

ly, "wars are long and, sometimes, warriors do not return."

The little girl bit her lip and she choked convulsively as tears ran from her eyes in a torrent of misery.

The young boy put his arms about his sister and tried to console her. "When our father returns," Mana said, "the people of the village will tell him how mean and cruel his sister has been to us. Before he left, I heard him ask her to be kind to us and to take care of us. When he returns, he will find out how she has used us as slaves in her household, and his anger will be great and terrible."

"And her wretched son, Umi, is just as cruel as she is," Noe sobbed. "Yesterday, I tried to beat the tapa smooth and even, but holes would come in it no matter how carefully I tried. She would not listen when I tried to tell her I couldn't help it. Then Umi took the tapa stick from my hands and beat me with it until my head ached and my arms were bruised and sore."

Mana was so moved by his sister's story that he leaped to his feet, walked to the edge of the cliff, and turned his back on Noe so that she could not see that he was crying. As he turned away, Noe noticed for the first time that he, too, had been the victim of Umi's cruelty. The boy's back was crisscrossed with ugly red welts. Noe laid her cool hand on the wounds and the boy turned around with shame brooding darkly in his eyes.

"Yes," he said. "Umi is a grown and powerful man now, but I too, will be a man some day."

"Auwe, they are devils!" said Noe. "They mean to kill us while our father is away so that Umi will be the young chief of Waialua. And when we are dead they will tell the people some lie to cover our disappearance."

Just then, a sharp ugly voice called "Noe-e-e!" The little girl began to tremble. "She will beat me again! Oh, Mana, what shall I do? She told me if I had not finished the tapa before the sun went down behind the mountain, I would be beaten." The little girl wrung her hands in fear. The sharp voice called again, this time nearer.

Suddenly, Mana turned and grasped his sister by the hand. "Come," he said, "she will not beat you again. The mountains are kinder than those with whom our father left us."

The two children crouched in the bushes until the woman passed. Then, breathless with fright, they ran wildly down the reverse slope of the mountain and into the deepening twilight. On and on, into the purple shadows they ran.

Night came and the two children found themselves deep in a forest surrounded by the grotesque shadows of trees. Frightened, sick, and desperate, they kept going. Finally, they came to a beach and flung their tired, aching bodies on the cold, damp sand. And for their lullaby that night there was the deep-throated song of the surf pounding on the shore.

When Mana awoke the next morning, he found his sister gazing out toward the sea with a look of hopeless misery on her tear-stained face. He forced a cheerful smile to his lips. "Please don't be sad, Noe," he begged. "We are alone and hungry, but we have felt such things before since our father went over the sea. Look, there are fish leaping from the pools in the coral, and those wet rocks are covered with juicy limu weeds. Rest yourself, while I get us a feast."

Noe's eyes brightened. "Oh, no," she said, "many hands make light work. I will go with you." Soon afterward, Mana returned with a fish still struggling on his spear. Noe had gathered an armful of tender limu weeds and tiny shellfish. The cihldren were starved. Since they had left home, they had eaten nothing but a few half-ripe berries.

The delicious white flakes of fish and the seaweed gave new energy to their bodies and new strength to their determination. That night, the stars reached down to kiss the innocent young faces as they slumbered peacefully on the leaves and grass Noe had gathered during the day.

For many days, they lived in this fashion. The ocean provided all the food they needed. By day, they raced gaily over the white sands, and by night, they slept beneath the open sky. They felt almost as happy as they had before their father sailed away with the king to make war on another island.

One morning, just before dawn, Mana awoke with a sudden start. There on the beach, silhouetted against the moon, he saw the hateful figure of his cruel cousin, Umi. He was looking down at the children's fishnet where it had been spread to dry in the sand.

Mana awakened his sister, and together the two children crept into the shadows of the forest, where they hid among the ferns and vines for several days, coming out only to eat a few berries and wild fruits.

In a few days, their courage returned, but they realized they could not return to their happy life by the sea. It was nearing the rainy season, and soon Mana was busy gathering pili grass to construct a hut to protect his sister and himself from the weather. Noe busied herself making new lauhala mats for beds. Together the children cleared a patch of land and a garden flourished through their combined efforts. To add to their food supply, Mana set traps in the sea near the forest to snare fish for food. Months passed and laughter found a place in the lives of the children again.

One evening they sat before the door of their hut. Mana played softly on his bamboo flute while Noe crooned a soft chant she had learned from her mother. The sun was a ruddy glow through the lacework of the trees, and the clouds overhead were tinted with the pastel colors of dying day.

Mana laid down his flute and spoke to his sister. "Noe," he said, "in a few days we can gather the roots of the taro. And with the mats and calabashes you have made, we shall find life easy, my sister."

"Yes," his sister answered, "and we have found peace at last. No longer do we fear the beatings and torments of our father's wicked sister and her ugly son."

But that night, the two children were awakened by the scorching heat of flames. Their hut was afire! Rushing out, they heard a fiendish laugh, and saw, by the light of the fire, the huge figure of Umi laying waste to the garden where they had spent so many long hours of toil.

For weeks they wandered through the mountains, hungry, sick at heart, and with the jeering laughter of Umi driving them on like hunted animals. On and on through the mountains they went, with Umi close at their heels. It was the season of water famine, and Hina had called the rain clouds to the windward side of the Waianae ridge. Finally, Umi drove the children into a dried-up valley where the mountains opened up to sea, and left them there to die.

It was a desolate spot. The grasses were seared and brown from lack of moisture, the leaves on the trees had dried and dropped off, leaving barren branches beseeching the sky. The stark gray rocks reflected shimmering waves of heat that hung in the wind-still air.

The children stumbled along the valley on swollen feet. Their heads ached from the rays of the unmerciful sun on their uncovered heads. Their tongues swelled from the awful thirst, and their lips dried up and festered with sun sores. Noe's eyes were blazing with fever.

"What's the use?" she babbled. "We plant, we weave, we cut and labor so hard. And for what? Look at your hands, the hands of the son of a great chief, calloused and worn with heavy toil; and for what?"

Mana sat down on a rock and, torn with bitterness, tried to think. Noe was stretched out on the ground beside him, half unconscious with fever. He shifted his body so that his shadow fell across her face.

As the boy was sitting there, Noe slipped into a delirium. She began to murmur strange, unconnected words, and to speak of her early childhood. Mana shook her.

"Wake up, sister!" he said. "You are having a bad dream."

Suddenly Noe opened her eyes. "Water," she croaked hoarsely. "Water, I tell you!"

"But there is no water," the boy sobbed miserably. Noe's lips were gluey with brown foam. Frightened and desperate, Mana sprang to his feet, looked at the heavens, and opened his arms in a pleading gesture.

"Oh, gods of the skies and the earth, cast your eyes upon thy stricken children! Bring forth the water of life, lest my sister die!"

The boy's prayer was answered. High up in the mountains the clouds thickened and grew dark. Out of the mist, a thunderous voice boomed and the call awakened Mo-o, the great green lizard, from his sleep in the earth. He tunneled through the earth and with a single blow of his great tail split the rocks asunder. A great flood of cool, crystal pure water sprang from the rocks and flowed into the dry stream bed near where the boy was sitting.

Hearing the gush of waters, Mana sprang alive and tears came to his eyes. Noe's life was saved and, where the stream flowed, new life sprang up. The trees would again be green and the berries luscious and sweet.

And there the warrior chief found his children. Before long he was at sea again, this time to carry his wicked sister and her son to exile on the Isle of Demons.

And the water still flows today from a spring in the rocks. It is still known to the people of the valley as the Well of Last Resource.

The Lost Princess

MANY thousands of nights have passed since that night long ago when a lonely little canoe tossed fretfully on the breast of the dark ocean. And wearily paddling the tiny craft was Haina Kolo, the wife of a great chief of Kauai who had gone to war amid the burning mountains of the island of Hawaii. Her heart was heavy. Sharp tears brimmed in her eyes and coursed down her cheeks. And as the canoe rose and fell with the rolling waves, her voice sobbed out a song of loneliness as old as womankind.

As Haina Kolo chanted her sad lament, the darkness of the night seemed to engulf her. A chill wind swept across the heaving ocean and chipped the waves into white-capped fragments that tossed the little boat around like a kukui nut on the water.

A child whimpered in the bottom of the canoe. Haina Kolo laid aside her paddle, tenderly picked up the little brown form of her son, and drew him close to the warmth of her body. She wrapped the veil of her long hair around the baby and softly began to croon a lullaby.

"Sleep, son of the great chief Loakalani. Sleep close in my arms, bathed by the tears that spring from my heavy heart. Thy father has too long forgotten Kauai —forgotten the wife who loves him—forgotten the son she bore him." Haina Kolo's voice broke and her eyes glistened in the starlight.

All through the night Haina Kolo held her tiny burden close to her heart, rocking back and forth in the cradle of the ocean and crooning softly each time the child awoke. It was nearly dawn when she looked with listless eyes toward the morning star on the horizon. She took her paddle and turned the canoe in the direction of the star, but a cold wave of fear crept over her. Had she lost the way to Hawaii? She looked at the empty water gourd and the empty calabash at her feet. No food and no water with the end of her journey still not in sight! She drew the naked body of her son closer to her and lifted her eyes to the heavens in silent prayer.

Overcome by a vast weariness, Haina Kolo drifted into a painless slumber as the magic brush of a new dawn swept the purple shadows from the sky. As she relaxed, the paddle dropped unheeded from her hand and floated away in the fast-running sea.

The day wore on and mother and child slept wrapped in close embrace. The canoe drifted aimlessly, its course directed by the changing whim of the sea. A playful breeze ran its soft fingers through the long, dark hair of the sleeping mother to reveal a face still beautiful and soft with the blush of youth.

But when the sun rose higher into the heavens, there was a low growl in the distance and a shadow loomed on the horizon. A great, ugly storm cloud crept across the sky and muttered angrily as it grew in size. Suddenly a snarling wind sprang from the dark horizon to leap upon the ocean. It struck the water like the flat side of a paddle, and the spray raced madly ahead of the curling waves.

With a quick jerk the canoe ripped over the crest of a huge wave, wallowed helplessly in the trough, and stood almost on end as it mounted another boiling crest. Haina Kolo, violently aroused, dragged herself painfully to her knees and searched frantically for her paddle. The child screamed with fright as the outrigger bounced like a splinter over the tormented sea.

Then Haina Kolo gasped. Coming closer was a mountain of water with its ragged crest reaching out green, clutching fingers toward the trembling outrigger! Haina Kolo braced heself and held her child closer as the wave rushed toward them. Viciously, the curling hand of the wave closed around the canoe and crushed it with a giant fist.

Haina Kolo, still clutching her child, struggled to the surface and struck out for the splintered bulk of her canoe, floating like a log in the angry water. All through the long hours of the storm, she clung tightly to the wreck. Again and again, the pounding waves tore her aching fingers loose from the canoe, but each time she found new strength to renew her hold. Toward the end of the day the skies cleared, and Haina Kolo saw an island looming darkly in the waning twilight. Mustering new strength, she began the long swim to shore.

How long she swam, she did not know — but sometime during the night her feet touched land and she dragged herself through the surf, still carrying the tiny, limp body of her son. She collapsed on the damp sand, with the tiny form still cradled in her arms.

"Lei Makani," she whispered, "open thine eyes. Speak to me." But the child never stirred. She pressed her warm lips against the cold cheek and continued to coax the still, brown body. Finally, she arose and made a nest for the little one from the soft grasses growing in the rocks above the beach. "Sleep on, my son," she said, "while I gather food to give thee new strength." Then half-sick with a growing fear that the child was dying, she turned to search for food.

A short while later, two fishermen approached the spot where Haina Kolo had so tenderly placed her child. They had caught nothing that day and they were worried by what the queen might have to say about their failure to provide fish for her table. The two men stared in astonishment when they came upon the tiny figure in its nest of soft grass. "Auwe, this is a strange fish to come out of the sea," said Niiu, who was the older of the two men. And as the men continued to gaze in wonder, the child moaned weakly.

Niiu took the child in his arms and smiled as the tiny body snuggled against his broad chest. He reached down and looked curiously at the slender necklace the child wore around its neck. The fisherman whistled softly. "The child of a high chief," he said in an awed voice. "Fish or no fish, we must take it to the queen." And off the two men sped to the queen with their strange catch.

When Haina Kolo returned to find her child gone,

she stared at the green emptiness of the nest with unbelieving eyes. At last, her face brightened and she called out, "Lei Makani! Lei Makani, where art thou?" Her voice echoed sweetly through every crevice on the rocky shore, but there was no sign of the familiar, laughing face for which she sought so frantically.

Then, when she heard no answer to her calls and found no sign of Lei Makani, she sank to her knees and remained staring out to sea. A look of growing horror crept into her eyes and her breath came in wracking sobs. For hours she continued to stare out at the wide blue ocean, but her eyes saw nothing, until the rising tide swept close and swirled around her knees. At the first touch of the water, she sprang to her feet and ran madly away from the ocean into the heart of the forest. Her mind was gone and she stumbled through the green shadows like a wild screaming animal.

For many years thereafter she lived deep in the shadows of the everlasting hills. And whenever a storm brooded over the ocean, it awakened a haunting memory in her mind and she would run swiftly down to the shore. When the fishermen heard her crying along the rocky shore, her piercing cries of "Lei Makani! Lei Makani!" were known to all as a warning that a storm was approaching. "The mad woman calls the winds," the fishermen would say and hasten to make ready for the storm.

At last there came to Hawaii a series of storms that raged over land and sea. For weeks the fishermen dared not venture forth, and constant rain washed out the taro patches. A great famine swept across the land and plague followed close behind. So many died on the island that the wailing never ceased from dawn to dark.

The cries of woe rose to mingle with the shrieking winds.

After the highest priest warned the queen that the storms and sorrow would not depart from the land until the body of the mad wahine of the mountains was laid upon the altar of the gods, the queen dispatched her messengers in search of Haina Kolo. They found her quietly weaving in front of her hut in the forest, and she came innocently with them to the stockade in the palace courtyard.

That night the high winds came again, and above the sound of the wind the voice of the mad Haina Kolo could be heard calling, "Lei Makani! Lei Makani!" In the sleeping house of the palace, a young chief stirred restlessly in his sleep when he heard the call. He rose and went outside, but the rain awakened him and he wondered why he had left his bed.

In the morning a guard reported to the queen that the mad woman had chanted a strange song of Kauai and the chief, Loakalani. "She called herself Haina Kolo, the princess," the guard told the queen.

The queen immediately recognized the name of the lost princess of Kauai. The swiftest runner in all Hawaii was sent after the high chief of Kauai. When he returned to the palace grounds, he found that Niiu, the fisherman, had come forth to tell the story of the child he had found on the beach.

The chief felt a flood of tears rise to his eyes when he saw the wife he had thought drowned in a storm many years before when she attempted a voyage from Kauai to Hawaii in search of her warrior husband. And when he saw his own likeness in the handsome young chief embracing his mother, he felt a great pride well up inside him.

The forest where the lost princess had wandered for so many years in lonely solitude is known to this day as the Forest of Haina Kolo.

Na Oahi O Kauai

ONE day I was sitting on the fence of the big corral at Waiawa, watching the kanaka cowboys handling some young colts, when I noticed a small man on a skinny horse riding towards us. As he jogged along the road he waved a friendly greeting. He was a stranger to me, and even my cowboys did not know him. He was coming from Mana and I presumed he was on his way to Waimea, but when he came to the big front gate he opened it and rode into the yard and up to us. He got off his horse, untied a bag that seemed to be quite heavy, and came towards me. He was a wiry little Hawaiian, and when I climbed off the fence and met him, he flashed me a smile and held out his hand.

"Aloha," he said. "Are you Elika, the brother of Agata?"

"Yes," I replied. Whereupon, he caught my hand and said, "Lucky am I today to meet you. I have heard of you for years. I knew your father Kanuka Makua, and your brother, and now I meet you! My name is Daniel and I have come all the way from Milolii to meet you. I am your tenant. I have been renting the valley of Milolii from your brother for $30 a year."

"I am glad to meet you," I said. "Have you come to pay the rent?"

"Oh, no," he replied shamelessly. "I haven't a cent,

but I brought you this." He opened his bag and rolled out a beautiful watermelon. He was a diplomat, all right.

We cut the melon. The two cowboys joined us and we all ate the delicious fruit. As we ate he told us of the difficulties he had met in trying to bring back to cultivation this once fertile and beautiful valley, lying in the little known Na Pali Coast and long since abandoned by its ancient inhabitants.

The melon finished and the cowboys having returned to their patient task of taming the colts, he now came to the real reason for his visit. He was going to have an old-fashioned oahi, he said, and would I and my four house guests honor him with our presence?

What an oahi was I hadn't the slightest idea, but he soon explained. An oahi was an exhibition of fireworks, like a Fourth of July celebration, but without the noise and risk of exploding bombs and firecrackers. When successfully carried out, it was a thing of magnificence and rare beauty. This sport was indulged in by the former kings and chiefs of Kauai to celebrate great events in the history of the island, and had been a custom from time immemorial.

An oahi required months of preparation. Two kinds of wood were used, the hau and the papala. The hau was easy to get and was cut into ten- or twenty-foot lengths. The bark was peeled off and then dried until it was as light as a feather. The papala grew in the high mountains and was hard to get, so it became the kings' special fireworks. It had a hollow core when dry and the flame ran through it as it fell, giving the effect of a shooting star.

These dried sticks were carried up the high cliffs to a ledge a thousand feet or more above the sea. On a dark night the men climbed up to the ledge, built a fire, and lighting the ends of the sticks hurled them like javelins into space.

The two most famous oahi places on Kauai were Kamaile peak, rising 2,500 feet over Nuuololo landing on the Na Pali Coast, and the high cliffs that tower over the wet caves at Haena.

The cliffs being concave, the trade winds are forced upwards, forming a sort of air cushion from which the blazing hau sticks rise and fall. The force of the wind and gravity together fan the burning end into a blazing ball of fire as the stick works up and down in the air and away from the cliff until it reaches the outer edge of the air cushion. There it comes tobogganing down, blazing fiercer and fiercer until like a great rocket it sails over the flats below and rushes out to sea.

"Have you ever seen an oahi?" I asked Daniel.

"No," he answered sadly. "This old custom has almost died out, like so many of the old Hawaiian customs. But I am going to revive the oahi to celebrate my son's marriage.

"It will be a real old-fashioned oahi," continued Daniel enthusiastically. "All you need are blankets, because there will be plenty of food, poi, fish, and sweet potatoes. My whaleboat will meet you at Polihale and take you and your party."

Of course we all accepted, and the next day found us at the end of the land. True to his word, Daniel had the whaleboat anchored just outside the surf. The skillful Hawaiians soon had us all on board, and with four sturdy men rowing, we skimmed along the shore, passing valleys that once had had large populations but now were empty. Finally we reached Milolii, where we picked up the rest of Daniel's family, and in a short time we were put ashore on a small beach lying at the foot of Kamaile.

A number of Hawaiians had come by boat from Hanalei and the scene was very festive. The food was delicious and, our hunger appeased, we turned to view our surroundings—a semicircle of towering cliffs with Kamaile at the center and a strip of sand with the ocean pounding in at both ends, making a veritable trap in rough weather.

With the luau over, and the sun sinking in the west, our host informed us that his two children, a boy of eighteen and a girl of sixteen, were starting for the top, where they had carried two hundred long hau sticks. They were a handsome pair of young Hawaiians. Armed with an old lantern, they started bravely to climb to the top, a task that would take them until dark. After the show they were to return to the beach. How they managed to do it is a mystery to me; the trail is bad enough in broad daylight but in the dark, with only a lantern, it seemed an impossibility. But do it they did, and seemingly with ease.

The sun sank into the west and the short tropical twilight soon faded. The night became black. Outside, the breakers moaned on the reef; the sea birds cried in the cliffs, and as we sat or lay on the beach we could dimly make out the huge black cliff whose top seemed to reach the stars.

Our host became unhappy. He kept walking up and down the beach muttering to himself. When we asked him what the trouble was, he explained that the wind had died down completely and, as a result, there was no uprush of air on which the firebrands were to coast down. The conditions were not right, but there was no way to notify his children up on the cliffs to wait. Anyway, how could he wait? All the people had to go home the next day. It was not like the olden days, when time meant nothing and there were no clocks. Then the king just called it off for a few days until conditions were right.

Suddenly someone shouted. Looking upwards we saw a tiny red spot. It seemed to be standing still. Then it began to blaze and come down the black face of the cliff, growing larger and fiercer every minute. Evidently some air currents were moving, for it began to zigzag down. It struck the cliff with great force, threw out a thousand sparks, and died! Near the top of Kamaile Peak, on a protected ledge, the two children had made a fire. As soon as a stick was burning they threw it like a spear out into space.

Rocket after rocket streaked into the air. Some came down almost to the beach, some stuck far up the cliff. A friendly akua must have heard the old fellow praying for wind, because a faint breath of air came in from the sea. The next few rockets caught the air as it blew up the cliff. They came out, coasting on the outer edge of the up-current. As they fell, they fanned themselves into great roaring balls of fire that seemed to be many feet in circumference. Like great rockets or meteors they soared over our heads and landed out in the sea.

The show kept up until the last stick had been hurled, and then the cliffs settled back to their usual peace. The spectators slept where they sat. The two firethrowers came safely down the steep cliff and in a very short time reported in camp. The show that evening at Nuuololo was the most amazing exhibition I had ever seen. I knew, too, that I would never be satisfied until I had had an oahi of my own.

In due time I laid my plans. I chose the high cliffs at

Haena as the scene of my party, because the place was easy to reach by land or sea. I managed to find five men who agreed to stage a real old Hawaiian oahi in July of the following year.

It took time to collect the hau sticks. Then they had to be dried for at least eight months, then collected at the base of the cliff, and finally carried to the top.

Time passes quickly in Hawaii and before long we were ready. All Kauai was excited. It had been many years since such an event had taken place. People from all over the island flocked to Hanalei and Haena, and the steamer, *Mikahala*, ran a special excursion from Waimea.

The evening of the exhibition arrived and we all sat at the foot of the sand dunes waiting for the show to begin. The wind was just right and the night was dark. Just as the huge shape of the mountain blended into the darkness, we heard a shout from the far peak. Looking up, we saw the first of the sticks starting on its 1,800-foot trip to the flats below.

Everyone began to shout as the ball of fire began to grow. It caught the air currents and began to roar and rise and fall, dart to one side, and then back as the air currents forced it out. We had a moment of terror when this ball of fire was coming straight toward us, but luckily it passed over our heads and went out to sea. Some of the firebrands stuck in the cliffs but most of them came down the whole way. Many fell on the flat, and all who were near made a mad rush to get bits of wood for souvenirs.

Finally the last stick was thrown, and when it had made its blazing trip to the sands the show was over. A faint halloo from away up among the stars told us that the end had come. The spectators began to seek places where they could spend the rest of the night. The steamer blew three farewell blasts, and the old flats of Haena settled back to the quiet, humdrum life of the present.

The spell and the sport of the ancient kings was over.

A Deal in Real Estate

HE WAS a thrifty old Hawaiian, and he and his wife had lived on the island of Niihau all their lives. He was a large, powerful man, who had always done his share of hard work; and whenever there was work to be done for the konohiki, or chief, the old fellow was ready and willing to help.

That piece of land on which he and his wife lived had belonged to his father and grandfathers from time immemorial. All the years the old man worked, he had only one goal — to own the property that he and his fathers had tilled for generations. Nothing else mattered as much as that.

Finally the great day came when the old man could approach the government for the land, and proud he was when he walked away with his royal patent. With tears in his eyes he showed the papers to his wife.

"Now," he exclaimed joyfully, "we own our land. It is ours for the rest of our lives."

And indeed the two old people did own their land, and the house on it, too. No one could turn them off.

The old man was getting somewhat feeble now, but

he was still strong enough to till his fields and catch his fish, and his wife was one of the best weavers of the famous Niihau mats. He was happy and content, and faced the end of his life with that calm philosophy enjoyed by the Hawaiians. When his time came, he would die, and his spirit would go to Po. His children would take care of the farm, even as he had done when his father died. Oh, it was a wonderful world!

And then a strange thing happened. A white family came to live on the lonely island. The old Hawaiian was told that they were now lords of the land because they had bought up the whole island. And he would no longer be a subject of the king, but must take orders from the white people. The old order was gone and a new one was beginning.

It was all very confusing to the old man. He sat and pondered in his simple way. He had known some white men in his day—some were good and some were bad. The island was big enough for all, he was sure of that. If they just left him alone on his little farm, then all would be well.

Things went on just the same for some time. Finally, when the new masters had finished building their home, they began to organize the natives living on the island. The white men laid down rules and regulations, too, governing the comings and goings of the natives. And then one day everyone was summoned to a great gathering to meet the new master.

Accordingly, the old man called to his wife and the old couple tramped over the hot road to the landing and met the family of whites. There were quite a lot of them—men, women, and children. They brought a great many cattle and sheep. They were industrious and sober, different from most whites he had met. He decided they were all right and welcomed them in his friendly manner.

The meeting was a mere matter of form, for all the other Hawaiians there were simply tenants at will, and the commands of the owners simply had to be obeyed, whether they liked them or not. But for the old couple, it was a different story. When it came his turn to agree, he firmly refused. Then the fact came out that the old fellow had his own rights and ownership. He was a freeholder with a royal patent. The trouble was, when the government sold the island it had forgotten the fact that there was one owner on it.

It was the newcomers, now, who were confused. They thought they owned the whole island, but behold, they did not. It was not enough that they had thousands of acres and this old man had only one or two. It was the fact that they couldn't get these, also, that took all the joy out of owning the rest. Before long it seemed as if the value of the old man's little holding exceeded in value all the rest of the island.

The family decided at once to buy him out. They offered him a fair price for his land, but he refused to sell. Why should he sell? The dream of his life had been to own his own home and land, and now they were trying to turn him out again into the world. Oh, no, he would live and die on his property, and that was all there was to it!

It seems as if he couldn't have been much in the way, but the trouble was that no road could be laid out, no fence could be built, without in some way having to cross his land. It was simply unbearable to the new owners of the rest of the island. He must be gotten rid of.

Every member of the family tried to persuade the old

couple to sell, but they turned a deaf ear to them all and continued to live contentedly in the little grass hut.

Several years passed. The white men never gave up trying, but their pleas fell on deaf ears. Finally, in desperation, one of the family called in a white man who lived on Kauai, known to the Hawaiians as Kanuka. He had lived many years on Kauai and spoke the Hawaiian language perfectly. Furthermore, he was well respected by the natives.

When Kanuka first heard of the proposition, he would have nothing to do with it. He knew why the old people wanted to keep their land. But the new owners begged him so earnestly to help them that finally he agreed to try and buy the land from the old man.

"Well," said Kanuka, "how much do you want to pay for the land?"

"One thousand dollars!" was the quick reply.

"One thousand dollars!" echoed Kanuka in great surprise. "Why, that's unheard of for such a small piece of land. You have really set your heart on getting it, haven't you?"

Kanuka was a notary, and in due time he prepared a deed to the land. "Now, one more thing," said Kanuka. "I think it will be better if you give me the money in silver dollars. One thousand big, shiny silver dollars."

The family were a little surprised at the strange request, but complied without a murmur. After all, Kanuka knew best.

He put the money in a bag and started off. He took a whaleboat, crossed the channel, and went directly to the house of the old couple. "Aloha," he called.

"Aloha," they responded, grinning happily over his visit. They too, knew him, and loved him. He entered their house, laid the sack at their feet, and told them all the news of Kauai.

Then he said, "I have come to buy your land."

The old people laughed at him. "You might just as well go along, Kanuka. We are sorry, but you are only wasting time."

Kanuka smiled at them, and putting his hand into the bag, he took out the silver dollars and piled them in stacks till he had one hundred, all neatly aranged on the table. "How about that?" he asked. "A lot of money for you two folks."

"No," replied the old man, "take it away."

Without saying any more, Kanuka piled up another hundred on the table. And as he piled up the dollars, he carried on a gentle monologue. "In Waimea Valley the natives live alongside a beautiful running river of sparkling sweet water. The women go out in it and catch shrimps and oopus and swim in it. All the valley is full of taro and the pake makes poi twice a week. Coconut trees grow along the banks, and you can have all the hauhau nuts you want for the asking.

"How about that?" he asked again.

"No," replied the old man; "you are wasting time."

Again Kanuka piled up one hundred dollars, and again. Thus the deal went on until he had piled up all the big shining dollars on the table. As he stacked them he continued, "In the village there is an old whaler named Salem Hanchet. He has opened a store, and in it you can buy new holokus made of bright calico. All the well-dressed women on Kauai wear them. For the men, he has good top-boots and denim pants.

"How about that?" he asked again. And the answer was the same. "No."

"That's too bad," Kanuka replied. "This is a lot of

money. You could buy yourself a new pair of boots and pants and many new holokus for the old woman, and button-boots for her to wear at church. You could live in ease the rest of your lives. But that is your affair, not mine. That is all. Aloha! I go."

Saying this, he opened the bag and started to sweep the whole gorgeous pile into it.

The old woman had been sitting in a corner all this time, never saying a word, but looking hard at the treasure. Suddenly she sprang up and grabbed Kanuka's arm.

"Stop!" she cried. "Those dollars are mine! Bring out your deed; we will sign. Here, you stupid old man, are you crazy? Sign the deeds, and I will sign."

The game was over. Kanuka was pleased, and the papers were duly signed and acknowledged. The thorn was removed, and all the families mixed up in the transaction were happy.

"You won't be sorry," smiled Kanuka as he left them.

When he reached the end of the path, he turned to wave, but the old couple had forgotten him. They were laughing and playing with their lovely new gleaming dollars.

Umi the Conqueror

NOW, Umi was the son of King Liloa of Hawaii, but he was born far from the king's house because his mother was not of equal rank; and he was brought up as a simple country boy.

Some time after Umi was born, his mother married a

countryman who was not kind to the little fellow. Often he would chastise him for no good reason at all, and this would make Umi's mother very sad.

One day when his stepfather had punished him severely, the boy's mother called him aside and said to him, "Umi, the man who has beaten you is not your father. Your own father is so mighty and powerful that it is dangerous for you to even go near him. But now I see that you must go to him, my son. Go to the king, who is your father. Go to him who dwells in Waipio, and if he should let you sit upon his knee, show him the things I now will give you."

As Umi's mother placed a loincloth, a necklace of the whale's tooth, and a war club in his hands, she told him they had been given to her by King Liloa.

Umi put on the loincloth, hung the necklace around his neck, and started off with the war club in his hands. As he started away, his mother gave him last minute instructions. "You must swim across the river at the bottom of the Waipio valley. The king's house is on the other side. Do not enter by the gate, but climb over the fence and go in the side door. When you are inside you will see your father. Several guards will be near him holding feather standards. Go and sit on his lap and tell him you are Umi."

Umi hurried away, for he did not want to see his mother's tears. Two of his boyhood companions joined him. One was Omaokamau and the other was called Piimaiwaa.

When they had crossed the river, Umi told the two boys to wait for him outside the king's house and, if he should be killed, to hurry home and tell his mother. Then he climbed over the fence and disappeared through the side door.

When the guards saw the strange boy, they chased him, but Umi ran to the king and sat down on his lap. Of course, the king didn't know who he was and let him fall to the ground. The guards would have killed Umi had the king not noticed the loincloth around his waist and the whalebone necklace.

"Who are you?" he asked. And the boy on the floor smiled up at his father and answered, "I am Umi."

Then Liloa took the boy on his knees and kissed him. "Where is your mother?" he asked. Umi told him that his mother was still at home.

The king told his courtiers about Umi's mother. Umi then became recognized as the king's son, and soon the sacred drum was beaten to let all know that the ceremony of adoption was to take place.

Now King Liloa had another son called Hakau, who was the rightful heir to the kingdom and who had been brought up near the king. When he heard the drum, he ran to his father. Then his father said to him, "This is Umi. He is your half-brother and he shall be under you, so do not worry about his coming."

But Hakau was jealous and did not like Umi. He treated his young half-brother very badly.

The king was an old man and knew he soon must die. He made over all his authority and all his lands to Hakau and willed his temples and images of his gods to Umi. When he died, Hakau took possession of everything.

The new king treated Umi so badly that finally he could stand it no longer. He called his comrades, Omaoamau and Piimaiwaa, and the three swam back across the river. They did not go near Umi's mother's house, but kept on traveling until they came to a spot where they decided to settle down and make a living. Umi's friends soon married. But they would not let Umi work because he was of princely rank.

One day a man named Kaoleioku saw Umi and recognized the form and bearing of a prince. Going to the house where Umi lived, he asked him if he were not King Liloa's son.

"Yes, I am indeed Liloa's son," said Kaoleioku. So Umi went to live with the man.

Soon Kaoleioku began to make plans for winning Liloa's kingdom from Hakau, and brought many, many men to learn the art of warfare.

Now Hakau was hated by all his people because of his jealousy and treachery. Whenever anyone—man or woman, boy or girl—was praised, the king would have them slain if he heard about it.

Two old men who had been councillors of King Liloa were badly mistreated by Hakau and one day decided to leave Waipio in search of Umi, whom they remembered well.

When they had come to Kaoleioku's house, they were given a great feast of welcome. A pig was killed and made ready for the imu. Chickens and fish were prepared. And when the old men tasted the food, they said, "How good is the feast that is set before us! It is a long time since we were so well treated by anyone."

After the big meal, the old men went to sleep. It was late in the afternoon when they awoke. The sun was setting over the mountains. Looking outside, they saw a procession of men coming up from the fields. The men ahead were very tall; then came the shorter men; and at last the boys of the party.

When finally Umi was brought before them, they bowed and said, "Oh, Kaoleioku, we have no way of making up for all that has been done for us. We have no possessions and no power. But we promise to help to give over to Prince Umi the great island of Hawaii."

"How can that be done?" inquired Kaoleioku. "Umi, son of Liloa, should rule Hawaii, but Hakau has men at his command and in battle would be sure to win over Umi. I have men here who will fight for him, but what would be a few against Hakau's army?"

The old men were not disturbed, but nodded wisely and said, "It is settled. Hakau is even now defeated."

Then one of them spoke up and explained. "A day is soon coming that is marked as a day for the gods. We two still have some authority in regard to the gods. When the day comes, we will send most of Hakau's men into the mountains to make a sacrifice. Then let Prince Umi come with his men, and he can easily win the kingship from Hakau."

Before the two old men left to return to Waipio, they gave final instructions: "We shall be five days upon the road, and on the sixth we will be back in Waipio. Follow with your men. On the day of Kane, be on the cliff overlooking Waipio. On the next day, which is called the day of Lono, descend from the cliff and come to where Hakau will be."

Umi and Kaoleioku made their preparations, and three days later set out for Waipio. On the day of Kane, they took their place on the cliff.

Now, the two old men came before King Hakau and declared that the day had come when his men should decorate the image of the god. Hakau sent most of his men into the mountains, as the old men advised.

Soon after, Umi and his men began the descent into Waipio, and when Hakau saw them, he cried, "What is this great procession? I thought this was the day set apart for the god Lono."

241

The procession came nearer and nearer and soon surrounded the king and his few men. Hakau then recognized Umi. Angrily he cried to his men to do battle and kill his half-brother. A fierce battle raged, but Umi came out victorious and Hakau was killed. Then Umi took possession of his father's house. The two old men became the new king's stewards.

Umi made Kaoleioku his chief councillor and his old friends, Omaokamau and Piimaiwaa, became his chief generals.

Not long after Umi's victory, he heard about the beautiful daughter of the King of Maui. He sent to Maui for her and soon Piikea, the lovely princess, had become Umi's queen. Together, they ruled Hawaii for many, many years.

When King Umi came to die, every man, woman and child brought a stone and placed it upon a great pile before him. Then six pyramids of stones, each one representing a district in Hawaii, were raised for him. And these six pyramids remain a lasting monument to Umi the Conquerer, the Great King of Hawaii.

Kahuna Business in a District Court

WHEN I took over the Waiawa Ranch, I found an old chap named Joe working as a milkman. He was a tall, gaunt old fellow whose education had been sadly neglected. He could neither read nor write, and when pay day came he would never take all his wages, but would say to me, "Give me ten dollars and keep the rest for me." Since there was no bank on Kauai, I was glad to accommodate him and carried his balance in the payroll book.

One day some time later he came and asked for his money, telling me he was going to quit. He gave no reason for his sudden decision, and I asked no questions. We checked up his work and found it came to $300. Not having that amount of cash on hand, I gave him a check on the Bishop Bank of Honolulu. He took it gladly, shook my hand, and left.

Several months went by. I had been elected as delegate to the Republican Convention in Honolulu and was all packed and ready to leave when a policeman rode into the yard.

"I wonder who's in trouble now," I thought as I watched him dismount. He stalked up to me and handed me a summons to attend the very next day. When I read it, you can imagine my surprise to find that I was the one in trouble. I was to answer to a suit in debt for wages due the plaintiff Joe, the old milkman, for $300.

I saddled my horse and rode into Waimea to see the judge. He was an old Hawaiian minister of the gospel, but knew no law and could hardly speak any English.

"Your Honor," I said. "Would you kindly postpone this case until next week? I am a delegate to the Republican Party Convention and I must sail for Honolulu tomorrow."

"Politics has nothing to do with me," he replied seriously. "This is a court of justice and you must be here."

"Well," I said, "I gave the man a check and it is in the Honolulu Bank. I must get it. If you hold court I will not be here, but I will simply appeal to the Circuit Court in Lihue."

"Oh, I see—that sounds different," he replied. He graciously granted a continuance for a few days and I left for town.

At the Honolulu Bank I found the check all right. He had cashed it at Silva's store in Eleele, Kauai, fifteen miles away, and it had been endorsed, Joe X, His Mark, by Manuel, Silva's clerk.

The day I returned to Kauai the case was called. I took my time book and checkbook and drove the five miles to Waimea. As I tied my horse to the hitching post, I saw that the Courthouse was packed. During the three days I was in Honolulu the plaintiff had evidently advertised his case well, for it seemed the whole village had turned out to see and hear the fun.

I forced my way through the mob and entered the courtroom. Every seat was taken and spectators lined the walls. The old judge sat on his throne, his face beaming. He had not enjoyed such a show since he had taken office.

As I entered the space reserved for attorneys and their clients, I sw old Joe, but he failed to notice me. Sitting beside him was his lawyer, who rose to greet me. He was tall negro—over six feet, I'm sure—and as thin as a rail. When he said, "My name is Jackson; pleased to meet you," he held out a hand that was enormous.

I bowed to the court and took a seat. The judge called the case and a hush fell on the eager audience. Mr. Jackson got to his feet and began to talk.

He spoke fervently of his downtrodden client, and as he warmed up he began to tell what terrible people employers were and how they robbed poor but honest men. Every few minutes he shook his long fingers in the judge's face. The judge was entranced, and the audience got its money's worth. Finally Mr. Jackson rested his case, and the judge turned to me and asked if I had any defense.

When I started to show my payroll as evidence, Lawyer Jackson stood up and shouted, "Judge, that is a book account and not admissible as evidence."

The judge threw it out. I began to argue, but the lawyer shouted and ranted and shook his big hands in the judge's face. As soon as I made a remark, he would start shouting again. I offered my checkbook as evidence and he went into a roar again. The whole time was taken up in what seemed an endless roar, and the judge finally suggested that we meet again next morning.

Since I saw that I would have to have Mr. Manuel of Silva's store in the courtroom, I telephoned him. He promised to be on hand.

I rode home and found my certificate of admission to the Massachusetts Bar and to the Hawaiian Bar and, though I was not practicing law but managing a ranch, I took them with me to court. Both certificates had big red seals on them and were very impressive looking.

When it came my turn to take the stand I spoke in Hawaiian to the old judge and said, "Judge, yesterday you didn't give me a chance. You let the lawyer for the plaintiff have his own way on every point. You threw out evidence that I knew was good. I know you think I am only a cowboy and ignorant of law, but if you look at these papers you will see that at least I have studied law and know a little about it."

He glanced at the bright red seals on my papers, then gave me a sweet smile and said, "Yes, I was mistaken. I thought you were only an ignorant cowboy."

At this point Jackson jumped to his feet and shouted, "Judge, I will gladly welcome the defendant into the Bar Association."

"What!" I exclaimed. "You know no law. Your strong point is noise."

A titter went through the crowded room. Lawyer Jackson collapsed.

Motioning to Manuel, I said, "Judge, here is a man I would like to have you swear in as a witness. Mr. Manuel, will you please take the chair."

The judge swore him in, and I produced the cancelled check and handed it to him. I asked him if he remembered anything about it, or if he had endorsed it. He took the check and gave it a quick glance. "Sure, judge, I know Joe, the plaintiff. He came into my store and I cashed it for him and gave him $300," he said.

Joe stared as though bewitched at Manuel, then looked at the check. He let out a fearful yell and with both hands held high in the air he dashed out of the court and ran full speed across the road, vanishing into Hofgaard's store.

His lawyer sat for a moment as if stunned. Then he jumped to his feet, walked up to the judge and, shaking his long fingers once more in the judge's face, shouted, "This court is bought. There ain't no justice here. I will appeal this case to the Supreme Court of the Territory of Hawaii." And out he dashed.

For a moment all was still in the courthouse; then the spectators began pouring out and only Manuel, the judge, and I were left.

"Your Honor," I said, "do you know that the plaintiff's lawyer accused you of being bribed? That is generally regarded as contempt of court. You should call him back and fine him."

"Oh," the judge said, quietly, "I can't do that. He was such a wonderful orator!"

"All right," I replied. "If you don't feel hurt, that's your business, but he demanded that I pay him a fee of $50. How about granting me the same?"

"Oh, Elika," he said, thinking I was serious, "you don't need the money, do you?"

"No," I laughed. "That's all right!"

Then like a child he turned and asked, "Well, Elika, what am I to do now?"

"Seeing that the plaintiff and his lawyer have both fled and abandoned the court and their case, why not enter a verdict for the defendant?" I suggested.

"Sure," he said happily. "I will do that."

I thanked him and we shook hands. As I stepped out of the courthouse into the yard I met Manuel, laughing so hard there were tears in his eyes. "Listen," he said; "that fellow Joe is shouting that you are a kahuna, a dealer in black magic and in league with the devil; for if you were not, how did you ever find out that he cashed his check away over at Silva's store in Eleele?"

I thought that was the end of Joe's case. But a few months later, a young lawyer friend in Honolulu notified me that Lawyer Jackson had actually entered a law suit against me for $300.

I asked my informant to look out for my interests. The case was about to be called when I received a letter from my lawyer. All it said was: "Lawyer Jackson was sitting in a chair near the entrance to the Supreme Court, waiting for his case to be called, when he suddenly fell over onto the floor and died. His case against you has been dismissed. Perhaps old Joe was right when he called you a kahuna."

The Ale Koko Fishpond

SOME distance from where the Huleia River flows into the busy harbor of Nawiliwili lie two fishponds — a small one on the south side that is, strangely enough, called Sister; and one on the north side, about which I am now going to tell you.

It is a large pond covering about thirty-five acres, and the wall along the riverside is over two thousand feet long and five or six feet wide at the top. It has a gruesome name — Ale Koko, the Rippling Blood.

One day, many years ago, I was riding along the rim of the high bluffs above the Huleia River with John Gandall of Lihue, who was my guide. As we came out on a point overlooking the valley, he pointed down.

"That," he said, "is the largest fishpond on Kauai, and that long wall, or embankment that shuts it off from the river, is the largest also. The old Hawaiians say the wall was built by the menehune."

So the little men of the forests and hills had been here, too. Here was another masterpiece of engineering. I must see it. We rode down a winding path and came out on the bank of the stream.

Near the end of the embankment was a small grove of coconut palms, and under them sat an aged Hawaiian woman with her snow-white head bent over her weaving.

"Aloha!" I called out. Slowly she rose and looked at me with dimming eyes. "Aloha!" she replied. "Who are you?" I introduced myself. "Ah," she said, "you are Elika, son of Kanuka, and you are a long way from home. Welcome to our river. Pehea ke nu hou — what's the news?"

"I saw your big fishpond and I hear it was built by menehune," I said. "I want to know more about its history. Perhaps you can tell me."

"Of course I can," she answered. "I was born here. Tie up your horse and come sit in the shade of my coconut trees, and I will tell you." So there we sat together, and as she continued her weaving, she talked in a low, sweet voice. This is what she told me:

"The story goes back for many, many years . . . hundreds, perhaps. It was told to me by my mother, who learned it from hers, and so the tale has been handed down by word of mouth through all the long years before we Hawaiians learned to write.

"This valley has always been a favorite place with the Hawaiians. The river is full of fish, and the kings used to come here to fish and to bathe in the clear waters.

"One day, thinking how nice it would be if he had a fishpond by the side of the river where he could stock small amaama, or mullet, until they grew big enough to eat, the king explored the valley for a likely spot. On the north shore lay a large lagoon, ideal for a king's pond except that it was too large and the distance from bluff to bluff along the main stream was too long. He finally chose a smaller lagoon on the south side and there he built a wall. But after many days of hard labor, a great flood came roaring down one stormy night and carried away the dam. The pond was useless. Terribly disappointed, the king gave up the idea of having his own private fish pond.

"Some months later, while he sat in his house thinking about the matter, he was suddenly confronted by a very small but very handsome man. He was furious. No human being dared enter his presence unannounced.

It meant instant death. How had this man, although small to be sure, passed the guards without being challenged? He was about to call his guards and order this rash intruder instantly executed, when the little visitor began to speak.

"'Your gracious highness, do not be angry with me. I, too, am of royal blood. I am the King of the Menehune. It grieves me to see such a noble man as you unhappy. I will build you a fishpond at any place you choose to designate. The only condition will be that you must allow my people to fish in the pond as well as your own men.'

"The King of Kauai was overjoyed. He knew about the famous ditch in the Waimea Valley and now the menehune would built him a lasting monument to their skill. He accepted the offer and led his guest up to the large lagoon.

"The King of the Menehune looked at the chosen spot. It must have caused him some misgivings. It was huge, but he accepted the contract and assured the king that it would soon be built.

"The King of the Menehune knew the retaining wall had to be built of rock. He sent his men to search the lands around Lihue and Kipu, but for miles around the land lay bare of rock suitable for his men to carry."

Here my old Hawaiian lady paused a moment, and then asked, "Elika, you know about the Nomilo Fishpond that lies near the ocean on the south side of Kauai half-way between Koloa and Eleele, don't you?"

I nodded. "Well, that was once a small hill," she went on. "But when Pele, our fire goddess, made up her mind to leave Kauai for Oahu, she had one last great exhibition. She caused the hill to erupt, and it threw up rocks and molten lava thousands of feet into the air. It must have been a glorious farewell party! Then the south wind came up from the sea and carried the rocks far inland and covered the lands of Wahiawa and Kalaheo with thousands and thousands of small black rocks about the size of coconuts. Then the volcano sank down into the earth, leaving a large crater from which all the lava had been ejected. That big hole filled with water and made the Nomilo Fishpond.

"In their search, the menehune found these rocks ideal for building the king's fishpond, but alas! many miles of rough country lay between Wahiawa and the chosen spot in the Huleia stream. Nothing daunted, the little King of the Menehune decided to use them. He lined up his men—and he had plenty of manpower! They stood facing one another but in a staggered fashion, so that when a man received a rock he passed it to the man in the other line. In that way, each stone zigzagged the many miles on its long trip to the wall, where other little men waited to receive it and place it in the wall.

"The night the King of the Menehune chose to build the wall was clear and beautiful. Thousands of tiny figures standing in the zigzagging line were moving silhouettes against the blue moonlit sky. When the king had given the signal, the rocks began to pass from menehune to menehune and without interruption down the long, long line.

"All night long the rocks raced along from hand to hand. It was a tremendous job, and the little men worked at breakneck speed, for the wall must be completed by dawn. The menehune always had to finish any job undertaken in one night, but if not finished then they never returned to go on with it.

"How they worked! But too soon the sky paled and

the sun crept over the horizon. There was only ten feet or so left to go. Over two thousand feet had been completed that night. But the king told them to stop work at once and to wash their hands. The sharp lava rocks had taken a fearful toll. Not a man in all the lines had escaped. All had lacerated, bleeding hands. They washed them in the water of the lagoon and the surface of the water turned blood-red.

"The King of Kauai was very pleased with his fishpond, and soon had the wall finished and the pond well stocked with fish. In memory of the heroic little menehune he named it Ale Koko, the Rippling Blood."

My old Hawaiian friend had ended the strange story. She turned to smile at me. "Did I tell you all that you wanted to know about the fishpond, Elika?" she asked quietly.

"Yes! Yes, indeed!" I said. "I am most grateful, and I thank you."

And so, through all the centuries the fishpond has furnished food for thousands of people, and even today it is stocked full, not only of amaama, but a large variety of other fish — moi, ulua, kaku, and awa, to mention only a few.

Happy New Year

IT WAS late in the afternoon. All my cowboys had gone home, and I was closing the office when I heard the musical tinkling of spurs. Who would ride up but Kapaholili. He was mounted on a handsome bay and around his hat he wore a lei of maile. I knew he had come from Kaholuamano, my cousin Francis Gay's summer camp high up in the mountains back of Waimea.

"Aloha, Elika!" he called out. "Here's a letter for you." And he handed me an invitation to visit a few days with my cousin.

What a break! I hadn't been on a good hunt for a long time. In a few days I was up in those wild hills, packing my old hunting rifle with me and followed by my three dogs.

The second day after my arrival, three boys rode into camp and asked to join in a cattle hunt as they had no meat at home. "If Kua Papiohuli, my old hunter, is willing to go you may go, too," my cousin told them.

The boys said, "We want Elika to go along also."

"I took that for granted," Francis replied. Then, turning to me, he said, "You want to go, don't you?"

"You bet!" I told him. And so Kua saddled up, called his dog, and we were off.

As Kua's dog came trotting up, I said, "Kua, when did you get that pup?"

"That's no pup," he answered. "That's Happy New Year, the best hunting dog on Kauai. He's one and a half years old, but he can bite a pig and hold him."

"I don't doubt it," I replied; "he is as big as a calf."

We trailed off into the woods, six men and eleven dogs. We made quite a cavalcade.

We had ridden for an hour and were jogging along the bank of the Waialae Stream when the dogs began to bay. Suddenly a handsome young bull charged out of a thicket and dashed off up the valley.

The pack of dogs was at his heels and we all came galloping after, in and out of the small gullies. The bull ran for half a mile and then stopped to fight the dogs.

Kua and I jumped off our horses and ran ahead. There he stood on a little rise, the dogs surrounding him with Happy New Year acting as leader.

Kua carried an old .38 Winchester, and when he put it up and pulled the trigger out it only clicked. By that time I was in line, and putting my bead on the bull's chest, I fired. The bull turned and fled into the next gulch. We jumped onto our horses and chased after him.

"Look out, Kua!" I yelled. "The bull is at bay!" But when we got to the top and looked down into the little valley, the bull was flat on the ground. Happy New Year had hold of one ear and was pulling for all he was worth.

"Look at my dog!" said Kua proudly. "He could have held the bull alone."

The bull was skinned and all the meat cut off, but the boys were not satisfied. "Only two bags apiece . . . not enough . . . get one more," they implored. We climbed out of the valley onto the wide ridge and rode toward the swamps and the land of the bog bulls.

We rode and rode until the visitors finally cried, "Let's go back and try another valley." But just then Kua discovered the tracks of a big bull. We kept on.

It was not long before the dogs scurried off into the jungle, and soon a terrible din started up. All eleven dogs were barking and yelping.

Kua and I ran into the jungle. It was an almost impenetrable mass of kalia branches. Kua got ahead of me and I heard his gun roar. And then a huge animal came crashing through, rushing straight at me.

I was standing by the stump of a dead tree, but in a second dropped to the ground. It seemed that the bull must hear my heart pounding, and his right foot was so close I could have grabbed it! I didn't dare move. I was afraid he would smell me and then try to crash through to where I crouched.

The dogs were at him again, and he turned and dashed back at them. I slipped out of the branches and ran into open swampy ground. Tall, smooth-barked lehua trees sprawled on the ground. Off to my left the dogs were barking. I couldn't see the bull, but I was afraid to cross the open space. I looked for Kua. Finally I spied him standing behind a tall tree.

With a crash the bull suddenly dashed out of the thicket and came charging into the open glade, his tail high in the air, his head low, and his huge horns trying in vain to strike brave Happy New Year.

He was a big fellow. He was old, fifteen or more years. His horns were broken at the tips and splintered back a couple of inches. Once he had probably been leader of a herd, but now he was a member of the bog bull fraternity, destined either to die of old age or be killed by some hunter.

Happy New Year was dancing along ahead of him, barking almost into his face, tormenting him; and the old bull had only one thought in mind—to kill that dog.

When he was about a hundred feet in front of me, I took a quick shot at him. He stumbled and fell flat, but then struggled to a sitting position. Happy New Year turned, and as the rest of the dogs grabbed at the bull's hind legs, he sprang right at the bull's head.

The bull swung his horns, caught the dog, and gave him a mighty toss. Up into the air flew poor Happy, yelling and howling like mad. He must have gone fifteen or twenty feet, described a big arch, and fell with a big thud onto the ground.

The bull then began to bellow, the terrible cry of an old bull when mortally wounded. The first time I heard it, I was so frightened I wouldn't go near the bull, but now I knew he was down and out. Kua dropped his rifle and climbed up into the branches of a tree, crying out to me, "Elika! Elika! Climb a tree quick or the bull will get you. You will be a dead man."

I watched the bull thrashing at the dogs. I was sure Happy New Year must be dead. Poor, brave, but foolish fellow! Suddenly out of the ferns he came, a hole in his side where the bull's horn had caught him, but still full of fight—though I noticed he grabbed the old bull by the tail this time.

The bull was still down. I ignored Kua and ran from tree to tree until I got quite close to him. The dogs were jumping all over him. He was thrashing at them with his blunt horns, and his huge old head bobbed wildly in every direction.

One tree was about ten feet from him. I jumped over to it, held my rifle pointed at his head, and waited my chance. As he struck at the dogs, they jumped back and for a second his head was free. I fired. He rolled over, measuring his great length on the ground. Just to make sure, I put another bullet into his head. The game old fighter was dead.

Kua climbed down from his tree. All he said was, "You're a lucky fool. I could see you spinning in the air like my dog."

"There was no real danger after he was first hit," I said. "I knew he was done for."

When we called to the boys, and when they saw the bull, they gasped. "He's a big one," they said as they eyed him critically, "but he is too old. His meat will be as tough as leather."

"Take it or leave it," Kua told them. "An old bull is generally more tender than a younger one."

Of course the dogs had stopped barking and now stood over the bull, their tails wagging over the success of the kill. Kua and I walked over to examine Happy New Year. The dog was lucky. The old blunt horn had ony broken the skin. The smooth sharp horn of a younger bull would have gone clean through and killed him. The dog didn't seem to feel hurt. In fact, he seemed to think that the whole success of the hunt had been entirely due to him. Perhaps he was right, for if he hadn't enticed the bull to charge into the open, I would perhaps not have managed to get in a good shot.

I stroked his head. "Good boy . . . good old fellow!" Happy New Year, smart dog, knew what I was thinking, I'm sure.

For the Love of Kaala

ALMOST a hundred and fifty years ago, Kamehameha the Great paid a brief visit to the island of Lanai. When the beloved ruler and his court landed on the beach of the little island, he was welcomed by a cheering crowd of inhabitants. The people gave the conqueror many presents — fragrant leis, finely woven lauhala mats, pigs, chickens, and the choicest samples of the fruits of the island. And among those who came to offer their gifts to the great king was Kaala, the most beautiful maiden of Lanai.

She was the lovely daughter of Opunui, a minor chief of Lanai; and her beauty made her a symbol of love in the eyes of many young men on the island. Even the mighty Kamehameha followed her graceful movements with pleasure as she cast a path of flowers before him.

But the most deeply moved by Kaala's beauty was Kaaialii, a young chief from Oahu, who was a member of the royal bodyguard. Kaala needed only a glance to see in the eyes of the handsome young man the fire she had stirred in his breast. Strange to say, she who had remained cool to the advances of the young men of Lanai found herself swept away on a tide of emotion by the young chief of Oahu. When she smiled at Kaaialii, a secret message passed between them and a love was born that shall live in the legends of Hawaii forever.

Before long, Kaaialii came to Kamehameha and begged the great ruler to grant him Kaala for a wife. The king promptly gave his approval but suggested that the matter be referred to Opunui, the girl's father. The young chief was delighted. He knew that his fame as a warrior had reached the ears of the people of Lanai, and he felt that his noble birth would be another factor that would receive favorable consideration by the girl's father.

But Opunui had other ideas for his daughter's future. He bore a secret grudge against Kaaialii which dated back to the battle of Maunalei, in which he had fought and been beaten by warriors led by the young chief. But more important than that, there was another suitor for Kaala's hand—Mailou, the bone-breaker, whose skill as a wrestler had won the admiration of Opunui.

But the thought of marrying Mailou caused Kaala no pleasure. She despised his cruel mannerisms and his ugly face.

Opunui was too wise to meet Kamehameha's request for his daughter with a blunt refusal. He had a great respect for Mailou's strength and ability as a wrestler, and his wily mind concocted a plan that he thought would defeat the aims of the young chief and secure a clear field for the marriage of his daughter to the wrestler.

Opunui appeared before Kamehameha and, bowing and scraping, he said, "Oh, Great One, you have brought a great honor upon my house by asking for the hand of my daughter in marriage to one of your great warriors. Your request has brought a great pleasure to the members of my household, but it has also brought a great problem."

Opunui's evil face took on a shrewd expression. "Some time ago," he whined, "I pledged my daughter in marriage to my dear friend Mailou. Surely, O Wise One, you understand how difficult it is for me to decide on a just solution to the problem. I am deeply impressed with Kaaialii's noble heritage and your royal sanction, but I feel that I owe a debt of honor to Mailou.

"With your permission, O Great One, I suggest that these two young engage each other in a contest — say a wrestling match. The gods shall give strength and skill to him who should be the husband of Kaala!"

The great Kamehameha suspected that Opunui had some wily scheme in mind; but he was too proud to admit that one of his warriors could be bested in a contest of strength by any warrior of the outside islands. "It will be done," Kamehameha said, and ordered one of the members of his court to make the arrangements for the contest.

As the day of the great wrestling match came near, the people of Lanai could hardly contain their excitement. The final arrangements had been made and it was agreed that no holds would be barred. The two men would be permitted to inflict any possible injury on each other as long as no weapon was used. It was to be a battle to the death!

For days before the contest, people gathered around the spot where the arena for the match had been built. At night, while the torches of the fishermen sent bright ribbons of light across the waters, the people gathered on the beaches to talk of the great battle. A fight between two warriors was one thing; but when the romantic prize was the loveliest flower of Lanai, it kindled public interest to a blaze of excitement.

Who would be the victor? That was a question in the minds of every person on the island, from the humblest fisherman to the great Kamehameha himself. Few of those who discussed the match gave the young chief of Oahu much chance against the great strength and size of the Lanai bone-breaker. Mailou, with his long arms, broad shoulders, and mighty limbs made Kaaialii look slender by comparison.

For Kaala, it was a period of frantic despair. She knew the great strength of Mailou and his fearsome reputation as a wrestler. Was she sending Kaaialii, the young chief she loved so dearly, to a terrible death? The wrestling skill of the young chief was her only hope of life. Many were the tales that the women on the island told of the many men that Mailou had killed and cast into the sea.

On the night before the battle, Kaala clung to her young lover in a tight embrace. She looked up at the handsome face, and with tears brimming in her beautiful dark eyes she said, "My dear Kaaialii, our love is yet so young. Auwe, if it were only possible to give the little strength I have to you."

Kaaialii kissed her trembling lips and tried to console her. When they parted, Kaala felt only slightly consoled by Kaaialii's cheerful confidence.

Every man, woman, and child on the island of Lanai gathered at the arena the next day to see the battle from which they knew only one of the contestants would walk away alive. The two men stood facing each other, Mailou flexing his mighty muscles and opening and closing his huge hands as if anxious to tear his opponent to pieces. Kaaialii, meanwhile, stood with a composed smile on his face. His arms were folded and he appeared completely relaxed. He made no reply to the taunts and insults that Mailou hurled at him.

Then the battle began! Mailou rushed at his opponent with a roar, his sharklike teeth bared in a snarl of hate. He sprang at the young chief's throat like a wild beast; but Kaaialii was on the alert and neatly sidestepped the rush. As Mailou fell headlong to the ground, the young warrior reached down and seized his right arm. With a skillful kick, he snapped the bone above the elbow.

Mailou howled with rage and sprang to his feet. Once more he leaped to the attack, and again he was pushed off balance and smashed to the earth. Another quick maneuver by the young warrior, and Mailou had his left arm broken as his right had been.

With both arms broken, the wounded giant rushed once again at Kaaialii, with his head lowered like a bull. This was his last charge. Kaaialii had him by the hair as he fell and, with a lightning blow, the might Mailou's neck was broken, and he lay a crumpled heap on the ground.

There was much rejoicing among the people of Lanai at Kaaialii's victory. Mailou, the bone-breaker, had been feared because of his strength, but he was a bully and the people despised him for his cruelties. The only regret was in the black heart of Opunui. He remained at the edge of the crowd muttering to himself, but he dared offer no further opposition to the marriage of the two lovers. Soon after the wrestling match, Kamehameha stood Kaaialii and his lovely bride before him, and hand in hand they were pronounced man and wife.

Kapahe, Captain of the Niihau Whaleboat

KAPAHE was a splendid speciment of Hawaiian manhood—tall and straight and strong. He was already past his prime when I knew him; but how I loved to hear him tell of the times when he was young. He had belonged to a club called "The Stranglers." A rival society was known as "The Clubbers." Both were warlike clubs that have long since been abolished.

"Did you ever kill a man?" I asked him one day.

"Yes," he replied. "I was traveling across the island on the old trail from Waimea to Wainiha. My sister's boy, a lad of ten, was with me. We were far up the mountains above Kokee in the deep forests when we met a man going toward Waimea. We had gone but a short way past him when my nephew said, 'Kapahe, that man is following us, but he is walking backwards.'

"I knew then that he wanted to fight me but did not want to appear as the agressor, as that might bring him bad luck. I did not want to fight him because I had the little boy with me and, besides, the other man was an older and more experienced fighter. But I knew I had to fight. I stopped and waited for him.

"We sat down on a log and began to talk in quite a friendly manner, though in our hearts we knew that only one of us would leave that spot; for under the code of our clubs, the fight was always to the death. We sat and chatted while all the time we were watching one another for a chance to attack.

"Finally a twig fell on the shoulder of the other man. For one brief moment the Clubber's attention was distracted, and in that second I had my arm tight around his neck and the fight was on. Wrestle, fight, and strike as he would, he was unable to break my stranglehold. As the fatal noose grew tighter, my opponent was slowly forced to the ground and killed."

Kapahe smiled at me as he finished the exciting story. "What did you do after that?" I asked, still curious.

"I then returned to Waimea," he told me. "If I had gone on to Wainiha, they would have known that I was the killer and my life would have been in danger. Soon after that fight, the secret clubs were broken up and I bought an old whaleboat and began taking poi and taro from Kalalau to Niihau, across the channel."

Kapahe told me many other stories. The one I liked best concerned a time when he was shipwrecked. He had sailed out of Kalalau with a load of taro, accompanied by an old Hawaiian couple who wanted to visit Niihau. When they were in mid-channel, they were caught in a frightful gale that came roaring down unexpectedly from the north. The old whaleboat battled bravely for a while in the foaming sea, but finally began to break up as the mountainous waves crashed against it. There was nothing to do but start to swim toward Niihau with the gale.

Kapahe and the old man and woman swam until darkness came, making little headway in the boiling waters. At last the old people told the younger man to go on and leave them, as he was a much stronger swimmer.

"No, I'll not leave you!" cried Kapahe, holding his arm about the tiring woman while trying to guide them on. For many moments they argued; but finally he listened to the pleas of the couple and decided to leave them, hoping to be able to make the distant shore and bring help back before it was too late.

He struck out toward land and soon the old people were left far behind. He heard them singing a hymn as he swam away, and by that token he knew they had given up their struggle with the sea.

All through the long, night hours he kept on, and just as the grey dawn broke overhead, he felt the reef beneath his feet. Barely was he able to drag himself out of the water, and when he had made the beach he fell into an exhausted sleep.

Hours later the hot sun awakened him. His throat was parched and his lips cracked from the seawater. Dazedly he looked around and, to his horror, soon discovered that he was on the uninhabited little island of Lehua.

If he were to live, it meant he must reach Niihau. His tired eyes looked across the treacherous channel between Lehua and Niihau. Could he make it? For a few moments he was filled with weariness and discouragement. Then, standing on the edge of the sea, he breathed deeply and plunged into the water, striking out with long, rhythmic strokes toward the far shore.

The tide and current carried him up the coast. He saw men fishing off the shore, but they didn't see him.

On he swam, until he finally managed to get ashore on a little sandy shore near Kii.

He crawled up onto the warm dry sand and lay like a dead man until some fishermen found him and took him to their camp. Soon his strength was restored by a good meal of fish and poi.

Not long after that, my grandmother bought Niihau from the king. And, since there was no other way of crossing the stormy channel between Kauai and Niihau, it became necessary for her to buy a whaleboat. She was in need of a captain for her new boat and sent for Kapahe, of whom she had heard a great deal. She hired him at once, and he held the post for many years. He was as trustworthy a man as one could meet, loyal and fearless. He became a famous sailor, and the feats of his strength and seamanship would fill many a book. How well I remember hearing this one incident in particular.

Kapahe sat in the stern on the boat one day, holding the long steering oar and chatting with his lone passenger, a haole fellow about his own age. Both were about the same size, too — Kapahe, a bronzed and powerful Hawaiian; the passenger, a strong and active Norwegian named Valdemar Knudsen.

All day long the boat had been trying to make the crossing from Niihau to Kauai, but headwinds and tides had carried her far westward. It was late in the afternoon and the boat was still moving slowly along the coast of Kauai, away down towards Barking Sands of Nohili.

It would still take hours of rowing to get to Waimea. The crew was tired; so was the passenger. As he gazed shoreward, it seemed that only a finger of surf lay between him and the beach. He decided it would be possible to swim in and walk the few remaining miles to his home.

Determinedly he spoke of his intentions to Kapahe. "Don't try it," warned the captain. "That surf is bigger than you think and the shore is not safe to land on."

But the passenger, who was an excellent swimmer, only laughed at Kapahe and paid no attention to his words. Kapahe's words went in one of the Norwegian's ears and out the other, and he undressed and dived overboard, unheeding.

"Good-by! Aloha!" the captain called as he turned shoreward.

The swimmer was soon inside the breakers and striking out bravely for the shore that seemed so near. On, on, and on he swam; but it was not long before he realized that he was no nearer the beach than he had been when he first struck the water. Swimming as strongly as he could, he finally began to tire. Still the beach had come no nearer. He tried to make it back toward the boat, but could make no headway. His strength was giving out, and he had just about reached the stage of exhaustion when something struck him with great force on his right. He turned over in the water, thinking that a big shark or ulua had hit him, when to his surprise he looked into the smiling face of Kapahe, the boat captain.

"Kanuka," he said, using a name the Hawaiians always called my father, "I was watching you, and I thought to myself, no white man can make that shore today in such a surf. I just jumped overboard and came to help you."

Kanuka smiled weakly and murmured "Mahalo!" Kapahe then struck out at a tremendous speed, pushing his passenger ahead of him, and in a few minutes the two men crawled up on the beach.

When they had rested a few moments, Kapahe said, "You're all right now. Aloha!"

And with that, he turned and ran down into the boiling surf, swam out to his waiting boat, climbed aboard, and waved a friendly greeting to the tired man on the beach.

Punia and the King of the Sharks

KAIALEALE, king of the sharks, lived on the far side of the island of Hawaii. He ruled over the ten other sharks, and together they lived under the sea near a cave filled with lobsters.

The old Hawaiians knew where the cave was, and they also knew that it held the biggest and best lobsters to be found. But how to get them? No one dared to dive down to the cave because Kaialeale and the ten sharks were always on guard, ready to devour any intruder.

Living nearby was a young lad named Punia, whose father had been killed by the sharks. Since his father's death, there had been no one to catch fish for him and his mother. True, they had plenty of sweet potatoes to eat; but often Punia would hear his mother sigh and wish aloud, "Oh, if only we had a fish or lobster to eat with these!" Punia made up his mind that he would find some way to get lobster for his mother.

One day Punia stood above the cave where the lobsters were. Looking down into the still, clear water he could see the sharks—all ten of them, and Kaialeale as well. They were all asleep, but when his shadow above them was reflected in the water, they awoke at once.

Punia pretended that he didn't know the sharks had wakened. Leaning over the water, he spoke loudly so that they would be sure to hear him. "Here am I, Punia, and I am going into the cave to get lobsters for my mother and myself. The king shark, Kaialeale, is asleep, and I can dive to the point over there and then get to the cave. I will take a lobster in each hand, and my mother and I shall have them to eat with our sweet potatoes."

Then Punia listened to the whispers of Kaialeale below the surface. He was speaking softly to the other sharks. "Let us rush to the spot where Punia dives and we will eat him as we did his father."

But Punia was a clever boy and was not to be caught so easily by the stupid sharks. He had a stone in his right hand, and when he heard what Kaialeale said, he tossed the stone far out into the water. Of course, the silly sharks rushed to the place where the stone fell, leaving the lobster cave unguarded. Like a flash, Punia dived down to the cave, caught his two lobsters, and was safely back on land before the sharks had returned.

Again he shouted down to the sharks. "Here is Punia with two lobsters in his hand, brought from the cave. Now he and his mother will have something to eat with their sweet potatoes. It was the first shark, the second shark, the third shark, the fourth shark, the fifth shark, the sixth shark, the seventh shark, the eight shark, the ninth shark, the tenth shark . . . it was the *tenth* shark with the thin tail that showed Punia what to do!"

When the king of the sharks, Kaialeale, heard what Punia said, he ordered all the sharks to come together and to stay in a row. One by one he counted them. All ten were present, but sure enough! Punia was right. Number ten had a thin tail.

"Aha! so it was you, Thin Tail," said Kaialeale, "that told the boy Punia what to do. You shall die!" Then the king of the sharks ordered the thin-tailed one to be killed.

"For shame!" Punia called out to them. "You have killed one of your own kind." Then he ran home to surprise his mother with the two lobsters.

Punia and his mother enjoyed their feast and, when the lobsters were all gone, back he went to the same place above the cave. As he had done before, he called out to the sharks: "I can dive to the place over there and then slip into the cave, for the sharks are all asleep at this time of day. I can get two lobsters for my mother and for myself to eat with our sweet potatoes." Then he threw another stone, but in another direction this time.

Splash! went the rock when it hit the water, and in an instant the sharks had rushed to the spot, leaving the cave unguarded as before. Again Punia dived down and grabbed two big, fat lobsters in his hands. In a matter of seconds, he was back in his place above the cave and waiting for the sharks to return. When they were once more swimming about the cave, he shouted down to them: "It was the first shark, the second shark, the third shark, the fourth shark, the fifth shark, the sixth shark, the seventh shark, the eighth shark, the ninth shark—it was the *ninth* shark, the one with the big stomach, that told Punia what to do that time!"

And so the days sped by and Punia continued to fool the sharks. Always, when he had returned to his place above the cave, he would name one shark: "The first shark—the second shark, the third shark—the shark with the little eye, the shark with the gray spot on the side — told Punia what to do!" he would call down to them. Each day, another shark was killed, until only Kaialeale, the king of the sharks, remained alive.

When Punia knew that all ten sharks were dead, he went into the forest and hewed out two pieces of hard wood, each one about a yard long. Then he found a stick of aulima to rub with and a stick of aunaki to rub on, so that he could make a fire. He gathered some charcoal and packed some food and, when he had put it all into a big bag, he carried it down to the beach.

Once more he stood above the cave that now was guarded only by King Kaialeale. Speaking in a loud voice so that the shark king would hear, he said: "If I dive now, Kaialeale will bite me and my blood will come to the top of the water. Of course my mother will see it and she will be able to bring me back to life again. But if I dive down and Kaialeale should take me into his mouth whole, then I shall die and never come back to life again."

Stupid Kaialeale was listening, of course. And he said to himself, "No, I'll not bite you, but I will swallow you whole, and then you can never come back to life again and I'll never be troubled with you any more. Yes, I shall open my jaws wide enough to take every bit of you in! Ah, yes! Yes, indeed, I shall get you this time!"

Punia was a bit worried. What if Kaialeale decided not to open his mouth wide? What if his trick did not work this time? Then, true enough, he would never come back!

But Punia was a brave boy. Taking the bag in his hands, he dove straight toward the gaping jaws of Kaialeale, and in a moment was locked in the shark's great mouth.

Quickly, Punia opened his bag and took out the pieces of wood he had cut in the forest. It was not long before he had the shark's jaws pried open and held apart with the strong sticks. With his mouth held open, Kaialeale went thrashing about in the water.

By this time Punia was inside the shark. There he kindled his charcoal fire and cooked the food he had brought with him. With the fire burning in his insides, the shark king could not keep still and went dashing all over the ocean.

Finally, he came near the island of Hawaii again. "If he brings me near the breakers, I am saved," said Punia, speaking out loud. "But if he takes me to the beach, I shall die."

Of course Kaialeale heard what Punia said. When he came within sight of the beach, he rushed in from the ocean and right up onto the land. No shark had ever been there before, and when he was once high and dry on the beach he couldn't get back to the ocean again.

Punia came out of the shark and called to the people, "Kaialeale, king of the sharks, has come to visit us!"

When the people heard that their great enemy, Kaialeale, was in their midst, they hurried to the beach with their spears and knives, and soon killed him.

From that day on, Punia and all his friends were able to dive down into the cave to get the lobsters. And every day, Punia and his mother enjoyed lobster with their sweet potatoes.

Glossary of Hawaiian Words

a'a, dwarf
ahu, thatching stick
akua, evil spirit
anaana, evil
awa, liquor distilled from
    peppery root
auwe, alas
hale, place, house
heiau, temple platform
holoku, gown with long train
hopapa, wrangling
ilianu, cold skin
imu, underground oven
kahuna, sorcerer
kaikamahine, daughter
kalia, native tree
kane, male, man
kapa, cloth of beaten bark
kapu, forbidden, tabu
keiki, child
kiu, northwest wind
koali, morning-glory
konohiki, landlord
kuala, prophet
kupuna, grandparent,
    ancestor
lei, flower garland
limu, seaweed
luna, overseer
maika, bowling game
malihini, newcomer
mele, song
mo-o, supernatural lizard

newa, war club
okolehao, liquor distilled
    from ti plant
oopu, small fish
opu, stomach
pahu, coffin
pake, Chinese
paniolo, cowboy
papehe, strike, kill
pilikia, trouble
pololu, long spear
punee, couch
pu ohe, shell trumpet
wikiwiki, hurry

272

TALES OF THE PACIFIC

JACK LONDON
Stories of Hawaii $4.95
South Sea Tales $4.95
Captain David Grief (originally A Son of the Sun) $4.95
The Mutiny of the "Elsinore" $4.95

HAWAII
Remember Pearl Harbor by Blake Clark $3.95
Kona by Marjorie Sinclair $3.95
The Spell of Hawaii $4.95
A Hawaiian Reader $4.95
The Golden Cloak by Antoinette Withington $3.95
Russian Flag Over Hawaii by Darwin Teilhet 3.95
Teller of Tales by Eric Knudsen $4.95
Myths and Legends of Hawaii by W.D. Westervelt $3.95
Mark Twain in Hawaii $4.95
The Legends and Myths of Hawaii by Kalakaua $6.95
Hawaii's Story by Hawaii's Queen $6.95
Rape in Paradise by Theon Wright $4.95
The Betrayal of Liliuokalani $6.95
The Wild Wind by Marjorie Sinclair $4.95

SOUTH SEAS LITERATURE
The Trembling of a Leaf by W. Somerset Maugham $3.95
Rogues of the South Seas by A. Grove Day $3.95
The Book of Puka-Puka by Robert Dean Frisbie $3.95
The Lure of Tahiti, ed. by A. Grove Day $3.95
The Blue of Capricorn by Eugene Burdick $3.95
Horror in Paradise, ed. by A. Grove Day and Bacil F. Kirtley $4.95
Best South Sea Stories, ed. by A. Grove Day $4.95
The Forgotten One by James Norman Hall $3.95

TRAVEL, BIOGRAPHY, ANTHROPOLOGY
Manga Reva by Robert Lee Eskridge $3.95
Coronado's Quest by A. Grove Day $3.95
Love in the South Seas by Bengt Danielsson $3.95
Home from the Sea: Robert Louis Stevenson in Samoa by Richard A. Bermann $3.95
The Norhoff-Hall Story: In Search of Paradise by Paul L. Briand, $4.95
The Fatal Impact by Alan Moorehead $3.95
Claus Spreckels: The Sugar King in Hawaii by Jacob Adler $3.95
A Dream of Islands by Gavan Daws $4.95

Orders should be sent to Mutual Publishing Co.
2055 N. King St., Honolulu, HI 96819. Add $2.00 handling for the first
book and $1.00 for each book thereafter. For airmail add $2.00 per book.

TALES OF THE PACIFIC

Order should be sent to Mutual Publishing Co.
1215 Si... St., Honolulu, Hawaii 96816. Add $2.00 handling for the first
book and $1.00 for each book thereafter. For airmail add $2.00 per book.